TROPIC HUSTLE

A LUKE ANGEL CRIME THRILLER

NATHAN VAN COOPS

Cover designed by Damonza.

Ebook ISBN: 978-1-950669-29-5

Paperback ISBN: 978-1-950669-30-1

Hardcover ISBN: 978-1-950669-31-8

To inquire about the availability of film or television rights, send email to: inquiries@nathanvancoops.com

TROPIC HUSTLE

PROLOGUE

FRANK ANGEL WALKED out of Union Correctional Institution in Raiford, Florida to a view of dark clouds and distant lightning. The palms lining the front walk shook in the wind and the scent of rain forecasted the approaching storm.

He decided it was his new favorite weather. It smelled like freedom.

Frank's breezy euphoria lasted the length of the sidewalk to the parking lot, then ended with the slam of a car door.

The finish of the '98 Chevy Caprice was a kaleidoscope of primer spots in four paint colors. The rims had none of the original hubcaps, but the woman that climbed out of the passenger door had enough shine to make up for it. Gold bangles adorned both wrists and huge hoop earrings were tangled in her cascade of dark hair. The crimson tube dress could have been painted on and rode high up her tan legs. She tugged at the hem twice, and Frank wondered briefly why she thought it was still her size, but after almost two decades inside, he wasn't one to criticize any view of a woman.

The hulking driver of the Caprice came around to slouch on

the front fender, a hand-rolled joint dangling from his lips. He spread his muscled arms wide. "Didn't think I'd forget about you, did ya, Frank?"

"You told me he was an old guy." The woman in the gold earrings cocked a hip as she took Frank in. "Looks pretty good to me."

"Didn't need to trouble yourself picking me up, Deacon," Frank said. "I'd have taken the bus."

"What kind of cellie would I be if I let you sweat it at a bus stop in a rainstorm on your first morning out?" Deacon pulled the joint from his lips. "Time for you to taste the good life, brother. Even this shit's legal now. You believe it?" He offered it to Frank. "Breakfast of champions."

Frank shook his head.

"He brought you Little Debbies donuts too," the woman said. "Made me get 'em for you from the Stop 'n Shop. Said they were your favorite."

"My first meal out of prison, and you thought to get me the same thing I ate every day *in* prison?"

"Isn't my man sweet?"

"Like taffy. And just as sticky."

Deacon lifted one foot and tried to shake a spec of fallen ash off the toe of his basketball shoes. When that failed he bent down and swatted it off. "Good thing we showed up this morning, huh, Frank?" he said when he'd straightened up. "If we'd have been here tomorrow like your message said, we'd have missed you."

"Leave it to the R&D guys to process you when you least expect it."

"Deke worried you were gonna ghost him," the woman said.

"Lyla, shut your mouth," Deacon said. "Don't insult my friend. Frank knows who it was kept him safe all those years we bunked together in C-block. Though he did do some pretty OG shit prior to gettin' in that helped his rep." He pushed himself off the fender, flicked away his cigarette and closed the distance to Frank in three quick strides. He stepped up onto the curb and draped one arm over his shoulder. Deacon kept his voice low as he breathed the smell of pot into Frank's ear. "But I didn't forget anything, did I, Frank. And it's time we take a drive and help you remember how to do some of that gangster shit again."

The weight of the muscled arm lay heavy on Frank's shoulders. He looked up at the sky and the oncoming storm and sniffed once more. He'd been wrong. Didn't smell like freedom after all. Smelled like a short trip on a merry-go-round with the doors of Union Correctional swallowing him again at the end of the ride.

Luckily, he knew one place where the sun would be shining. And one man he could count on for help.

He stepped off the curb, out from under Deacon's grip, then made his way to the Caprice. He held the rear passenger door open for Lyla while Deacon walked around to the driver's side. Lyla gave him a wink as she slid into the back seat. He knew she'd also be the one carrying the gun.

Frank climbed into the front passenger seat and slammed the door.

It was going to be a long drive south.

But he was out. And if he played this right, soon he'd have the best part of his life back.

After one important stop.

ONE

ENGINE OUT

"YOUR ENGINE JUST QUIT. What are you going to do?" I took my hand off the throttle control and waited.

In the seat beside me, Taylor McMaster, a nineteen-year-old commercial pilot student and someday airline pilot, watched the needle on the tachometer gauge plunge to idle speed with her eyes wide.

"Shoot. Now?"

"Emergencies don't happen when you're ready for them."

She tightened her grip on the control yoke and swore under her breath. She'd doubtless done dozens of simulated engine failures in her training to this point, but a single-engine aircraft going quiet always has a way of elevating the heart rate.

The plane we were piloting together was a 1970s model Cessna 185. Taylor had climbed in at daybreak enthused about starting tailwheel landing practice, but I liked to see how a student's basic skills stacked up before trusting them with the controls of a new-to-them airplane. Plus I was on my second cup of coffee and I was feeling punchy.

"What's your first job?" I prompted.

"Uh, airspeed. Pitching for best glide," she said, pulling gingerly back on the yoke.

Taylor's hesitation before acting had already cost us a hundred feet of altitude, but I was happy to see she was getting herself together. After pulling the nose up to the horizon and decreasing our descent rate, she finally got her head out of the flight deck to look outside. "Next is best landing place."

We were two-thousand feet up and had just overflown a beauty of a field for an emergency landing, but I kept my mouth shut and waited to see if Taylor would spot it.

"That doesn't look bad." She pointed toward a pasture a mile ahead of us.

"Now is the time to decide," I said. "Get a good look."

"I'm going for it." She fumbled for a checklist with one hand, while fighting the pressure on the yoke with the other. Trimming the elevator would solve the pressure problem for her, but she hadn't thought of that yet. "C is for controls and comms," she said, listing the third letter of the engine-out ABCs.

While she rattled off more items from the checklist, I looked out my passenger-side window and surveyed a herd of cows grazing in a meadow.

We were east of Tampa Bay in the once-rural landscape stretching toward central Florida. Pastures were still plentiful, though housing developments encroached from every direction. Below us, a half-mile distant, I spotted a horse-rescue I'd once visited with my niece. The owner, a bristly pinecone of a lady named Harriet Stubbs, had made it her mission in life to save every retired racehorse she could from slaughter and had harangued and tongue lashed every racehorse owner she could find in order to do it.

Despite the spit and vinegar she exhibited toward the adults unlucky enough to land in her crosshairs, Harriet had a soft spot for kids and hosted an annual summer camp around humane horse husbandry and trail riding.

As we overflew her pastureland, I spotted Harriet herself and what appeared to be a half-dozen grade-schoolers on sedate mounts meandering their way across a field toward the eastern woods. The morning sun shone on what was shaping up to be a pretty fine day—if we could avoid crashing and burning in a hayfield.

Out the front windscreen, Taylor's chosen landing point was approaching fast and the power lines she'd failed to spot from altitude were looming large. Even if we cleared them, an irrigation ditch divided the target property in exactly the spot we'd touch down. It would likely shear our landing gear off in a landing.

"Uh, Luke. I think I have a problem."

"You're running out of altitude for making turns. What's your plan?"

"Switching fields." Taylor cringed as she said it and banked left, pulling up involuntarily as she tried to make another rugged pasture to that side. The stand of fifty-foot pine trees looming ahead was going to have something to say about it. The stall horn screeched a warning in our ears as Taylor gritted her teeth and hung on.

"Okay. My airplane," I said, once it was clear to both of us that we were going to end up in the trees. "Let's go around." I pressed the throttle in with the index finger of my coffee-holding-hand as I nosed over with the control yoke and the engine roared to life once more. The added thrust gave us the airspeed we needed to climb. We cleared the trees with a hundred feet to spare, and I banked the plane right again as we ascended.

"What would you do differently the next time?" I asked, relinquishing the controls to Taylor now that we'd achieved a safer altitude.

"I'd pick a different field. Or maybe have a better backup?"

I pointed to her checklist of to-do items she'd run though during the descent. "Those are great, but shouldn't detract from the pilot's number one job: getting the aircraft safely on the ground."

"I should have spent more time on the emergency field selection."

"Options only narrow when you get lower. We can always lose altitude, but it's impossible to get it back."

"Want me to climb back up and do it again?" she asked.

But an unusual scene distracted me out the window. A pair of dust clouds were forming to the south—three vehicles on a dirt road moving fast. Two police vehicles with lights on were responsible for the second dust plume, but the origin of the first was a pickup truck an eighth of a mile ahead of them, careening haphazardly along the road. At intervals, a man stuck his head out the passenger side window and looked back at the cops. And even from my altitude the finger gestures he threw out were easily recognizable.

"Hang on a second," I said to Taylor, and took control of the aircraft again.

"Okay, your airplane," she said, putting her palms up and leaning back in her seat. As I banked right, she spotted the vehicles. "Oh wow, is that a car chase?"

"Never know what you'll see in rural Florida," I said.

The fleeing Chevy pickup truck was an old model with big tires and a tackle box and a couple of fishing poles in the back. Maybe they'd been out on the river early, but something about the way the truck was swerving gave the impression that these good ol' boys may not have gone to bed yet.

I'd certainly seen my share of sunrises after long nights in my time, but I hadn't made the choice to run from cops in a long while. It was a dumb move, yet people pulled over for DUIs weren't always in a state to see the futility of the plan. Even so, as the truck made a sharp turn and barreled into a farmer's field, one couldn't help but admire their enthusiasm.

I couldn't hear the sirens of the police cruisers, but even from the air the scene evoked modern-day *Smokey and the Bandit* vibes. The Chevy's big tires tore huge ruts in the dirt as it rocketed over the recently tilled farmland, and it was clear the moment the police SUVs tried to follow that they were going to have a tough time. The street tires of the SUVS served well on paved city roads and well-enough on backroads, but going off-road was a different matter. The Chevy's wide tread and all-wheel drive torque had it widening the gap every second.

There was a vague satisfaction that came from seeing this fox outrun its hounds. Everyone loves an underdog story. But as I was about to peel away from the scene playing out below us, I noticed the wide dirt trail the maverick Chevy had chosen as its next path of escape. The battered old truck had careened out the far end of the rutted field and was now headed through the woods on a dirt road turned horse track. The same horse track I'd seen Harriet Stubbs and her gaggle of grade-schoolers recently enter from the far side of the woods.

"Aw, shit," I muttered.

I banked toward the woods and overtook the racing truck. The joyriding idiots showed no sign of slowing, and as I watched, the driver flung an empty beer can out his window, missing the truck bed and sending it bouncing along in the truck's dusty wake. The woods were sparse enough in sections to allow some visibility, but with the twists and turns, my hope that the truck would have the time to spot the danger ahead was slim. If anything, it looked like they were speeding up.

I flew on past an open glade toward the woods in search of Harriet and her summer camp riders. It didn't take long to spot them, still moving at a snail's pace along the old dirt road. The timing was the absolute worst. The truck would barrel though the glade and into the woods before they'd reach the clearing. And with a bend in the road ahead of where they'd meet, the riders would never see it coming.

"That truck's going to run right into them!" Taylor exclaimed from beside me, tuning in to the danger on the ground. "Can we warn them?"

I slurped the last dregs of my coffee, then tossed the cup over my shoulder into the back seat. "Take a break for a minute. I'm gonna try something."

"Uh, okay."

I executed a side slip and banked low over the trees for a better look at the rider group and popped the window open, waving one arm out the window while attempting a "go back" gesture. But the couple of kids that spotted me only waved in reply.

Any lower and I'd be in danger of spooking the horses. A galloping herd with scared fifth-graders hanging on for dear life was no one's idea of a good plan so I continued into a left turn and set my sights on the only remaining option. Stop the truck.

"Wait, what are you doing?" Taylor asked, suspicion in her voice as I lined up for the trail ahead.

"Might want to hold onto something. This could get tight."

The wingspan of the Cessna 185 was thirty-six feet. The distance from tree to tree on either side of the dirt road was no more than fifty. The term "threading a needle" came to mind.

"You can't be serious," Taylor said.

"Good news. If we die, I won't charge you for this flying lesson."

The plume of dust from the speeding truck gave evidence to its approach. It would be on the riders in under half a mile.

"How can you stop them?"

"I'm becoming a visual deterrent."

"Visual deterr— I did not sign up for this!" Taylor blurted out. But she was already tightening her seat belt.

The truck entered the far side of the glade and zoomed toward the woods on the near side. I wouldn't have time to catch it in the open. So I used the only option I had left. I pulled the power out and dove the plane, dipping beneath the tree line and skimming the dirt trail at about five feet of altitude.

"You're playing chicken with a truck?" Taylor said. "We're not going to win."

Her math checked out. Thirty-two hundred pounds of aluminum airplane with a zero impact safety rating versus a seven-thousand pound Chevy Silverado was a lousy matchup. Plane versus anything was a losing proposition, so while I wanted to reassure her about my plan, I was too busy not hitting trees.

I throttled forward and took the bend in the road doing sixty-five knots. Slower would have been easier but airspeed is life.

The truck came around the bend in the opposite direction doing at least fifty miles per hour.

"Don't worry, I've done this once before," I said. "They'll swerve."

Maybe.

We were close enough to see the driver's eyes go wide in his head. Big truck or not, the element of surprise is a potent ally. At the last moment, the driver locked up the brakes and wrenched on the wheel, careening off the road and through a stand of stubby palms—rods and tackle flying in all directions.

I pulled on the yoke and climbed, noting a vague thump from the right wingtip as we clipped a pine branch—but we stayed airborne.

My gut clenched from the increase in G-forces but they eased once we leveled out above the trees. I banked hard right and took a look back at the results of our efforts. The Silverado was in the trees but hadn't collided hard with any. Both the driver and the passenger stumbled out of the doors, irate and bellowing. The driver shook his fist at us.

A quarter mile down the road, the police cruisers raced into view.

Taylor had turned a shade of pale I'd never seen before. Her eyes were closed, her hands were on her stomach, and she seemed in need of a pep talk.

"I never knew a situation where blabbing to the police ever helped my mood. What do you say we bug out? Call this enough of a lesson for one day."

One of her hands went to her mouth. "I think I'm gonna barf."

"Dare you not to."

On the ground below, Harriet Stubbs and her parade of grade-schoolers had found the accident scene. A few looked up and watched us fly away.

I waved.

I hoped none of the kids had good enough eyes to spot our registration number.

Some good deeds were best left anonymous.

Like Batman.

I smiled.

In the pilot seat, Taylor got the window open just in time to lose her breakfast into the slipstream.

Some of it didn't make it out.

Gross.

Bet that never happened in the Bat-plane.

Evidently, hero work wasn't all it was cracked up to be. But still, it beat an office job.

Life was good.

I had nothing to worry about.

"YOU MADE Taylor McMaster throw up during a flying lesson?" my ex-wife said from the speakerphone on my desk. "Seriously, Luke?"

I couldn't see Cassidy Angel furrowing her brow and frowning, but I sure could feel it, all the way from Boston.

"It was a tiny amount," I clarified. "And I cleaned it off the side of the plane already. No harm done."

"She's never going to want to fly with us again." This prediction came from Elsbeth Miller, my part-time office assistant and accounts manager, who was seated in one of my office chairs. Both women had apparently been waiting to ambush me the moment I walked in the door. I'd hoped for a quiet post-flight wind down in my hangar office, but that wasn't happening.

I considered explaining the circumstances with the summer campers, but the less these two knew of my methods, the better.

Whenever Cassidy and Elsbeth got into conversations without me, I always knew I was in trouble. A single mom and second-generation no-nonsense Italian-American, Elsbeth pulled no punches and shared none of my levity in running the business.

"You're going to need to find better hobbies than scaring off our students," she said. "Otherwise we'll all be out of jobs."

"Things aren't that dire," I said. "We're just in a transitionary period of spending."

"Oh good. Maybe we'll be *transitioning* to other jobs then," Elsbeth said, with a lot of arching of eyebrows involved.

Cassidy piped up from the speakerphone again. "We've been discussing the costs from the Mallard this month. 'Dire' might actually be the word for it."

I winced but tried to keep my voice upbeat. "Every plane needs its TLC. Good news is, I think we're almost done."

"Not in the eyes of the FAA," Cassidy countered. "Until we get the registration issues settled, there's no way we'll be able to use the plane on a charter certificate. And if it's not making us money, it's a liability, not an asset."

"The bottomless money pit is what I call it," Elsbeth added.

I walked around my desk and took a seat in my office chair. From there I could look out into the hangar and beyond to where *Tropic Angel*, my 1940s era Grumman Mallard, sat on tie-down. It was an immense plane compared to the usual general aviation aircraft we worked on, and the cost of repairing it lately had been daunting. But it was also a piece of Angel family history. Having it back in my life had patched a place in my soul I couldn't have filled any other way.

"I know you love the plane," Cassidy said. "But if we don't get the ownership issues sorted with the FAA, something will eventually have to give. We can't keep shoveling money down that hole."

"Forego paying my salary again this month," I said to Elsbeth. "Keep that in the company coffers."

"You don't pay yourself enough as it is," Elsbeth replied. "Fat lot of good that will do us."

I rocked in my office chair. "We've had more people interested in tailwheel training lately. That's a plus."

"In a lease-back plane where most of the rental fee goes to the owner," Cassidy countered.

"And you're more useful in the shop turning wrenches," Elsbeth said. "From a profit standpoint, you're slower than Reese so we get to charge more hourly."

"Am I supposed to take that as a compliment?" I asked.

"She just means you're the main *attraction* in this shop," Cassidy said. "People come in to chat you up while you're working, and that's half the fun for them. If we could keep you in the hangar and get Reese to stop ripping through her projects so quickly, we'd actually make more money."

"Stellar service at a fair price is going to keep customers coming back for years. Any other shop would kill to have Reese."

"All we're saying is that we need to find some ways to make better margins, pronto," Cassidy said. "And up the shop rate."

I scowled, and Elsbeth cocked her "I told you so" eyebrow at me. Raising labor rates had been a conversation we'd batted back and forth repeatedly of late. Now I was being tag-teamed.

"I'm scouting for another mechanic to bring aboard," I said. "Might increase our capacity some."

"But as long as we're a small shop, there are only so many planes you can fit in the hangar to work on," Cassidy said. "We're never going to be like Bayside Maintenance unless you get more hangar space and good luck with that at a field like Albert Whitted."

"I enjoy being a small shop," I said. "Tight crew, high quality work, casual lifestyle."

"No money," Elsbeth added.

I sighed. "I'm okay going up five bucks an hour on the shop rate."

"Needs to be fifteen to match Bayside." Elsbeth crossed her arms.

"So let's go ten for now," Cassidy said, ever the negotiator. "Then everyone is happy."

Elsbeth did not look happy, but she stopped glaring at me quite so hard.

"Elsbeth, would you mind excusing us?" Cassidy asked. "I'd like to speak with Luke privately."

Elsbeth made a noise that was something akin to affirmation and pushed herself out of her chair. "I have a pile of parts invoices to *not* pay, anyway." When she opened the office door, my cat, Blackjack, came sprinting in, almost tripping her. Elsbeth frowned at the cat but then let herself out. Her heavy footfalls sounded on the stairs.

"That woman is the bane of my existence," I said when she was gone.

"You know you need her," Cassidy said from the speaker. "She balances you out. Unless you want to be the one doing all the inventory spreadsheets and payroll."

I shivered and shook my head. "I love Elsbeth. Let's keep her forever."

Blackjack hopped up into my lap and started purring while simultaneously flicking her tail at me in annoyance. We enjoyed a love/hate dynamic that only she understood.

There was a long silence while I wondered if my cat was going to bite me in the chin and then Cassidy spoke again. "We need the Mallard cleanly in your name, Luke. I didn't want to spook Elsbeth any more than she already is, but without it up and making money in the next month, we can't float this business. I spoke to another FAA inspector this morning and they're still a hard no on our charter certificate without a clean bill of sale. According to them, it still belongs to your dad. I think it's time you had that conversation with him."

"Like hell. I'm not doing that unless we've exhausted every other option."

"We're there, Luke."

I frowned.

"Can you take me off speaker?"

I picked up the phone handset. "Let me have it."

"Last time I saw you, there was a big bag your brother gifted you. Have you dipped into it?"

"No. My family doesn't give gifts. They attach strings. And I'm done being shackled to their choices. That bag doesn't exist."

"I figured you'd say that. Was just thinking there are a lot of problems a big bag of money could solve. You might have to make a hard choice there soon."

"This business will survive longer without my family's involvement than with it. We'll find another way."

"I know we had talked about my coming down to train for a type rating on the Mallard on my weeks off."

"I'm still all for that," I said. "We can get you on the water anytime you want. You'd be a natural."

"It's just not a good time for it right now."

Blackjack was kneading my left leg with her claws and I had to pick her up to get her to stop. I cradled the phone with my shoulder. "Your flight schedule fill up?" Cassidy's captain job with the airline was notoriously flaky about her hours.

"There's just no point in it, Luke. If Archangel is headed toward bankruptcy, then I need to be flying all I can with the airline to salvage my finances. I've sunk too much into this business as it is."

"That outlook is a little extreme, don't you think? We still have the insurance payout coming in from the loss of the 206. That will boost us out of the red."

She sighed. "I got the numbers on that. It's going to be low, Luke. Much lower than we expected."

I froze halfway through removing Blackjack from my lap. I held her suspended from her armpits while that news sank in.

"I've done the math. If we can't get the Mallard on a charter certificate, I don't see how we get out of this. You can't sell it, you won't let it become derelict, and keeping it operational will sink us. That's the reality."

Blackjack meowed. I lowered her the rest of the way to the floor and then gripped the phone handset. "Are you saying you're . . . what? Done as a partner? Wanting out?" Something in the pit of my stomach tightened and didn't release.

"I *want* to stay." Her voice was tentative. Expectant.

Waiting for what? For me to get upset and tell her off? For me to say no problem, I'll just go sort things out with the one guy I can't stand the sight of? I stared hard at my desk and did neither. I massaged my temples with my thumb and middle finger. "Whatever you need to do to get your finances straight, do it. I understand. I can handle things on my own."

"Luke, I know you're doing the best you can. And I'm sure you'll find another job if this business doesn't work out. You're very capable. I just think we need to be realistic about the future. And it might not be Archangel anymore."

I squeezed my temples tighter, till the colors stopped swirling in the backs of my eyelids. I was drifting in darkness. An ocean with no edges.

"Luke?"

My cell phone buzzed in my shorts, pulling me back to earth. I tugged it from my pocket and read the number. I only knew one person I liked with that area code.

"Sorry, Cass. I have to take another call."

"Okay." Something in her voice gave away her disappointment. Whatever she'd been expecting—wanting—I hadn't supplied it. "Call me back?"

The cell kept vibrating on my desk. "Sure. Will do."

"Okay."

I replaced the handset in the cradle and stared at it for a long second, then took a breath and accepted the call on my cell just before it went to voicemail. "Earl. How you doing, old man?"

The voice on the other end sounded far off somehow. "Luke?"

"Aunt Margie? Is that you?" I sat up straighter.

I heard a sniff. "Earl's asking for you. He hasn't got long. Best come soon."

The call ended as quickly as it had come. A silence far louder than the words that had preceded it.

I lowered the phone and set it next to my landline. Two phones for two separate methods of devastation.

My cat stared at me from the floor, golden eyes questioning.

It wasn't even noon yet and my day was already shot to hell.

I looked out the window at the old Mallard. Then I blew the air out of my cheeks and addressed the cat. "Earl's dying."

The cat meowed and rubbed her whiskers on the leg of the desk. She didn't give a shit about anyone named Earl.

But I did.

And all the people I cared about kept leaving me.

THREE
INITIAL CONTACT

REESE WINTER HANDED me a spare quart of oil to stick in
the back of the Cessna 185. "How long do you think you'll be
over there?"

"Hard to say." I checked my watch. It was early afternoon
now. I'd given Reese the key to my Jeep in case she needed to use
it. "I hope to be back tonight, but I'll keep you posted. I won't
leave you in the lurch long."

She'd already replaced the plane's right navigation light lens
I'd smashed with the pine tree branch this morning. I asked a lot
of Reese. But her covering my ass in a hard time was nothing
new. We'd both said goodbyes to too many people. I'd never had
to explain obligations around death to her.

"Take whatever time you need. You sure you don't want me
to keep Murphy?"

My dog sat in the back seat of the Cessna panting happily in
expectation of the flight. As much as he loved spending time with
her, I knew which way he was voting.

"It's a dog-friendly scene over there," I said. "He'll fit in."

The Florida summer heat stuck my shirt to my back and

Reese was standing in the sun, so I left it at that and climbed into the 185. I got buckled but left the door open. "Our luck is going to turn around soon. I can feel it."

"We're already lucky," Reese said. "You're still flying, aren't you?"

"True. Can't complain about that." I gave her a thumbs up and she waved to Murphy before walking back toward Hangar 4.

I watched her go, my hand on the ignition switch, taking in the sight of my best friend and best mechanic walking into the place that meant far more than any building I'd ever known. It was a city-owned hangar that I merely leased, but the Archangel Aviation sign that hung on the back wall was a badge. The idea that it would ever have to come down to make way for a more profitable business hardened my resolve.

Not on my watch.

I cranked the engine on the 185 and it came to life with a satisfying rumble. I adjusted the throttle and watched the oil pressure gauge, then released the brakes and tapped them again for a quick test. Then I was on the roll. Reese was right. Being behind the controls of a machine like this every day was all the luck I needed.

Ground control instructed me to taxi to Runway 7, so I did my run-up checks on Taxiway Alpha and called the tower. The controller cleared me for takeoff and I eased the Cessna 185 onto the runway in a smooth turn. A last wiggle of the rudder pedals got the plane's nose and tail in alignment, and I pressed forward on the throttle. The rumble of the Continental IO-550 engine turned to a roar as all six cylinders sucked in 100 octane fuel at nearly 2700 RPM. The engine gauges looked good, all temps and pressures in the green.

As the speed built, I pressed on the yoke and the tail of the 185 came up. The torque and power of the engine tried to turn me left like always, but some steady right rudder and a bit of aileron pressure straightened that out. Now I was driving down the runway on two wheels in a thunder of thrust and horsepower. The airspeed looked good, so I rotated, easing back on the yoke and breaking the runway's grip on the big bush tires.

We were airborne.

Murphy gave a happy bark from the back.

"Me too, buddy," I said, relishing the feeling. I tapped the brakes to get the main wheels to stop spinning and enjoyed the climb past the control tower and over the blue-green water of Tampa Bay. Water stretched out across my windscreen for miles. I rocked my wings in a quick salute to the tower, then turned on-course to the east, adjusting my manifold pressure for the climb.

Tampa ATC controlled airspace above twelve hundred feet, so I kept the plane at a thousand feet as I crossed the bay. Sailboats dotted the water, a regatta of small craft zigzagging through mild waves. The skyline of Saint Petersburg receded behind me and I passed south of MacDill Air Force Base, its long runway quiet for the moment, but with a contingent of KC-135s easily visible on the ramp.

The stacks of the power plant loomed to the northeast and the city of Tampa lay sprawled at the top of the bay, but my heading kept me nosed toward the eastern horizon. A herd of manatees bobbing amid the seagrass was the last bit of bay scenery to take in before I was back over land, heading toward Florida's interior. Once Interstate 75 vanished beneath my wings, I crossed into farmland.

Out from beneath the focus of Tampa's ATC, I was free to climb, but I stayed low anyway, buzzing over citrus groves and strawberry fields. Huge agricultural sprinklers worked to irrigate the land. Cattle meandered across pastureland and chewed at fresh grass sprouted from the recent summer thunderstorms.

Today's weather threatened to the south and north, a couple of thunderheads building as distant dark cells, but nothing to deter me from my current course. I flew on through sunshine and only mild thermals, working my way ever east.

The GPS in the plane showed several airports on the moving map ahead, but my destination didn't appear.

The property belonging to Earl and Margery Warner was a ranch that had diminished in size over the years, but the land still hosted a long, straight section of dirt road carefully cleared and tended with a tattered orange windsock at one end.

The strip wasn't officially registered as a private airport because Earl was of the opinion that what the FAA didn't know wouldn't hurt them.

I made a wide turn around the field, judging the wind and taking in the sight of the old farmhouse. A pair of dusty pickup trucks sat in the drive, one of which bore a law enforcement logo.

I pulled the throttle back and reduced power, then dipped left and dropped into a spiraling turn for the dirt runway.

The 185 could be heavy on the controls. Its oversized engine and sturdy frame made it rugged but not sporty. It still felt good coming down on final approach, and when the main wheels impacted the dirt, they rolled with a satisfying crunching noise till the tailwheel touched down and I slowed to a taxi speed.

Murphy was standing in the back seat now, tail wagging, and he snuck a quick lick to the side of my face when I pivoted to check on him.

"Almost there, buddy," I said, wiping my cheek. "You'll have some new turf to pee on shortly."

Margery's bruiser of a dog, Brisco, came bolting out the unlatched screen door and tore across the yard to meet us. I turned the 185 off the road and up the driveway, mindful of the dog. The big mutt had enough sense to stay well clear of the airplane while it was running, but it stood nearby and barked. When I turned into the grass of the yard and shut down, Murphy whined and nudged the door with his snout.

"Fine. Go say hi." I popped the door open, and the dog launched like a missile. I pulled my headset off and watched as the two dogs met in the grass. Hackles went up, and they froze, stiff-legged in front of each other for a long second, but then Murphy's wagging tail gave away his enthusiasm, and they set to the business of sniffing each other and goofing off. By the time I got out of the plane, they were tearing circles around the yard.

The door swung open again on the front porch and a figure appeared. A tall, formidable woman in a sheriff's department uniform. When she stepped into the afternoon sun, I recognized her lean lined face as that of Earl's younger sister, Gail. She appraised me from the steps and offered a tilt of her chin. She held a green glass bottle of beer in one hand. Behind her a younger man appeared, this one spindly as a cowpoke. He wandered to the rail beside Gail, moving with a slight limp, and a grave expression on his face. Technically, his name was Earl Warner Junior but all his life I'd never heard him called anything but EJ. He likewise gave me a nod.

I stopped in the yard ten yards from the porch and the three of us stared at each other in silence.

Gail finally spoke. "All the family's black sheep back together at once." She took a swig of her beer. "God help us."

FOUR

READBACK INSTRUCTIONS

"NICE TRUCK," I said, nodding toward the Ford.

"Property of Monroe County," Gail replied. "But I get to drive it till they come take it back." She pointed the neck of her beer bottle toward the 185. "That yours?"

"Borrowed it from a customer."

"Got any of your own left?" EJ asked. His voice had gained a raspy quality to it like he'd marked each of the days since I'd last seen him with a pack of cigarettes.

"I've got an insurance claim for a 206 I sank in the Gulf of Mexico recently. Does that count?"

"Heard a rumor you had your dad's old Mallard back," Gail said.

I shrugged. "Sort of. Pending some registration issues. The FAA is giving me grief about it."

"Guess we're a regular Who's Who of success stories, huh?" Gail mused.

"You aren't retiring from the sheriff's department loaded with wealth and glory?"

Gail snorted. "If I wanted to make a fortune, I chose the wrong side of the law."

"How's Earl?" I asked.

Her jaw clenched.

"Fuck that cancer," EJ said.

I didn't have any argument to that.

"Heard he asked to see me."

Gail moved aside on the porch and I ascended the steps. She was nearly my height. Taller than EJ. Maybe it was the badge, but I'd forgotten how intimidating she could be. She held the screen door open for me.

Murphy was behaving himself. He and Brisco lay panting happily in the grass beside a hole one of them had dug and they seemed about as pleased with themselves as dogs knew how to be, so I followed EJ through the screen door.

It was an old farmhouse with even older smells. Someone had burned a pot of coffee recently so that scent had layered itself over the residue of old nicotine and a long history of baked goods. The furniture had lasted thirty years—enough for several generations of dogs to come and go and imprint their shapes in the couch cushions.

Margery had always kept the place tidy despite the dogs and kids that had run rampant through the house. But now the home sat in a vague state of neglect. An antiseptic smell lingered in the air. Age. Decay. The sour potpourri of illness. Margery descended the stairs at the back of the sitting room and took us all in from the landing. She managed a tight-lipped smile, but it never reached her eyes.

She made it to the ground floor and trundled toward me. My adoptive aunt had lost weight since I'd seen her last. She'd never been slim, a matron of the Wagner family with broad hips who'd acquired a grandmotherly pear-shape in her forties. But now her housedress hung looser about her, her shoulders slumped forward by degrees. Her arms opened and I gave her a squeeze, noting the bones of her shoulder blades protruding.

"How're you holding up?" I asked.

"Pitifully, no doubt. But EJ And Gail came in yesterday to be here with us and Kat got to talk to Earl on the phone last night. Said her goodbyes. She'd have been here too, but Earl talked her out of it. Wanted her to finish her work on the ship."

Earl and Margery's daughter, Katherine, did marine science aboard a research vessel someplace out west. California maybe. I nodded and let her break loose from my hold on her. She went to Gail and gave her a hug next. "I so appreciate all your faces around. Only thing better would be if the boys were here."

"I'll get 'em here for the service," EJ replied. He had two sons I knew of from a failed marriage. I guessed the boys must be teens by now.

The mention of a service seemed to jar Margery. The inevitability of it. Her eyelid twitched. "Yes. I hope you will."

If EJ noticed her reaction, it didn't show on his face.

"You can head up there," she said to me, patting my arm. "He's been asking for you." She regarded the stairs as one would a mountain. A mountain she must have climbed innumerable times in the preceding weeks.

"I'll go up with you," EJ offered, and led the way. The slight limp gave away his one artificial limb from a farm accident in his youth, but it didn't slow him down much.

The stairway ascended to a hall with a carpet runner and several bedrooms, the first of which on the left was Earl's. EJ paused in the hall before opening the door and addressed me. "He ain't got much left."

"I won't tax him."

EJ opened the door.

I'd come to see Earl only a matter of weeks before, but even in that time he'd shrunk. The man in the adjustable hospital bed wasn't much more than a skeleton now, his hair thin. Margery had combed it, and his face was shaved and clean. He had on a plaid cowboy shirt that was visible above the bedclothes. Dressed to go somewhere. Somewhere better maybe.

His eyes were sunken when they turned toward me but they brightened in recognition as I approached.

"Luke. Good. I needed you to come." His voice came with a rasp of effort, but clearly audible.

"Wouldn't miss an excuse to see you," I said.

"I'm waiting for my departure clearance."

"You ready?" I reached for his hand and gave his bony fingers a gentle squeeze.

"Almost. Tell EJ to shut the door."

I turned to find Earl's son still lingering in the doorway. EJ heard the comment though, and after a nod to me, stepped back into the hall. The door eased closed behind him.

"That's good," Earl said. "You and I need to talk in private."

"What can I do for you?"

"You can carry on a job."

I nodded slowly, but didn't follow his logic yet.

"When your daddy went away, he asked me to keep something for him till he got out."

"Saw a bunch of his old junk you had in the barn in boxes."

"This is different. He trusted me with a secret. One I've kept for him for nearly twenty years."

I narrowed my eyes. "If it's a secret of Frank's, I doubt I'm the one he'd want hearing it."

"There's no one else." He took a long inhale. "Your brother's in the wind. No way to reach him. Your daddy's getting out. Told me it was soon, and I sure wanted to see him one last time, but I don't think I'm going to make it. I left a message for him, letting him know I was on my way out. But they record all his calls. Couldn't tell him much if I wanted to."

"Tell him what?"

"Where I put . . . his treasure."

I shook my head. "Don't tell me Frank dragged you into one of his nonsensical tall tales."

"This wasn't nonsense." Earl reached for a framed photo on the bedside table. It was one I'd seen many times. Earl and Frank, arms over each other's shoulders, standing in front of *Tropic Angel* on a lakeshore. "We had the best times together, me and your dad. You remember Costa Rica? Best memories of my life, my family and yours together. Didn't surprise me he had something put away that the feds couldn't find. Showed up here that night after the accident. He asked me to keep it safe for him while he was gone. To hide it someplace so even he wouldn't know where it was while they had him inside. He didn't know what they might do to him in there to get it out of him."

"Drug money?"

"No. Not drug money. It was his. His and your mama's. Called it their retirement fund."

"Any money he made was ill-gotten gains. All of it illegal. If the government was supposed to seize it, then they probably ought to. I don't want to be dragged into it."

"I wouldn't ask you to do this if it wasn't important." He stared me down. "Your daddy mightn't have been a perfect father but he was my best friend. And when I told him I'd take his secrets to the grave, I meant it. A man is only as good as his word. But I'm one foot in that grave now. And I never asked anything of you. Far as I'm concerned, it was my duty to do what I did to see you had a roof over your head that year after your momma died and Frank went away. So don't think I'm asking this of you as repayment. You don't owe it to me. But I'm askin' you to do it.

Askin' man to man. So I can go, and know the thing I promised my friend will get done."

I hung my head and exhaled. But then I reached out and retook his hand.

When I met his eye again, he nodded. "Good. Now I'm gonna tell you how to find it."

FIVE
CLEARED FOR DEPARTURE

I PICKED the photo of Earl and Frank off Earl's lap and set it back on the nightstand. Then I stood at the bedside looking down at the man who'd only ever been generous to me. He seemed at peace now, eyes closed, resting after our conversation. I could tell it had exhausted him, but now he appeared unburdened. Even a hint of a smile on his face.

I rarely envy the dying. But there is something to be said for reaching the end of a journey. He'd done his duty to his kids and more. Seen them off on their way and had plenty of adventures of his own in the meantime. Standing there looking down at him, I couldn't help but recall Earl in his vital years—all the way back to when I was a kid, splashing with him in the waves in Costa Rica. Him chasing my brother and me down the beach in fits of laughter. Digging among the rocks and giving the sea creatures we found ridiculous names.

Then our times in the back of his Super Decathlon. Earl had been the first to show me what an aircraft could truly be capable of. He'd hang the plane from its prop with the rudder deflected and fly it sideways while facing almost straight up. Tail slides and

Cuban eights, outside loops and hammerhead turns. He could do it all. And I'd watched and admired every maneuver. There was no feeling like it.

Born into a family of pilots, it was hard to pinpoint the exact origin of my love for aviation or its usefulness, but Earl had been the man to show me that it could also be an expression of unadulterated joy. The way he'd whoop into the headset mic at the completion of a particularly satisfying stunt never failed to put a smile on my face.

"Hope the skies are blue where you're headed, Earl," I said.

I doubted any conscious part of him heard me, but his closed eyelids moved some. Maybe he was seeing his way onward.

Beside Earl's prone hand on the bedsheets was the fine-tipped purple Sharpie he'd had me fish out of the drawer in the nightstand.

"That's your key," he'd said. "To the secret." He'd given one last sly grin. "X marks the spot."

I tucked the Sharpie into my pocket. The door to the hall had come ajar again so I slipped out silently. I met EJ coming down the hall from the bathroom.

"All done in there?" he asked. "About time he took his meds."

"Pretty sure he's asleep."

"He say what he needed to?" EJ hitched his thumbs in his pants pockets.

"For what it's worth."

"Guess I best check on him." EJ eased past me and entered Earl's room, leaving me to find my own way down the stairs.

Gail had a pot of coffee brewing and offered me a cup when I reached the kitchen. We managed through a bit of small talk about planes and her law enforcement job down in the Keys, while Margery got out the sugar packets and creamer.

"You and Earl mend fences?" I asked Gail. "Seem to remember you two having a fractious relationship."

"He had a few things he wanted to say," Gail replied. "Dying men often do."

"There's no need to dredge up the past here," Margery interjected. "Water long under the bridge."

"Ever the peacemaker, huh, Marge?" Gail said. "Luke's a grown man now. Able to see our family with all its warts." She filled my coffee cup for me.

"Not my place to pry," I said. "Was just curious."

"My brother and I have had our differences over the years," Gail said. "But we were close when we were younger, and being his little sister still counts for something—disapproved of or not."

"Family is family," Margery said. "We should leave it at that."

I took that as my cue to keep the conversation on lighter topics.

But my coffee cup was still half full when EJ called downstairs.

"Mama, he ain't breathing right."

Our contingent from the kitchen filed back up to Earl's bedroom, me at the rear, and when I reached the door, I could make out the sound EJ had yelled down about.

Earl's breaths were fewer and farther apart, long pauses followed by open-mouthed gasps. Margery took a seat next to him and squeezed his hand. Gail did the same on the far side of the bed. EJ stood with his hand on his mother's shoulder while I lingered near the doorway.

Margery cried but her grip on her husband's hand didn't waver. She talked him out, murmuring her love, and that it was okay. He could go if he needed to.

Gail's eyes glistened but she kept her tears in check. She stayed at her brother's side and used a handkerchief a few times to wipe her nose. It took about fifteen minutes. Each pause between Earl's breaths getting longer. Finally, after one last gasp, his chest stopped moving altogether.

Margery dipped her head and pressed her face to Earl's side, muffling the low keening cry that escaped from her throat. EJ rubbed circles on his mother's back. Gail said, "He's gone."

I eased out of the room and gently closed the door behind me, leaving them to their grief.

SIX

ARRIVALS

I SAT AWHILE on the front porch steps throwing a stick for the dogs. The pair fought over it and played a game of tug-o-war, blissfully unaware of tragedy.

After a few minutes, I got up and walked to the barn, knowing what I'd find.

The rollers on the barn door squeaked when I opened it, motes of straw dust swirling in the beam of daylight I'd introduced. The smell brought back memories of preflighting the Super Decathlon, my teenage self wiping dust from the stabilizer and leading edges, the anticipation of flight speeding my heart rate.

The space the Super Decathlon had occupied was vacant now, but the wooden barn floor still had an oil stain where the engine had leaked on it over the years.

The pile of my father's belongings sat in the horse stall where I'd last seen them—a stack of dry-rotting Rubbermaid bins and a few mildewed cardboard boxes. I'd poked through them on my last visit, wondering what could possibly be of value in the accumulated junk.

Now I knew.

I pulled lids off containers and rummaged around with purpose this time, thumbing through the books and tossing aside old headsets and yellowed plastic chart plotters. In a matter of five minutes, I had the items I'd been told to acquire: a Miami sectional chart, a yellowed airport facilities directory of the southeast, and a metal kneeboard. All were innocuous items any pilot over a certain age might have lying around. Modern pilots had all but forsaken these in favor of iPads or other phone-based apps, and with good reason, but the old ways did come in handy when your tablet's battery died.

The cache I'd acquired was nothing of any value. The chart was long expired, the facilities directory renamed and superseded by newer editions, and the metal kneeboard had three holes drilled into it, making it a hazard for a pilot trying to write a note. A sharp pencil tip might puncture the paper and plunge into your thigh mid-flight. But thanks to Earl I knew the holes would serve a purpose.

The silver kneeboard was standard size, six and half inches wide and about nine and a half high, with bits of common aeronautical information like light signal meanings printed on it. The oddly drilled holes in the board were about an eighth of an inch in diameter, probably done with a #30 drill bit.

Unfolding the sectional chart, I scanned both sides, finally locating the purple dots Earl had made down in the Florida Keys. One dot sat on Key West. The second marked Marathon. The two airports were common enough destinations for general aviation airports. But when I held the kneeboard over the chart and oriented it, two of the holes lined up with the purple dots. The third hole showed a tiny spot of land. An island.

I stared at the island a long moment, then folded the chart back up and clipped it to the kneeboard.

I was about to dive into the old facilities directory when a cacophony of barking interrupted me. Brisco was going nuts about something, and it sounded like Murphy had joined in.

I pocketed the facilities directory, carried the kneeboard, and headed back outside to see what the fuss was about.

A car was coming down the long drive from the street, an old model Chevy sedan that bounced its way through the ruts and finally turned up the driveway. The guy in the driver's seat was big. No one I knew. Once parked, he sat there talking to someone in the passenger seat, but the glare on the windshield obscured my view.

Murphy trotted closer to investigate while Brisco kept up a steady barking at the driver's side door. Finally the passenger door opened and a man climbed out. His once shaggy head of hair was now grey and cropped short. The years behind bars had leaned him and disposed of his tan, but standing there in the open daylight, there could be no question.

It was Frank Angel.

My father.

He gave Murphy a brief pat on the head before coming around to face Brisco on the far side of the car. The sturdy dog kept its distance, out of breath, but still punctuating the air with barks from deep in its diaphragm every few seconds. Frank studied the Cessna 185 in the yard, then walked up the porch steps and knocked at the screen door. The door swung open and he was admitted.

He hadn't seen me.

I let out a breath I hadn't realized I was holding. My sunglasses hung at the neck of my shirt and when I went to slip them on, I found my hand was trembling.

"Knock that shit off."

Admonishing my traitorous appendage seemed to do the

trick. My hand steadied and I finished donning my sunglasses. Then I made for my plane.

Around the time I reached the near wing of the Cessna, the driver of the Chevy got out. He wore black jeans and a baggy gray tee-shirt, with white-and-blue high-top sneakers. From the back of the car emerged a looker of a woman with dark hair wearing not enough of a dress.

The pair appraised Murphy and the still-barking Brisco cautiously, not making a move toward the house yet.

"Murph!" I shouted. "Here!" My dog obeyed immediately, sprinting to me happily with his tongue hanging out. Brisco seemed satisfied he'd done his duty by the trespassers and came plodding along toward me too.

The big muscled guy in the high-tops shouted across the yard. "Who are you?"

"Nobody," I called back. I opened the door to the 185 and tucked the sectional chart, kneeboard, and old facilities directory into the passenger-side seat pocket. I looked over the interior of the plane, making sure nothing was out of place, then headed for the engine cowling.

"Oh wow, you're Frank's boy, aren't you?" the woman said. "You look like him."

"You guys got here too late," I said. "Earl passed about an hour ago."

The woman turned and smacked the big guy in the shoulder. "See, Deacon. I told you we shouldn't have stopped so many times on the way down here. Now Frank didn't get to see his friend in time."

"I look like I give a shit?"

She screwed up her face and scowled at him.

"Go up there and see if these people have a beer for us or something," he ordered, and gave her a shove.

The woman teetered once in her heels on the uneven surface, but then found surer footing on the steps and clomped up them. She wagged a warning finger at the guy as she climbed. "You break my new Christian Louboutin's I'm gonna jam a heel in your eye."

The guy she'd called Deacon scoffed. "Don't pretend that knockoff K-mart shit's fooling anybody." He then went back to staring at me. "Why'd I never hear about you coming to see Frank? He was in a long time and I known him most of it."

"Good. Then you can ask him." I went back to preflighting the engine. The oil level looked fine so I wiped the dipstick off with a rag and screwed the cap back tight.

"Guess you never been inside. Never known how much it matters to have your family visit."

I turned and squared up with him. "You done whining about Frank now, or you need to run your mouth some more?"

He narrowed his eyes.

We were roughly the same height, but he had some heft to him. He clenched his jaw while he sized me up.

"Why don't you two just whip your dicks out already?" the woman on the porch said. "Need me to get you a ruler?"

The screen door finally opened and Gail Wagner took in the scene. The woman who'd arrived with Deacon took a step backward. Even in her heels she had to look up to Gail. Gail addressed me first. "Margie wants to talk to you before you take off." She eyed the other two cautiously, but then held the door open for them also.

"I'm Lyla," the woman said with a smile, and offered her hand. Gail merely grunted in reply.

I watched the two newcomers file inside and rested my fists on my hips.

Gail waited.

Earl's words ran through my head. "You don't owe it to me. I'm askin' man to man."

I sighed.

He was wrong. I did owe him. So I climbed the steps and went back inside.

SEVEN

EXCESS BAGGAGE

SIX PEOPLE WAS a lot of bodies to fit in Margery and Earl's living room. Walking in as the seventh felt like trying to squeeze an extra egg into an already full carton. Margery was seated, as was Lyla-the-Looker in her non-farm attire. She perched straight-backed on the edge of her armchair, chest out, hands in her lap and wearing a polite smile, a contrast to Deacon who was lounging on the sofa with an arm up along the top of the cushions. He regarded Gail in her sheriff's department uniform coolly, then licked his thumb and wiped a smudge off one of his sneakers. The Wagners all stood, conspicuously leaving Earl's favorite recliner vacant.

Frank Angel also stood when I entered the circle. He seemed unsure if he should come closer.

"Been a long time, son."

"Not long enough."

His blue eyes blinked and a muscle in his jaw twitched. But that was it. We held each other's gaze in silence.

"Luke, your father's my guest, same as you are. Let's keep it civil," Margery said.

I shrugged. "Of course. Doesn't bother me. I'm leaving in a few minutes anyway."

Margery acted like she didn't hear me. "Earl would have loved seeing you both under our roof again. Like old times." She turned to the newcomers. "Their family and ours go back a long way."

Lyla nodded politely. Deacon yawned.

"Where will you be staying now, Frank?" Margery asked. Her eyes flitted to me again.

"I'll figure something out," he said, though he was staring at Gail as he said it. "They give you a referral to a halfway house once you're out. That's an option."

"First Frank's coming on a road trip with us," the bruiser on the couch interjected. "Me and Lyla gonna take him on a tour of all his old favorite spots. Ain't that right, Frank?"

"Something like that," Frank replied.

EJ had been quiet till now, but he piped up with a "Where you headed, Frank? Down south, maybe?"

But Frank didn't meet his eye. His gaze seemed unfocused, thoughts elsewhere. He turned to Margery. "I apologize again for not getting here quicker—in time to see Earl. I tried all I could."

Margery offered a sad smile. "Earl always knew where your heart was, Frank. He never doubted your friendship for a moment. Took it with him."

And then Frank did something I hadn't seen since I was a kid. He closed his eyes and pinched the bridge of his nose. When he opened his eyes again, a tear fell down his cheek. He wiped the tear away. "I apologize. First day out and it's been . . ." He trailed off and tried to pull himself together. "Might I use your restroom for a minute?"

"You take all the time you need, Frank. God knows this is a day for tears. You remember where it is?"

Frank nodded, avoiding looking my way, and moved slowly into the hall that led to the west side of the house.

Margery turned her attention to me. "A father is still a father, Luke. And he's served his time. My Earl was no saint, nor me, but he and I always agreed that if you want peace in a family, you've got to make it."

All eyes in the room were on me.

I hadn't come for a lecture.

"Aunt Margie, I'm grateful you called and gave me a chance to say goodbye to Earl. But this is a family affair. I'm going to leave you and yours to grieve in your own way. And if there's anything I can do to help with a service or memorial or whatever you decide to do, I'll be available."

"And your daddy?" Margery asked.

"Deacon and Miss Lyla here sound like they've got grand road trip plans for him. Who am I to interfere?"

Deacon stared languidly from the couch and Lyla gave another of her polite smiles. When I turned to the door, it was Gail who had the sharpest look for me. Maybe she thought I ought to be a better mourner. She could think what she wanted. EJ lifted his chin as I walked past him, but that was all the reaction he managed. But he was the one who followed me out the screen door to the porch.

When the door was shut behind us, he finally spoke up. "You ever seen someone die before, Luke?"

"A few times."

"Is it always like that? With the gasping and the hard breathing?"

"Not always, but that's a pretty normal way to go. I doubt your dad felt it, if that's what you're worried about. He was already checked out. His body was just a few minutes behind."

"What was it Dad wanted you for? Must have been something important if he only held out till he told it to you."

"Nothing that important. But I appreciated the chance to say goodbye. Take care of yourself, EJ. I know Aunt Margie is relying on you now more than ever." I rested a hand on his shoulder, then jerked my head toward the dogs who were laying in the sun on the sparse lawn baking like potatoes. "Make sure you let Brisco see Earl at least once before the undertaker comes. A dog should know when his master has passed. He'll understand once he gets in the room."

EJ nodded.

There wasn't anything else to say, so I strode through the afternoon sun to the Cessna 185, Murphy on my heels. I had to boost him up into the back seat with a sheep carry method, but once there he seemed happy enough, immediately setting to sniffing the seat crack.

I climbed into the pilot seat and had the engine cranked over and rumbling in a matter of a minute. While I was checking the instruments and monitoring the engine's rising oil pressure, Deacon emerged from the house, looked around the porch, then walked out into the yard to watch my slow roll. His eyes didn't linger on the plane long. After a brief scan of me and Murphy and the cars in the driveway, he turned and stalked across the yard toward the barn. He didn't look happy.

I took the 185 down the slight hill of the driveway and onto the road. It was a short runway in either direction, but with the added horsepower of the larger cylinders, I knew the plane had the guts I needed. Even so, when I spun the tail around and got moving on the runway, it took several seconds longer than usual before the tail came up. I had to re-trim the elevator and wait longer than was comfortable, but finally the 185's tires were free of the earth. I held the plane low, capitalizing on the ground effect like a pelican over waves, then pulled up to clear the trees at the end of the road.

Margery and Earl's property receded out my left rear

window as I made my turn west toward St. Pete. I climbed to two hundred feet, reset the flaps and trimmed for a three hundred feet per minute climb before pulling one earphone of my headset away from my ear and shouting over the engine noise.

"You can come out now, Frank. I know you're back there!"

Murphy had his head resting on the seat back and when Frank's face appeared above the edge, the dog licked him in the eyebrow.

"Didn't want to pop out and startle you on takeoff. Could've scared you into stalling it."

"You don't think I know what a tail-heavy center of gravity feels like? Get out of the baggage compartment already so I can get this thing level."

He rose up and threw a leg over the rear seat, squeezing past Murphy. "You want me up there with you?"

"Right there is fine. That way I don't have to look at you." I adjusted the elevator trim again for the weight shift and went back to scanning outside for other aircraft.

Frank found a headset in the back seat and put it on so he could talk over the intercom.

"I had to pry myself loose from those two barnacles, and you were the first flight out. Figured you wouldn't mind if I tagged along."

"I *do* mind. But it's too hard to throw you out of the plane and fly at the same time, so you can sit back there and be quiet."

"Good. You don't plan to take me back to Earl's, do you?"

"You're that scared of that guy?"

"Scared? Hell no. He's slowing me down."

"One of your prison buddies, I take it?" I leveled the plane off for cruise flight and aimed toward Tampa Bay in the distance.

"Deacon has the idea I owe him protection money from inside. Thinks he can leach me now that I'm out."

"Looked none-too-pleased that you dipped on him. Won't be long till he puts together where you went."

"Might take him a while. You can sell tickets to an airshow with the amount of things that go over that man's head."

"And that sex kitten he showed up with?"

"Lyla. Yeah, she's a wildcard. With harder edges than she lets on. But . . . they don't have a plane."

"Don't worry. As soon as we land, you won't either."

"Come on, son. I could use your help. Why do you think I came straight to see you when I got out?"

"You went straight to see Earl. And I know why."

"Of course. A dying man gets some priority. Can you fault me for that?"

"You expect me to believe your friendship with Earl was your driving motivation? I saw that move you pulled on Margery. The squeezing out a fake tear nonsense just so you could get away."

"Hey, I'm plenty broken up about Earl passing."

"But more broken up that you missed your chance with him."

"What are you talking about?"

"He *told* me. About the buried treasure mission you sent him on. Hide your 'retirement fund' so even you didn't know where to get at it?"

"He told you that?"

"What did you think? Did you expect Landon was going to show up when they called? He's too much like you—off making his own bad decisions. So I'm the one who gets stuck with your messes. Like always."

"Where'd he say he put it?"

"He wasn't that specific. But he told me how to figure it out."

Frank was quiet for a while in the back, his hand working through Murphy's fur. "I sure missed having a dog. Keeping an animal around is good for your soul. Helps you see things clearer."

Murphy's tongue was hanging out and he panted happily at the compliment.

"Don't think you're getting what you want from me just by being nice to my dog."

"If you don't want to help me, that's fine. I'll figure things out on my own. Hell, just getting to be up in the sky like this again is all I needed. After so many years in that hellhole, you have no idea how good this view looks. When we get back to St. Pete, I'll leave you alone. I know there's no reason you need me around. I'll jet out and you won't even have to see me, if that's what you really want."

I kept my eyes forward, not giving him the satisfaction of a reply. His comments reeked of a guilt trip and I wasn't about to fall for it.

The thrumming of the six-cylinder engine droned on, and we flew with nothing but the occasional radio chatter from ATC on the airwaves.

I had a feeling Frank was waiting for a reaction, but I wouldn't give him one.

Out the window, Saint Petersburg's downtown skyline loomed on the far side of the bay. Frank's eyes were on the airport as we crossed over the shallow water and entered the downwind approach for Runway 7.

When I was midfield, I looked back again. He was sitting straight, posture tense, focused on the ramp in front of Hangar 4.

He adjusted his microphone to his mouth again. "Don't tell me . . . You've really got it here?"

He'd seen it. *Tropic Angel.*

The grin spread on his face. "That's my plane!"

And just like that, I knew there was no way I was getting rid of Frank Angel.

EIGHT

THE BUOYS

I SPUN the Cessna 185 around in front of my hangar and cut the engine. Frank was out of the plane faster than I'd seen any man his age move. But when he hit the tarmac, his walk slowed, easing toward the big Grumman seaplane like she was a horse he might spook.

His figure beside the antique aircraft was a sudden reflection from decades past and left me vaguely unmoored, as though someone had dug up a time capsule of my dustiest memories and dumped them onto the ramp in front of my hangar.

I hadn't been prepared to feel any way in particular about him being out, but now that he was here in reality and the memories were surfacing, I wanted to shovel everything back in the hole. A pit in my stomach told me that wasn't going to happen.

Frank Angel.

He stared at the old airplane—not touching—just absorbing it.

It was a lot of plane, magnificent in its shape and design. It bore a legacy no one knew better than the man whose name was still on the old registration papers in the logs. The man who finally stretched out and rested his hand on the hull.

This was going to be a problem.

I climbed out of the 185.

Murphy leapt to the ground behind me and trotted happily over to the neighboring fence, checking his usual pee-mail inboxes and leaving responses.

My hangar door was closed, my crew gone home for the night. I checked my watch. Half past seven. Murphy would be getting hungry.

And what the hell was I going to do about my newly homeless father and the treasure hunt he'd landed me in?

I walked over to the Mallard. Frank had moved around to the left engine nacelle and was inspecting the dirty cowl flaps.

"This thing always did love to drip oil. Marking its territory." He ran a hand over the landing gear strut. "I still can't believe Landon got it out of that jungle."

"*I'm* the one who flew it home—at significant personal expense."

"You don't operate a Grumman flying boat to get rich. Everything on them is an expense."

"This plane needs to be on my charter certificate if it's going to earn its keep."

"She'll get you passengers, that's for sure. They'll come for the nostalgia, then complain about the lack of baggage space. You hire a hot enough stewardess, that will fix most of the complaints."

"We call them flight attendants now. And passengers are used to minimal bags. It's the lack of wi-fi they gripe about."

"Rumor is, that's all anyone does anymore. Look at their phones?"

"They're a blessing and a curse."

"You leave a man behind bars nearly twenty years, he comes

out a dinosaur. But a plane like this? One that's been around longer than any of us? This levels the scales. Makes me feel like maybe there's still a place for fossils like me to be appreciated."

My dog came over and nudged my hand.

"I've got to tie the 185 down, then get Murphy home and fed. What's your plan here?"

"Besides ogling this beauty?" Frank raised his eyes toward the western sky and pointed. "The gulf's still that way. Sun still sets. I figure I'll try to make it out to the beach to catch it going down. I've got some gate money and I'm sure there's a cab I can flag down somewhere."

"You don't have a phone to call one."

"Then I'll find a phone booth."

I sighed. "No. You won't." I pointed to the parking lot. "That old Jeep over there is mine. Get in and I'll give you a lift to Gulf Boulevard and leave you somewhere."

"Don't put yourself out."

"You're lucky Murphy likes sunsets too."

Frank patted the hull of *Tropic Angel,* then wandered toward the parking lot as directed. I took the headsets from the plane, then pulled the sectional chart and facilities directory from the pocket of the passenger seat.

I considered taking them with me, simply giving them to Frank and just being done with the whole thing. But I tucked the items under the rear seat and locked the cabin doors.

Frank had waited nearly twenty years for his retirement party. He could wait a little longer.

Once I had the plane tied down, I met my father at the Jeep and climbed in. Murphy sat in the back, his eyes bright and eager. The Jeep fired up with a burbling rumble.

On the way up First Street, Frank stared at the skyline and whistled.

I knew what he was thinking. Saint Petersburg looked

nothing like it had the last time he'd seen it. At least a dozen high rises had sprouted up and now cast long shadows.

"I don't recognize any of these bars," Frank said as we cruised Central Avenue.

"Mastry's is still there." I pointed.

"It better be," Frank said. "Babe Ruth drank there."

"You and The Babe good friends, were you?"

"I drank with plenty of old salts every bit as cool."

"Bet they drink somewhere else now."

"You have anyplace at the beach you can take me that I'll remember?"

"The Undertow is still around."

"Yeah, that will work." He lounged in the passenger seat and took in the ever-evolving city as I switched to First Avenue North and continued west into the sun.

It took twenty minutes of driving, but finally we made our way down Gulf Boulevard and pulled into the sandy lot of The Undertow. The place managed a locals-only dive bar vibe despite being savvy enough to attract the tourists. The physical bar itself had one of the most unique features: a built-in lazy river for rubber ducks that drinkers could use to float messages to each other or conduct duck races to see who bought the next round. Bartenders wore bikinis and looked good in them, and for fifty dollars they'd even hang upside down from a rail on the ceiling like some half-naked angel, and pour a shot straight into your mouth from on high.

Frank took one look at the scene and smiled. "Yeah, this is all right."

"Is getting drinks out here going to violate the terms of your parole?"

"You already looking for ways to send me back?"

"Will it take two drinks or five? Does it need to be liquor or can I shitcan you with a beer? I'm fuzzy on the terms."

"I'm not on parole. I did my full bit. So make mine a margarita. I'm going out to the beach."

He strode off through the thatched cabanas and disappeared.

A few of the bikini-clad bartenders cooed over Murphy, scratching his chest with their fingernails and telling him what a good boy he was. He was in heaven. One girl even went into the kitchen to fetch him a snack.

By the time I got a Modelo with a lime in it for myself and Frank's margarita, a cook came out of the kitchen with a bowl of rice and some grilled chicken strips and set it in front of Murphy. My dog appeared to be in good hands, so I left him there to enjoy himself and went to look for Frank.

I found him out at the water's edge, staring at the horizon. His eyes were watery. He wiped them quickly as I approached.

"Just leave that there for me. I'll get to it," he said, pointing to the margarita. Then he pulled his shirt off. "I'm going in." He stripped down to his boxers, garnishing a look of curiosity from a pair of older women passing by. But they didn't seem to mind staring.

Frank left his clothes in a neat pile on the dry sand, then waded out into the low surf. The sandbar was wide so it took some walking, but eventually the water was deep enough and he dove, vanishing under for several seconds, then coming up with long freestyle strokes toward one of the buoys. His steady rhythm and excellent form made short work of the distance. When he reached the buoy, he stretched out with two fingers and set it wobbling, then cut south and headed for the next one.

I settled onto the beach and sat, nestling Frank's drink in a mound of sand and nursing my beer.

I expected Frank might swim in after hitting the second buoy, but he made a turn around it and headed back to the first for another lap. The sun settled lower on the horizon and Frank just kept swimming, lap after lap. The sun was touching the water by the time he finally dripped his way back onto shore.

He plopped down in the sand next to me. "I see you drank my margarita."

"Your ice was melting and it was going to ruin it. Did you a favor."

"Felt good out there. I can't swim what I used to, but it'll come back. You remember swimming the buoys together when you were a kid?"

"Sure. You used to make me do a mile if I wanted ice cream on the way home."

"It was good discipline for you. You still do it?"

"Every other week or so. Not at twilight, though. Sharks are more active this time of day. Was thinking one might nab you and take you off my hands."

"Sharks are just the dogs of the ocean. There's a few you have to watch out for. But most are friendly enough, just curious. Can't help it the only thing God gave them to greet the world with is their teeth."

"I'll stick to playing with the land-dogs."

"Don't think I'd ever get sick of this view. You live a charmed life, son. I'm happy for you."

A few beachgoers were out snapping selfies, taking advantage of the flattering lighting. They steered clear of us.

Frank brushed the sand from his knees. "Listen, I could use your help to find what Earl put away for me. It would mean a lot. And of course I'd cut you in for a percentage."

"Figured that was coming. I don't want your money."

"You must need something."

I frowned at him, then sighed. "What I do need is for you to sign over a bill of sale for the Mallard, so it's officially in my name. That's it. That's all I want."

"That's all, huh?" He looked back at the horizon. "It's a hell of a plane. What if I still want it?"

"The FAA pulled your license. They're never going to give it back. What are you going to do with a plane? Besides, you owe me something."

"Lot of people seem to feel that way. I probably do owe you. But not yet. First I need you to help me settle a few things. You help me with that and *Tropic Angel* is yours. I'll sign it over free and clear."

"No bullshit."

"I'm not lying to you."

"We'll see." I stood and dusted myself off, then collected my empties.

"You getting me a fresh margarita?"

"I'm going to look for Murphy."

"We have a deal?"

"You screw me over, I'm going to find a lonely spot in the gulf to dump you for your ocean dogs. See how friendly you think they are then."

I walked up the beach and left my father sitting in the steadily cooling sand.

There was no doubt in my mind that the arrangement I was getting myself into was going to come with a steeper price than advertised. A devil never negotiates the front end of a deal. He waits till your back is turned to plunge the knife.

But the son of a devil learns a few tricks too.

We'd see who stuck who in the end.

NINE
NO FLY ZONE

"TREASURE," Reese said. "You know what kind?"

She was standing at her toolbox in front of a Beech Bonanza that was in for a cylinder change. Steam still rose from my morning cup of coffee and I'd brought her one too, to help with the discussion. The rest of my crew was only just arriving at Hangar 4, punching in and slowly getting at least the idea of work started. Tyson was focused on finding a playlist to set the soundtrack of the day, and Rip was yawning while petting the cat over at the break table. Reese was the only one who'd actually touched an airplane or tools so far this morning, but that was typical. We had a chill morning atmosphere at Hangar 4 that emphasized quality over work speed, at least until 8:30 when Elsbeth arrived on scene to glare at us and crack the whip of productivity.

"Earl called it Frank's 'retirement fund,'" I said, "so I'm eighty percent sure it's not just moldy bricks of cocaine. But I could be wrong."

"You could ask him." Reese lifted her chin toward the

Mallard. Frank was out there in the morning sunlight poking around *Tropic Angel*'s new folding boarding steps.

"Hasn't come up yet as a conversation topic."

"How'd he like staying on the boat last night?"

"Said it felt like a floating hotel. No character. But good for Hank if that's what he liked in a catamaran."

"Strong opinions for a guy just out of prison. What else did you talk about?"

"Not much. I put him in the port cabins and told him to stay down there till daylight or I'd make Murphy bite him."

"Fat chance. Murphy's too good of a boy. Also, it doesn't seem like your dog hates your dad as much as you do."

Murphy was out on the ramp following Frank with interest, a tennis ball in his mouth. Frank accepted the ball and chucked it, and Murphy raced after it with his tail wagging.

"Not Murphy's fault he doesn't know the history. Frank's a lying asshole who only looks out for himself."

"You don't think prison could've changed him?"

"Can't change what he did. Sooner I'm rid of him the better."

Reese opened the airport facilities directory and thumbed through pages. "What did you make of this?"

I had the sectional chart open too and had showed her how the kneeboard indicated an island between Marathon and Key West.

"I figure Earl must have hidden the whatever-it-is on this island and somehow the pages in this book give us the specific details."

"Coordinates?"

"Could be. Earl wasn't exactly Dan Brown. I don't think whatever he set up will require a doctorate in symbology to decode. Said the key to the whole puzzle was a purple Sharpie."

Reese flipped through the facilities directory and found a page with purple ink on it. "He circled just the letter M in

"Com," and the R in "Runway" on this page." She flipped a few more. "Then this one is a number."

"That's what I'm saying. I think I just piece it all together and hope it makes sense."

"You mind if I take some pictures? Sounds kind of fun."

"Knock yourself out."

She got out her phone and took photos of the marked pages, then flipped through looking for more. "He said he'll sign over the Mallard once you find this treasure of his?"

"Supposedly. Says we need to wrap up a few loose ends, whatever that means."

"Who else knows about the treasure? You expecting trouble?"

"Not sure, but the big bozo he showed up with at Earl's wasn't driving Frank around out of the goodness of his heart. Guy could've had dollar signs tattooed on his forehead."

"Deacon. The prison buddy."

"Yeah. And his girlfriend. Lyla. Keep an eye out for those two. Wouldn't be shocked if they show up here looking for Frank."

"Want me to send them in another direction?"

"Not sure it matters. It's a seven-hour drive to Key West by car. We'll be there in an hour and change. With any luck, we'll find this treasure he's after, sort whatever fiasco it involves and be back before those two even make the Seven-Mile Bridge."

"You get that plan at the optimism store on your way in this morning?"

"Three more holes in my punch card and they give me a free reality check."

"You might get that anyway."

"Probably. Keep the shop from catching fire in my absence. With any luck I'll come home tonight with a plane we can actually use to make money."

"Don't forget your treasure map." Reese handed me the sectional chart and the airport directory. "I'll text you if I figure out the puzzle before you do."

"That's cheating because I have to fly."

"I have to work. You could try *that* sometime."

"Sounds tedious."

I picked up my coffee and walked out to the plane. Murphy came running and trotted along in my wake, but I had to tell him to stay.

"You guard Reese and the shop for me," I said. "And keep the cat from eating all the snacks." He canted his head at the word snacks, but looked disappointed. "I'll be back soon."

The day was already warm, humidity thick in the air, and we'd all be sticky in an hour. Good time to gain some altitude.

"You hit the head yet?" I asked Frank. "The lav on this thing is still a hassle."

"I'm good. Let's get in the wind," he replied. He nodded toward Reese. "Is she your girl?"

"She's my friend. And she's got a girlfriend."

"Ah. You seem close."

"We served together. She saved my life, so we're like family. Closer in our case."

Frank chewed his cheek but didn't reply.

I climbed aboard *Tropic Angel* first and left Frank to raise the boarding stairs. I was in the pilot seat working through the starting checklist when he poked his head through the keyhole-shaped entryway. He made a move to put a foot over.

"Uh uh." I put a hand up. "You're in the back. You ride passenger princess this trip."

"A Mallard's better as a two-pilot bird."

"You're an unlicensed pilot with almost twenty years of lag. I'll manage."

"You don't think I remember how to fly? It's still my plane."

"Then you should enjoy seeing the back of it."

Frank gave me a sour look, cast one last forlorn glance at the flight deck instrument panel, then disappeared aft.

I had the big radial engines rumbling a few moments later and taxied away from the tie down.

Some new students from the flight school were out preflighting a Cessna 172 and gawked as we went by. *Tropic Angel*'s wingspan was almost double that of their school planes and sat high enough to clear their wingtips.

The little planes rocked in my prop wash as I swung out to the runway.

Whitted tower had given me Runway 7 for departure despite a stiff crosswind, and once airborne I wagged the wings in salute as I turned southbound.

By the time I had the gear up and trim set, I was on the radio with Tampa approach and climbing through their airspace. They directed me to three thousand five hundred feet for the start of my southeast leg along the shoreline and promised me higher once I was past the inlet to the bay.

I relished the climb.

The engines hummed smoothly and the air temp dropped as we gained altitude. A Grumman Mallard could do over two hundred miles per hour as a max speed, but at altitude I eased the throttles back for cruise and it settled in around one-eighty. At that airspeed we'd make short work of the distance between Saint Petersburg and Key West. Being a twin-engine flying boat also added safety to over-water operations, meaning I could cut the corner and spend more time over open water than most recreational land planes were comfortable with.

Tropic Angel was happily sucking down avgas and the skies were clear, but I had a steady nagging in my gut that had nothing to do with my lack of breakfast. I glanced over at the empty co-pilot seat.

The broad flight deck had controls that *were* easier to manage with a co-pilot.

But a pilot and co-pilot form a partnership based on trust. I'd have to manage the extra workload alone, because I was confident the only person aboard this plane I could trust right now was me.

TEN
CAYO HUESO

THE SOUTHERNMOST POINT in the continental US saw seaplanes aplenty in the heyday of Pan Am, but *Tropic Angel*'s prior contributions to the islands were suspect. My father and a few dozen others were the only ones who could put a number to the illegal cargo shipments they'd offloaded at miscellaneous Keys in the area, and if the county sheriffs had been around, there was a good chance they'd helped offload for a cut of the action.

The Conch Republic had never been a place that abided by the same rules as the rest of the continental US. They'd even had the cheek to secede and declare war on the US in 1982 for one minute as a statement protesting a roadblock on Highway A1A. The official weapon of the war was a stale loaf of Cuban bread cracked over a Navy officer's head and a vague threat of conch fritter bombs from a biplane, so the damage from the dispute was minimal, but the legacy was long-lasting.

Of course, the name Key West was a mistake, like many places in Florida, a butchering of a previous pronunciation. The Spanish had named the place Cayo Hueso, or "Bone Island" after discovering bones from Calusa Indians there. And it was "west" but by no means the farthest west. Other Keys and the Dry Tortugas sat as much as seventy miles farther out and many were visible from my position in the air. But most people had long since ceased to gripe about the misnomer.

As a young teen I'd hung around outside Captain Tony's place while my father bargained his services indoors. I'd roamed the streets of Key West getting into trouble alongside my brother as he grifted tourists and sweet-talked pretty girls. I shared a first kiss under a palm tree with a young suntanned local beauty with sand in her hair. I hadn't remembered to get her name, but I did remember the way she tasted like coconut lip gloss. The island held more memories per square mile of terrain than nearly anywhere else I'd hung around, if you discounted Army bases, but this trip I wasn't looking to dredge up memories. There was another history in Key West that concerned me more. Frank Angel's personal history.

Frank had spent a lot of time in the Keys, and his way of life involved people with longer memories than mine. I held some hope that time had torn the web he'd woven and scattered it to the wind, but webs are sticky, even when broken, and they are always dangerous to things that fly.

My plan was to land at Key West first, then figure out the rest of Earl's instructions to navigate to our final destination. The island was in view out the windshield now, a gem in the blue-green water dividing the gulf from the Atlantic. I'd had the flight deck to myself for most of the trip. It was only when I had Key West in sight that Frank's head reappeared in the entryway.

"They're still flying that damned blimp, huh?" He pointed east to the tethered airship "Fat Albert" in the distance that was used for drug interdiction and border protection. "I always hated that thing. You landing Runway 9?"

"Last time I checked, you need to be buckled in for landing."

"Wanted to see the islands. View back there is shit."

"Who knew ex-cons were so high maintenance." I adjusted my angle of descent some, in order to lose more altitude.

"When we land, there's a guy I need to go see. Set up a few things," Frank said.

"What sort of business is he in?"

"Kind of guy who knows everybody. I need to reconnect with a few friends from the old days and he might be the one to help us out."

"Is he on Key West proper or one of the other Keys?"

"He'll be around somewhere. We'll find him after we land."

"Let me guess, he owes you money?"

"He's a former business associate."

"How do you know he hasn't flown off in your absence?"

"I've kept tabs on him. Has a boat down here and a swanky place on the water somewhere."

"Reward for his life of good deeds, no doubt."

"Should make him easy enough to find once we're on the ground."

"Buckle up, then. I've got it from here."

Frank disappeared aft again, and once I was sure he was seated, I banked on course for the left-hand base leg to Runway 9. Out my pilot side window, the rest of the highway-connected Keys were laid out toward the horizon in a sea of turquoise. I pulled Earl's sectional chart from the side seat pocket where I'd stashed it and opened it up to the part that showed the purple dots. The island that the hole in the kneeboard had indicated lay off to the east on the horizon near Sugarloaf. I suspected we'd be headed that way soon. I put the gear down while the control tower cleared me to land on Runway 9.

The pretty island below beckoned, whispering promises she had no intentions of keeping.

Four minutes later, *Tropic Angel*'s tires chirped as they

touched the pavement. We rumbled onto the FBO ramp and a line guy came out with orange plastic wands to direct us to a tie-down space. We were far from the only seaplane. A beautiful turbine Kodiak, a Grand Caravan and a De Haviland Beaver all rode high on floats nearby, but a few heads poked out of neighboring hangars to watch us taxi up anyway. A Grumman Mallard was a rare bird with a classic appeal that was hard to argue with. Frank was right. People would show up for the nostalgia.

When I swung the folding stairs out, Frank descended first at a casual pace.

I called to him once he hit the ground. "You even still need me from here or are you good to find your friend on your own?"

"You said you'd help me. That was the deal, right?"

"What other part do I play besides pilot in this plan of yours?"

"It's a two-person job. You'll be useful." He walked on toward the Signature Flight Support building. I watched him go and frowned.

Once I was on the ground, I borrowed a lineman's step ladder to close everything back up.

Key West lay waiting beyond the fence.

As I followed my father up the stairs and into the FBO building, someone was playing Caribbean steel drum music over the speakers, but Frank's brow was set in a look of determination and focus I knew didn't bode well for a relaxing good time.

Decades behind bars was a long time to dwell on a plan of action. And I knew from that look that more than one scheme of his was in motion. I filled out the FBO arrival forms and stalked back down to street level, where my father lingered at the curb.

Before climbing into a waiting cab, I took one last look through the fence to the ramp where *Tropic Angel* sat in the midday sun. The sight of her steeled my resolve. It was going to be my name on the registration once this all worked out. So now I had to make it work out.

ELEVEN

A DRINKING TOWN WITH A FISHING PROBLEM

"I'M LOOKING FOR THE MOOCH."

We'd been into seven bars up and down Duval Street plus visits to Lagerheads and Hogs Breath Saloon. Every bartender had given Frank the same blank look when he asked the question. This girl at least had a smile on her face.

"The Mooch. Is he an old white guy who wears Guy Harvey fishing shirts and tips like shit?"

"Could match that description," Frank said.

"Then take your pick." She waved a hand to encompass the clientele. "I've got a zillion of those."

Frank turned back to me with a frown. "This isn't the place."

"What did you expect? That bartender just finished grade school. She's not going to know any of your friends."

We eased back into daylight on Duval.

"The Mooch is around here somewhere," Frank said. "I know it."

"Shocking as it may seem, we're gonna need the guy's real name." I had my phone out and had done some cursory Google searching, but not surprisingly, 'The Mooch' hadn't turned up helpful results.

"His name's Tony B, like bravo. But we had at least eight Tonys in the scene back then. So we always called him 'The Mooch' on account of how he never wanted to pay for shit."

"B is for Baker? Bradbury? Brown?"

"I can't remember that part. I told you. We had too many to keep them all straight."

I put my phone away. "Thought you said you kept tabs on this guy."

"I did. My man Ziggy checked up on him a month ago. Said he was still down here. Saw him out at the bars." He waved a hand to encompass the street.

"Probably wasn't at one in the afternoon. Where's this Ziggy now?"

Frank frowned again.

"Off island?"

His jaw clenched and he glared at the passersby, then at his feet.

"He's dead, isn't he. Geezer kicked off. That's it?"

"Coulda been a few months ago, I guess."

I took my sunglasses off and pinched the bridge of my nose. "Okay. Let's start this over. Are we positive this Mooch is still alive? Or did he go the way of Ziggy?"

"I can't help it Ziggy died on me. He smoked a shit-ton of weed. I'm surprised he made it as long as he did. But The Mooch was young. He's my age."

"Real spring chicken then."

"He didn't have a state of Florida correctional facility health program to keep him spry. Old boy did like to eat. But I know he's alive here somewhere. That bastard was too crooked to die."

The sound of a small aircraft engine penetrated the ambient noise and we both looked skyward.

"Piper Cherokee?" Frank asked, squinting at the plane.

"I think it's a Beech Sundowner."

"You might be right."

We watched it fly out of view, then I returned my attention to our terrestrial problems.

"What if we ask Earl's sister, Gail? She's been with the sheriff's department in Monroe County for years. If this guy is as shady as he sounds, he's probably on her radar. She can help us locate him."

"I'm not dragging her into this. Plus, Gail's a cop. And not the type of cop who is going to be on my side."

"Meaning, what you have in mind won't be legal. When we find this dude, The Mooch, how exactly do you see the conversation going?"

"We're gonna talk to him and then he's gonna answer some questions for me. Plus do me a few favors, like broker a deal with a buyer I have in mind."

"So this treasure of yours isn't a liquid asset. What's his motivation to help us?"

"He'll be plenty motivated when he sees us. But since you mention it, I was thinking we'd stop by a gun store too. Maybe pick something up for our personal protection."

"What's wrong with you?"

"Some of the guys we'll be dealing with probably have security. Someone we might need to convince in an assertive way. We'll need to look the part."

"Convince in an assertive way. That a term you made up in prison?"

"No. In there, they'd say we're gonna molly whop someone's ass," Frank said. "But we're just making an impression. It's for show."

"No one is letting you buy a gun."

"But you can. You have a concealed carry permit, right?

Veteran, all that? You can pick up a handgun same day in Florida, no problem. I looked it up."

"So that's why you brought me along."

"No. But it doesn't hurt our cause, you being a tall tough-looking guy who happens to have a gun on him, does it? Improves our image. Makes it less likely they'll try something."

"You want me to be your damn muscle, tweak this guy into giving you whatever he owes you, is that it?"

"I'm not asking you to hurt anybody. All I need is for him to have the idea that you might work him over if he tries to screw us."

"Unbelievable. I'm not going to shoot anyone for you, Frank."

"When have I ever shot anyone? All those years flying and running cargo for the cartels, I never carried a gun. I don't know anything about guns. It's only after getting out of prison that I'm needing one. Irony, huh?"

I shook my head. "What if this creep has his own son whose life he's ruined that he's conned into carrying guns and hanging out with him? You consider that option, genius?"

"Hey, who taught you to fight as a kid? You think I did a bid that long with my corn hole intact without being able to answer a chin check? I'm plenty capable of handling myself. But since we have an *arrangement* and you're along anyway, you can back me up. Or just stand there for all I care, but I'm improving our odds. Thinking smarter, not harder."

"That's not the phrase."

"You know what I meant. If you knew this guy, kind of people he deals with, you'd be as cautious as me."

"The only shady person that I know he's dealt with is you, so I don't blame him for being skeptical. The sooner I'm rid of you, the happier I'll be."

"So we pick up a gun. Improve our odds. You want the Mallard in your name, don't you?"

"But I have my limits. Don't think you can dangle that carrot in front of me and I'm going to jump through every hoop." I peeled away and made for a scooter rental building on the corner.

"Where are you going?"

"I'm getting us a ride. Unless you want to walk to Stock Island. It's the closest place with a gun store."

"Glad to see you're coming around to the idea."

"Only because it might be handy in case I get to use it on you. Pretty sure the FAA will let me register the plane if I inherit it too."

MOST OF THE way through completing the rental agreement on a scooter from Island Time Wheels, my phone rang. I finished signing my life away on the waiver, then picked up the keys and answered my phone.

"Luke? Can you hear me?"

"EJ? What's going on?" It sounded like he was driving.

"You got a minute? Mom wants me to check on you and see if you know where Frank is."

I peered out the rental office window to where Frank was browsing around the golf carts. "I've seen him. He's fine."

"He leave with you yesterday? That dude that was here with him was pissed. Gail had to kick him off the property and now Mom's worried."

I held the phone to my ear with my shoulder and scribbled another initial on the rental form. "Deacon say where he's headed?"

"Going to find Frank. That's why Mom's worried. Is he with you?"

"For the time being. We're down in the Keys dealing with

something. Hoping to be back in Saint Pete tonight, though." I finished the form and handed it to the girl behind the counter. "If that guy comes back around, let me know. But I doubt he'll hassle Margie if Gail's there."

"Gail took off too. Headed back to Marathon for work. Won't be back till we do the funeral."

"When's that?"

"Depends on you and Frank. Mom wants you both there."

"I wouldn't make any plans around Frank. Who knows if he'll stay out of prison that long."

I held up the keys and made eye contact with the girl behind the rental counter. "We good?"

She gave me a thumbs up. "Unless you need the lesson?"

"I can figure it out."

"You sound like you're busy," EJ said. "What are you doing in Marathon?"

"We're in Key West. Wasting my time, most likely."

"All right. You need any help with what you have going on? I've got some friends down there if you need anything. You need a place to stay?"

"Don't worry. I can handle it. Hoping to not be here that long. I'll catch you later, EJ. Tell Aunt Margie not to worry."

I hung up and bumped my hip into the door to open it, setting a bell jingling.

Outside, Frank was lingering near the sidewalk. He'd had to borrow clothes from me this morning. It was a faded Hawaiian shirt I didn't wear much and some shorts I had been planning to donate, but it was still odd seeing him in them. It struck me that he didn't look dissimilar to how I remembered him from my youth, and that made me consider that my post-Army wardrobe choices may not be as independently chosen as I'd suspected. Good reason to go shopping soon.

"You at least get us a big one?" he asked.

"If you're picky about your transportation, you're welcome to walk."

"When I was young they used to say riding a scooter was like screwing a fat chick."

"Whole lot of fun till your friends see you on it? Yeah, I've heard that one. When I was twelve, and probably from you. It was a terrible joke then. But don't worry, from what I can tell, you don't have any friends left anyway."

"An old school man would'a rented us a couple of Harleys."

"Maybe the old school man is the one who still has his driver's license."

I pressed the lock button on the key fob and a nearby turquoise scooter beeped.

"Oh goodie," Frank said. "It has rainbow stickers on it."

"When in Key West . . ." I said, and climbed aboard the scooter, rocking it off its kickstand. I fired it up and its motor sputtered to life, sounding like an overworked weed whacker.

Frank squinted at the machine from behind his borrowed sunglasses, then walked over and slung a leg over the seat, settling in behind me. He found the hand holds and got his feet on the pegs.

"There's probably a place around here I could get you a pretty blonde wig to wear back there if you want one," I said.

"I'm plenty pretty enough."

"Way to keep up that body positivity. You learn that in 'how to readjust to society' class?"

"No, but the prison queens told me. They also called me a wolf, which I'm ninety percent sure was a compliment. Hanging with those guys was great for my self-esteem."

We launched away from the parking lot and buzzed out into weekday Key West traffic on Duval which mostly consisted of day-drinking pedestrians and tourists also careening around on scooters and golf carts.

Trop rock classics like Last Mango in Paris and Red Solo Cup emanated from bars we passed. The day had turned typical Florida muggy and the breeze from the scooter's acceleration was a welcome form of air conditioning. I quickly found my way to the side streets and headed west toward Old Town. The bungalows wore painted wooden shutters, and white picket fences were ubiquitous. Along these side streets, the town held onto its abundant southern charm.

"Turn left up here," Frank shouted in my ear. "I want to check something."

I made the turn and rode till the street intercepted the perimeter fence of the above-ground cemetery. "You planning to read names on tombstones for your buddy or make yourself a reservation?"

"The Mooch owned a lot of property in this area. A guy I knew took care of one of his places. Might still be here." He pointed right and I followed the perimeter of the cemetery, circumnavigating the outer fence via Olivia Street, then another left on Frances.

"I think it's up here," Frank said. "The next side."

I made one more left, this time onto Angela Street which more closely resembled an alley. A sign warned that no trucks were allowed, and the street was too narrow to permit parking. The homes along this stretch were overgrown with jungle plants and palms. Perhaps the residents preferred to block out the view of their dead neighbors.

"Slow down. This is the place."

Only a rusty tin roof was visible beyond the foliage. A chain link gate hung on rusty hinges, but the rest was a wall of plants.

"I'll check if anyone is here."

Frank climbed off the scooter and I killed the motor. A sign warned I wasn't allowed to park there but I was hoping this visit would be brief. Frank unlatched the rusty gate in the low fence and forged into the jungle of a yard beyond. I followed at a slower pace.

Eccentric decor littered the yard, glass bottles dangling from tree branches on twine, wind chimes and strange bundles of sticks piled on stumps. An old stop sign was screwed to the weathered wood siding on the porch, the sign itself decorated with a faded bumper sticker that read "Where is Bum Farto?"

The reference to Key West's vanished drug-smuggling fire chief from the seventies wasn't a ringing endorsement of whoever lived here, but the question had also adorned T-shirts and drink cozies for decades.

A wicker coffee table on the porch held an ashtray and a glass pot pipe. The pipe had burned out but the smell still lingered.

Frank pressed the door buzzer, which did nothing. Then he banged on the edge of the dilapidated screen door instead.

Barking and squawking erupted from inside and a fuzzy footstool of a dog appeared, its yips and yaps coming at a frequency I prayed was unsustainable for long. The dog did its darndest to rupture our eardrums until a thick black woman in a muumuu appeared from the dark interior and squinted at us through the screen. She pushed the dog aside with a pantyhose covered ankle. I guessed her age to be somewhere between eighty and two-hundred. Coke bottle glasses magnified her cloudy eyes, but I had my doubts she could see past the end of her nose. The African grey parrot on her shoulder had no trouble spotting us, however, and made its displeasure known by opening its beak and spreading its wings in warning.

"What do you want?" the old woman said, addressing the question either to us or to the great outdoors in general.

"Ma'am, I'm from the utility company," Frank said, affecting a sort of Texas drawl. "Looking for the owner."

She squinted harder at the screen door. Her hazy gaze shifted like she was trying to echo-locate him. "You need to talk to my son. He's working."

"Tony B still own this house?"

"Fat Tony? Jerome knows about that. You'll have to come back later when he's here."

"When will that be, ma'am?" Frank asked.

"After work. When he brings me my medicine."

"Fat Tony," the parrot squawked.

"Where's Jerome working these days?" Frank asked.

"His job take him everyplace," the old woman said. "Sometimes the square."

"Mallory Square? With the tourists?" I asked.

"Fuck the tourists," the parrot interjected.

"No! You don't use that filthy language, Poppers," the old woman scolded, wagging a finger at the bird. It opened its beak like it wanted to take her finger off, but must have thought better of it.

"Jerome teaches my bird dirty words when I'm asleep. Thinks it's funny."

I interjected, "Do you have a phone number for your son, Mrs . . . ?"

"You find him when you find him. He always changes his phones. But if you see him, tell him we outta coffee creamer and he needs to bring me some."

"We'll stop back another time, ma'am," Frank said.

"I'll tell my boy you came by. He won't like it but I'll tell him."

The parrot said, "Go home, motherfuckers."

"I'll whap you, Poppers. I'll do it," the woman threatened, her hand upraised again. The bird spread its wings and opened its beak once more and this time dropped a poop on her shoulder. The front door slammed shut before we could see what the old woman did about it.

Frank turned to me and shrugged.

I sighed and stepped off the porch, idling back through the jungle to the scooter we'd left in the road and noting the slip of colored paper already stuck to the handlebars. I read the parking ticket and swore, then turned my attention back to the house. "Well, that was a pointless excursion," I said.

A car drove by so we moved nearer the cemetery fence to get out of the way.

"You think that old lady recognized me?" Frank asked.

"You've met her before?"

"Probably twenty years ago. She looked ancient then. Same damned bird too."

"I'm not sure that woman could recognize herself in a mirror unless it was close enough for her breath to fog the glass."

"I didn't want her to recognize my voice."

"So you know this son of hers? Jerome?"

"Yeah, I know him. He runs a fishing charter and dive boat for tourists, or says he does. Back in the day he ran a scam selling fake fishing licenses, and tickets for fishing tours that didn't exist. Once he made enough money, he graduated to actually having a boat and using that to overcharge people for tours instead of just standing them up at the docks. But I think faking it made more money."

"Sounds like a charming guy."

"If we don't run into him at the docks, we'll probably find him in Mallory Square tonight. It's his prime hunting ground."

The sunset festivities at Mallory Square were a long tradition. Street performers were abundant, with magicians, acrobats, and musicians all making a bid to part tourists from their money. Most were honest performers trusting their audiences to drop bills appropriately into buckets before seeing their grand finales, but there were always a few on the fringes of honest work and some who couldn't spot that line if they tripped and fell over it. Jerome sounded like the latter.

"Around town they used to call Jerome 'Big Tuna,'" Frank said. "From the time one of his charter customers caught him sneaking a pre-caught fish onto a hook during a black fin tournament. The client was so furious he pushed Jerome overboard. Someone on the charter had to reel him in with a life preserver, and it started the joke that he was the biggest fish his customers ever caught."

"And you're sure he still knows The Mooch?"

"The Mooch handled everybody's business back then. He was the one we all went to when we needed our money cleaned. My guess is Jerome would still be a client."

"Using the laundry service."

"The Mooch owned a bunch of businesses around town, or claimed to. Must have kept up a convincing enough show that the IRS never came for him. Here I spent almost two decades inside just for flying planes. He was walking around a free man that entire time, his books cooked so crispy they'd give you cancer just reading them."

"What makes you think a guy that crooked is going to give a rat's ass that you're out of prison?"

"He'll care. Because there's a chance he might be the reason I went away to begin with. And I'm going to put a gun in his face and find out."

FRANK ANGEL'S feet kept up a steady rhythm on the dusty road as he jogged behind the scooter, shouting.

"Would you stop already!"

I'd climbed aboard the scooter and gone almost a full block with him running behind. I finally stopped at a cross street long enough to look back. Frank jogged the remaining fifty feet to me panting and out of breath.

I shook my head and yelled over the noise of the scooter's exhaust. "I knew you were a piece of shit, Frank. It's my own damned fault for ever agreeing to bring you down here. Now I find out this whole thing is just a stupid revenge fantasy? What are you going to do? Kill the guy? And drag me back to prison with you?"

"The Mooch is the one you should be mad at. If you'd let me tell you the story, you'd be on my side."

I cut the engine and glared.

"The story? All you've ever done is tell stories. You need me to recap the highlights? How about the time you took Landon's first car to Rhode Island on a smuggling run, lost it, and told us drunk teenagers stole it." I swung my leg over the seat of the scooter and closed the distance. "Or the time the county cops were hassling you so you made us change schools and told us it was because of a lice infestation. That ring any bells?" I was in his face now. "Maybe it's all too fuzzy because it fades compared the big lie. How you let Mom die to save your own craven neck." I put both my hands on his chest and shoved him so hard that he tripped backward and landed flat on his ass in the road. "You bring me down here for revenge? I'm the one who deserves revenge!"

He groaned from the ground, then propped himself back to his elbows. "There it is. I wondered when you'd finally get that out."

"You think this is a joke?"

"No. I don't." He pressed himself up to sitting position and paused, brushing his hands off. "You're mad. I get it. Want me to stand up so you can knock me down again? Or you want to kick me while I'm down here to save you some time? You're bigger now. Tough-guy soldier. I'm the old man. Gotta show me the order of things. Teach me what a rotten dad I was. Is that it?"

"Fuck you and your condescension. You talk about wanting to point a gun in someone's face and see if they're responsible for putting you away? The only one responsible for that is you. So point it at yourself. Feel free to squeeze the trigger while you're at it."

Frank gave me a long stare and picked a fleck of gravel from a scrape on his elbow. "You're done with our deal then? Gonna leave me here in the road? I can fend for myself, you know. But that's not what you want, is it? Felt too good to knock me down. I bet you want more of that satisfaction. Trust me. I get it. You don't think I've had time to dwell on my injustices? Years of going over it? The hate gets to be like its own person, someone you talk to at night, make promises to. You want to hear some of the promises I've made?"

"Get up."

"For what? Oh, right. So I can be your punching bag. You can hit me all you want, it's not going to bring her back."

"I'm not going to hit you, Frank. You're not even worth the busted knuckles." I turned back to the scooter. "Let's just go home."

"That's it? You give up on your dream that quick? What about your plane?"

"I told you. I have limits."

Another departure from the airport flew overhead. We both looked up and watched it cruise towards the horizon.

"That one's definitely a Piper," Frank said, his voice subdued. "Saratoga."

"Cherokee Six," I grumbled. "That landing gear doesn't retract."

"Ah. Right." Frank got to his knees, then to his feet. "Okay. One meal."

"What?"

"I don't care where. You pick. We sit, we eat, I explain. When we're done, and you've heard me out, and if you still want to leave, we'll go. And when we get back, I'll still give you your signature on that bill of sale."

I studied him. "Why on earth would I believe anything you have to say?"

"I'm not asking you to believe me. I'm only asking you to listen to the story." When I didn't reply, he held his hands up and gestured to the city around us. "We've come this far, haven't we?"

The cemetery behind him sat as a testament to a long history of tragic decisions made on this island. One more wouldn't change anything. I checked my watch, then sighed again. "One meal, then you give me the signature, and I never have to see you again?"

"Preferably a place I can get a decent piece of fish. But your pick."

I climbed aboard the scooter and started it back up.

"I'll take that as an agreement," he said and hustled to get on behind me. Once he was settled, he said, "And I do appreciate you not slugging me."

"Yet," I said. "I still haven't ruled it out." As I rolled on the throttle, I added, "But this had better be one hell of a story."

FOURTEEN

SERVING TIME

THE SERVER at the restaurant lingered around the table and rested a hand on Frank's shoulder when she laughed. Her hair was dyed dark to hide her grays and she wore a lot of makeup, but the corners of her sharp blue eyes crinkled sweetly when she smiled.

"And you, honey?" she said to me. "Can I get you something from the bar?"

"I'll stick with the Arnold Palmer," I said.

She hadn't needed to write anything down, her posture and easy smile giving her away as a veteran of the service industry. But when Frank beamed his best grin back at her, she seemed to have trouble recalling she had other tables.

"You say you're not even going to stay one night in town? After flying down in a plane? Seems a crime. And you'll miss all the nightlife."

"Best part of my day so far has been right here with you," Frank said.

"Then you must be having a dull day," she said. "We'd better liven it up for you! I'll be right back with those drinks and we'll think of something."

When she walked away, Frank's eyes followed her.

"A buddy of mine once said, 'The hardest part of being an old man is getting used to looking at old women.' But I can't say I'm minding it so far."

"Think you can keep it in your pants long enough for us to eat?"

"You try existing for twenty years off distant memories and magazine pictures, or the occasional good-looking lawyer visitor, and see how you like it. But I guess you've had your run of bad luck too. I noticed there's no wedding ring on your finger."

"You don't need to worry about me. I'm fine."

"Your mother always hoped you'd grow up to have some kids. Said you were the sweet one and you'd make a great dad. Give us lots of grandbabies."

"Let's lay down some ground rules for this conversation," I said. "Rule number one is you're not going to talk about Mom."

"You want the story, don't you? You don't think she's tied into this?"

"Not if it means you disparaging her memory. I'm not going to sit still for that."

Frank sipped from his water glass and set it back on the table cloth. "Fine. I'll leave her out as much as I can."

Sherri, our server, reappeared and delivered my iced tea and a beer for Frank. "You ready to put something in?"

"You read my mind," Frank said with a wink.

"I meant an order," she said, turning pink.

"So did I. Where is your mind?"

"I'm gonna have to come back to you." She flattened her apron and turned to me. "He's naughty, this one. How about you, sweetie? What can I get you?"

"I'll take the mahi sandwich special."

"Sweet potato or regular fries?"

"A salad."

"I wish I had your self control. Are you two related? You look so much alike."

"My son," Frank said. "When he admits to it."

"Handsome always runs in the family. I have a boy myself. I raised him all on my own, but he still looks and acts just like his daddy. Nature versus nurture, right?"

"Luke here grew up a better man than I ever could've been. All without my help."

Her hand brushed his shoulder. "Well, you must have done something right, honey."

"One of these days I might." He handed her the menu. "The sandwich special for me too. Extra sweet potato fries. He's the only one at the table with self control."

She beamed down at him. "Now we're having fun. I'll put that in for you." She wagged a finger at him. "The order." She was smiling as she walked away.

Frank turned his attention back to me. "What?"

"You done now? Or am I going to spend all day waiting?"

"I'm getting around to it. I forget how impatient everyone is on the outside."

"Gotta take advantage of our brief lulls in dedicated service."

Frank took a long draught of his beer, then set it down. "All right. You should know it was going to be my last run," he said. "Out clean and going straight after."

"I don't believe it for a second, but let's pretend I do. Keep going."

"The Mooch was the key to the deal. He had my ticket to a new setup with your mother and to getting you kids out of danger. She and I had it all worked out that—"

I held up a finger. "You agreed to leave Mom out of this."

He sighed. "Fine. I had it all worked out. We . . . I just had to do this final run for the cartel. A cake walk flight up from the Yucatan to these Miami guys to drop half, then do a plane switch and on up the coast to the Carolinas with the other half of the load. First part went fine. Low and fast, did it in my Aerostar without a hassle. We unloaded here at the airstrip on Sugarloaf. No problems. But part two was in another plane. An Aztec The Mooch had come up with, and he swore it was fit to fly, but I'd never seen a bigger pile of rusty bolts in my life, and I'd flown some ragged-out hardware in my time. I almost refused to go. But your mother insisted that—" He caught my glare and paused. "I decided to do it. Against my better judgment. And sure as shit we weren't more than fifty miles into the flight when I lost both engines. One after the other, like they were on a goddamn timer. The investigators later claimed it was water in the fuel and put it down to pilot error for me not checking, but that's bullshit. I sumped those tanks personally before I left, so if there was water in there, it got in after we took off."

"Rainy weather and no fuel caps?"

"Bright sunshine. Not a cloud in sight."

"Flew through a flock of magic water fairies then?" I asked. "How could you explain that?"

"I've been thinking it over a long time. I still don't know for sure, but something went wrong with that plane that sure as hell wasn't coincidence. And based on who knew I was going up that day, The Mooch is one of my most likely suspects."

"Why would someone who works with the cartel sabotage their own run? And he would've known you could still land it."

"But they timed it so I'd be over the Everglades. He knew where I'd go down, and that's why the county cops were all over us when we landed. The feds too. Someone tipped them off that the plane was going down. Otherwise they never would have been there that fast."

My mind went back to the newspaper article. A photo of the

downed plane among the mangroves. The shocking photo of my mother's bloodied face the police had shown after. My jaw clenched at the memory.

"No matter what you say, it's your fault she was there, and it was your fault you didn't put the plane down in a way she could have walked away from it. You got out. She didn't. That's still on you."

"I'm not arguing it isn't. But you know that if the deck hadn't been stacked—" He froze because Sherri was back with our lunch order. She paused at the sight of my face. "Everything okay over here?"

I gave her a tight-lipped smile and accepted the plate.

"Just telling war stories," Frank said.

"You tell me if you need anything else," she said, brushing her hair behind her ear with one finger.

"We won't," I said. "Just the check."

"No dessert? We have fresh-made Key lime pie."

When Frank shook his head, Sherri reached into her apron and set a clipboard with the bill on the table in front of him, then faded reluctantly back to the kitchen. I noticed she'd already scribbled her phone number under her name on the bill with a little heart where the dot in the i would be.

I waited till she'd left, then leveled my gaze at my father again. "You lied to the police and said you weren't there when Mom died. Blamed the whole thing on her."

"Someone set us up. Not me."

"You left her there to die."

"You weren't there."

"She shouldn't have been either!"

We glared at each other across our fish sandwiches and I noted a few other patrons looking our way. I lowered my voice. "You've never taken responsibility for a thing in your life. Not your family, not your decisions, not your chickenshit cowardice that day. And if you think I'll ever want anything to do with you again in this lifetime, you're dead wrong." I pushed my chair away from the table and stood.

Frank spoke up at me. "You asked me to leave Lucia out of this. Out of respect. To protect her memory. And I have. For nearly twenty years I've sat behind bars taking all your hate. Sure, I've made bad choices. I screwed up. But you're a grown man now and not a kid. And a grown man should know the truth. Tell me right now which way it's going to be. Do you want me to keep protecting you, and your childhood memory of your mother, and all that it means to you, or do you want to know the truth?"

"You lie all the time."

"Not about her. Not to you. You really think your mother, as smart as she was, as clever and beautiful as she was, you think she let a guy like me fool her into doing anything she didn't want to do? Out of the two of us, who do you think had more brains?"

I clenched my jaw, then sank slowly back into my chair.

"The last thing your mother said to me—the thing that made me go—she wanted me to finish what we'd started. She took my hand, looked me straight in the eye and said, 'Frank, don't let this be for nothing.'" He rubbed his own hand over his face and down his stubbled chin. "So, that's why I left. Why I lied to the cops to stay out of it as long as I could. Why I tried to keep going for you boys. Because it was what she wanted." He gave a big exhale. "And that's the truth. So now I'm gonna eat this sandwich," he said. "When you're done giving it some thought, you let me know. Then you can tell me what you want to do about finding the person who really got her killed."

FIFTEEN

GUN SHOW

I WALKED into McIvey's Stockade alone and in a mood to be. The place had few windows and fewer charms, but a gun store is a gun store. The racks of firearms along the wall were a no-nonsense blend of shotguns and AR-style rifles, with several glass display cases of handguns along the wall. Central shelves held survival and camping gear, some fishing tackle, and up front sat a six foot long cannon on a wooden-wheeled stand. It wore an orange sign that read NOT FOR SALE.

Get your cannons elsewhere. Got it.

Part of me didn't even want to be here. But another part of me needed to be. It was a war in my mind whose victor I still couldn't predict. Frank's story from the restaurant had scratched at a place I'd been trying to heal for twenty years. If what he'd said about my mother's last wishes was true, it chafed against the story I'd told myself, eroding the foundations of a decades old wall I'd built to keep Frank out. Because the ideas of Frank and honesty didn't mix in my experience. He'd betrayed us and taken away the best part of my childhood—the mother I adored. But he was correct that she was smart. Her eyes were open. Did I really know how deeply my mother was involved in Frank's plans, or even what it was about him that made her choose their life together?

The guy behind the counter looked familiar in the way gun store employees often do, a gray-haired retiree from some other career who now liked to spend his day packing a pistol and talking about it. He gave me a congenial nod and got to business. "Something particular you're looking for?"

"Peace and quiet mostly."

"They do say a well-armed society is a polite society. Not sure about quiet though."

"Then I'll settle for a pistol. Preferably a 9mm semi-automatic. With an extra magazine."

He reached into the glass display case and started setting things on top. "We have a special going on. Buy a gun and get a free promo holster you can use for three of these Glocks, the Smith and Wesson, and two of these Sig models. Would have to make sure I have the holster style you like still in stock because they've been popular." He opened the slide on a Glock 43X and pushed it to me across the counter. "You have a preference on double action or single action for the trigger?"

I picked up the Glock and double-checked that the chamber was clear, then surveyed the piece. "Okay if I dry fire it?"

"Won't hurt it. But I appreciate that you asked first."

I rested a hand on the top of the slide, keeping it from slamming home as hard when I released it, then sighted along the gun toward the floor before dry firing, I kept the pressure on the trigger after and let it out slowly, feeling the resistance and where it clicked to a lighter pull. The trigger action was smooth and the tension close to one I owned at home. I dropped the mag out and reinserted it and felt satisfied.

The store employee offered a few more options and I repeated the process with a Kimber Micro 9, a Springfield 1911, and finally settled on a Sig Sauer P365 model like one I already owned.

"Hard to go wrong there," the guy said. "It's a solid gun and a compact concealed carry. You said you want two mags?"

"That's right."

"I'll see if I can find an extra for you. Shouldn't be too much trouble."

I wandered down the aisle a bit, leaning over the counter and studying the boxes of ammo in the cabinets behind. "I'll take two boxes of that Speer 9mm. Then one of these." I plucked a box from a rack that was accessible to customers and brought that over to the counter.

"See, that looks like your standard nine millimeter round, but believe it or not, those are actually blanks. Got a bunch in because some production company said they were shooting a movie down here. The movie must have folded though, because they backed out on the order. You want a third box of the Speer?"

"No. I'd like these."

"Oh, okay. You do film work too?"

"More like illusions," I said. "I won't ask to load a mag with live rounds in the store, but would you object to me loading a mag with the blanks?"

"Not planning to fire it inside are you?"

"Nope."

"Then as long as you pay for them first, I won't make a fuss. I'll expect you to take the live rounds elsewhere to load though, unless you're inside the range."

"Understood." I pulled a debit card from my wallet and handed it to him, along with my ID.

He got to work with a scanner and the keypad on the

computer doing the paperwork and even rang in a veteran discount, but when it came time to swipe the card, he frowned. "Says it declined. I tried twice. You have another credit card?"

I checked the total and grumbled. "Yeah. Hang on." I begrudgingly handed over my Archangel Aviation company card. "Try that one."

He swiped it. "Looks like that one went through just fine. Sometimes these machines are finicky."

His comment was appreciated but I knew the issue likely lay with my card balance and the lack of paychecks I'd been allocating myself. I accepted the card back and started bagging things up.

"I'll carry this one out empty," I said, picking up the original mag and showing him. "I won't need the packaging." I collected the complimentary appendix holster that came with the purchase, then stuck that and the gun with the empty mag in the waistband of my pants. "I'm on a scooter at the moment," I explained. "The less to carry, the better."

The salesman shrugged and observed as I loaded the second magazine with the blanks and took the rest in a reusable shopping bag with the store logo on it. I left the remaining packaging on the counter.

"Hope you get some good use out of them. You perform any of your illusions around here? It's not one of those bullet catching tricks, is it?"

"I always try to avoid catching bullets."

"You and me both, brother."

I gathered my acquisitions and walked out, feeling the man's eyes on me the entire way.

Outside, I squinted in the daylight till I found my shades and slipped them on. I'd left Frank to his own devices, needing a break from our conversation at the restaurant, but he was around here somewhere. The neighboring area included a marina and a bar/restaurant with a thatched roof facade for its tiki bar. If there was a more stereotypical Florida street than this stretch offering guns, boats, and beers, I hadn't seen it.

Before going in search of Frank, I stopped where I'd parked the scooter and arranged the rest of my purchases. The magazine loaded with blanks went into the gun and back into my waistband while I pulled the second mag from my front pocket and loaded it with live 9mm rounds. Before I tucked it away again, I took a moment to remove my pocket knife and make a noticeable scratch on the bottom. Seemed like telling the two mags apart at a glance might be a trick worth knowing.

The rest of the ammo went in the scooter's storage compartment which I locked with the key and felt satisfied it would stay there.

Frank had been walking toward the bar last I'd seen him, so I headed that way, but halfway there I spotted him on the marina docks instead. He was talking to some guy with a fishing boat and pointing off in the distance. I paused and watched. He was pointing northeast, out toward Boca Chica Key and beyond. He waved his arm around some, then stopped when he saw me.

Where are you trying to go, Frank?

I had five bucks said it was an island I had marked on an old sectional chart from Earl.

I kept walking, making my way toward the marina. By the time I'd made it through the gate, Frank was on his way back.

"What was that all about?" I asked as he got closer.

"Seeing if I could procure us a boat."

"You haven't even found where The Mooch lives yet. What good will a boat do you?"

"A boat's always good for the Keys. Anywhere you go around here is close to water. Plus we'd be traveling in some style."

Sounded like bullshit but I let it pass. "We've got a turquoise rental scooter. That's all the style we need right now."

"I thought of another place The Mooch used to own in town. The guy on the dock said it's still around. There's a chance he might be there. I figure we check that out next. You get what else we needed?"

I reached under my shirt and pulled out the pistol, then switched my grip on it and offered it to him. "You owe me five hundred bucks."

"Five hundred? You couldn't buy something cheaper?"

"You asked for a gun. You got one. If you wanted cheap, I could've brought the one of these I already own at home."

"If I'd have asked you to bring a gun along from the start, you wouldn't have flown me down here."

I considered that. He was probably right.

"Just take it." I offered the holster as well.

"I didn't say I wanted to be the one to carry it. You're the one doing the intimidation. And I just got out of the clink. It's not a good look for me."

"You want to wave a gun in someone's face, you carry it. Or I can return it right now and get my money back."

Frank looked around once to check the area, then accepted the gun and holster, tucking it behind his hip under his shirt. "So you're in this all the way then?"

"No. I'm in this till you screw it up and get yourself shipped back to prison. And I won't be going with you. If this guy, The Mooch, is really the asshole responsible for Mom being dead, then he and I are going to have more than words. But if you turn out to be the one full of shit, I'm going to find the fastest way to put you back in Union and make sure you stay there."

Frank put his palms up. "I get it." He straightened his shirt. "What did you think about the boat idea?"

"Unless it's free, forget it. This venture is already costing me too much. If we need to get somewhere on the water badly enough we'll take the plane."

"That'd be real subtle."

"You want this thing done? Let's get it done. Subtle be damned."

"All right." Frank frowned toward the scooter. "So much for style."

SIXTEEN

FAKE IT

"YOU'RE SURE this is the address?" I asked, taking in the view of the building from the parking lot we'd arrived in. "This place is a strip club."

"There's no business like show business," Frank said.

"I'm not sure this is what they mean by that."

"Seems like it would apply."

The two story building was pressed against the sidewalk across the street, not far from the cemetery we'd visited earlier. It featured a sun-faded awning over the staircase and bad paint on the walls of the gaudy tourist trap of a store below, but that likely didn't bother anyone during the nighttime hours.

"The Mooch owns this place?"

"Plenty of cash to wash."

"For more reasons than one. If we go in there, is anyone going to recognize you?"

"Why would anyone recognize me in a strip club?"

"I don't know, is this a place you hung around and did business back in the day?"

He frowned. "In all your life have you ever known me to visit a strip club?"

"I was a kid. I had no idea what you were getting into while you were gone other than most of the time it was illegal."

"Doesn't mean I was paying strange women to wave their tits in my face. Why, is this the type of place *you* hang out?"

"Never been in one."

"But since I'm your jailbird dad, I must have, huh? I see."

"After the way you hit on that waitress at the restaurant, pardon me if I'm having trouble gauging the limits of your libido."

"If you spent decades without the benefit of feminine conversation, you'd miss it too. You miss a lot of things, like making a woman smile. Doesn't make me a Lothario. And I never disrespected your mother by going into a place like this while we were married. The fact you think I would tells me you didn't know our relationship as well as you think."

"I stand corrected. Want me to refer to you as Saint Frank from now on?"

"I didn't say that and you know it."

"Maybe San Frank-o. You could be the patron saint of old narcos."

"Okay, enough. But you do make a good point. If I go up there, they might know I'm after The Mooch and tip him off. You should probably go."

"You've never besmirched your holy name in a strip club, but now you want me to."

"*Down these mean streets a man must go who is not himself mean. Who is neither tarnished nor afraid.*"

"Don't quote Raymond Chandler at me."

"Just seeing if you've kept up with your reading."

"I always do the reading." I pocketed the keys to the scooter. "I doubt this place is even open in the mid-afternoon. You couldn't think of an address where to find this guy during daylight hours?"

Frank squinted at the sun overhead. "Maybe The Mooch is nocturnal."

I left my father behind, forging across sparse traffic to the far side of the street. A wrap-around balcony surrounded the second floor of the old building. I took the wooden stairs two at a time and reached the top with only a minor spike in heart rate. The club was quiet, no music. Closed as suspected. A sign on the wall posted the hours starting at 8 p.m. The door stood open, however, and a young Hispanic guy was having a go at the floors with a mop. He looked up when he saw me. "Sorry. We closed."

"I'm looking for the owner."

He shook his head. "Sorry. No English."

I switched to Spanish and tried again. "I'm looking for the owner of this place. Man named Tony. El jefe."

"Tony? No. El jefe, sí. In the back." He pointed.

A doorway sat open to the left of the stage. Dim light emanated from the hallway beyond.

All the original windows were covered, leaving the patch of sunlight coming in the door as the only natural light. The overhead can lights were all odd colors and bathed the floor in weird patches. Made me realize why the cleaning guy wanted the door open.

The shiny bronze poles on the stage stood vacant and forlorn. Not a bare breast in sight.

I walked down the hall to the back, my footsteps echoing from the walls. The manager's office sat at the far end and when I reached the doorway, he looked up from his desk.

"Who the hell let you in?" he asked.

It wasn't Tony. This guy was barely thirty but with a mustache and mutton chops fit for a tour in the Civil War. His sleeveless shirt repped a name I vaguely recognized as a WWE wrestler and the guy himself looked like he might be at home in a ring. He sat squished behind the desk, the laptop he was using comically small for his huge hands.

"I'm looking for Tony B."

"What for?"

"I'm collecting for Girl Scouts of America. Tony owes us for a lot of cookies."

He chuckled.

I was hilarious.

I took a few steps into the office and looked around to give him time to size me up. I still had a pair of toothpicks from the restaurant. I pulled one out and stuck it between my teeth. I held up the little plastic wrapper. "You got a trash can?"

He pointed to the corner. "What's your business with Tony?"

"He told me to deliver something to him last night but I got held up," I said. "I'm trying to catch him today instead, but he didn't say where he'd be. You know where he is?"

"You a new driver?"

"I'm a pilot, actually."

"Pilot? What happened to Jimmy?"

I stuck one hand in my pocket and still worked the toothpick with the other. "Jimmy must be busy. I'm filling in."

"Why haven't I seen you in here before?"

"I usually hang around the airport. This time Tony said come talk to him directly."

"What's your name?"

"Ray." I picked up one of the business cards he had on the desk. It had a silhouette of a girl upside down on a pole. "If he's gonna be here soon, I'll hang around, otherwise I'll come back."

"I'll text him. He's probably at the house." He picked up his phone. "He's not usually in here till late."

"Gimme the address and I'll go by there. Save him the trip."

"Just sit tight."

"Gonna have to go there anyway."

He started texting. I nudged a cardboard box of flyers on the floor with my toe. The office was cluttered with them. Junk mail, a wall calendar written on with Sharpie, a wipe board with a schedule beside it, dancer names in columns by shifts. All the unsexy parts of running a club.

He finished texting and stared at his phone waiting for a reply. When none immediately came, he set the phone down exasperated. "Probably in the pool." He pushed away from his desk and stood. "I gotta piss. Don't go anywhere." He got up and stomped down the hall.

He left his phone.

Don't mind if I do.

I peeked down the hall, then slid around the side of the desk and picked up the guy's phone. But I was immediately faced with a passcode screen. Locked. Damn. But his laptop wasn't. It was an Apple product, and the toolbar on the left had a messages app. With any luck it was connected to the phone.

I clicked the talk bubble icon and waited. The chats popped up. Sure enough, the last text he sent was there.

>> Some pilot guy is here asking for you. Ray. You want me to send him over?

He'd sent it to a Tony Brewer.

Bingo.

I copied the phone number into my phone, then found Mutton Chops's number and saved it too. I could run The Mooch's number through a property records website, maybe get a hit on an address that way.

I was about to close the chat when a response came back.

"Who the fuck is Ray? What's he want?"

That wasn't helpful. The message had appeared on the lock screen of the iPhone too. I picked the phone up and swiped the notification away and then deleted the chat from the laptop. I had no idea if that would remove it from the phone though. I was guessing not.

Time to go.

I closed the message chat on the laptop and slipped back around to my side of the desk just before Mutton Chops entered the doorway. He wasn't alone. A busty black-haired woman in a too-tight T-shirt and sweatpants followed him in.

"Ray, this is Sapphire, she's the shift manager for the girls tonight. She's got a car, and needs to go see Tony today anyway. When Tony gets back to me, maybe you can ride over with her. She'll introduce you."

"Actually, I just had a message from him," I said, holding up my phone and pretending to read a text. "I guess Jimmy told him my name was something different and he got confused. But it's all sorted now. I'm supposed to head over." I rattled off Tony's phone number. "That's him?"

"Yeah. That's his number."

"Cool. Then we're set." I slipped my phone back into my pocket.

"You got the address?"

"Not yet, but Sapphire does, yeah?"

Sapphire was compact, like a gymnast. Black braided hair that hung down her back. She was chewing gum and putting off a disinterested vibe as she looked me over, but her eyes were bright and intelligent. More there than she was letting on.

I gave her my best smile. "Ready when you are."

Sapphire turned on her heel and headed back down the hall. Mutton Chops gave me a final once over, almost like he was going to say something, but yelled down the hall instead. "Move your ass, Saph, I need you back here pronto."

"Fuck you, Craig," she called back.

He looked at me and clenched his jaw.

"Sassy women run the world," I said. "I can see why you like her."

He grumbled something inaudible. Maybe she was his Elsbeth and did his bookkeeping. Everybody needs one.

I followed her out before Craig had a reason to change his mind.

Downstairs, Sapphire made a beeline for a car parked on the same side of the street I'd used. I gave her a 'hold one minute' gesture with my finger and cruised over to where Frank was loitering near the scooter. I tossed him the keys.

"Where we headed?" he asked.

"Follow us. She's taking us to The Mooch. Right now."

"Wait, does he know we're coming?"

"Everyone is gonna know something is up soon. I lied my ass off in there. We've got a short fuse till this blows up on us."

"Damn it. We were trying to sneak up on him, not barge in the front door."

"Beggars can't be choosers, Frank. We're making progress. Let's go."

"I still don't have a driver's license."

"Then you'd better not get caught. Maybe make yourself some happy scooter memories to relive in prison just in case."

SEVENTEEN

TAILDRAGGER

"WHO'S THAT OLD GUY?" Sapphire said when I sank into the passenger seat of her Firebird.

"A pain in my ass," I said.

"I know a lot of those." She started the car. After her third twist of the key, the engine caught and fired.

The vintage Firebird looked to be from the 80s. The interior was worse for wear but still classic.

"I like your car. But you need a tune-up. Sounds like you have an exhaust leak too," I said.

"You want to pay for that?" she said. "I drive it till it stops moving or something falls off, then I fix it. Like a normal person."

"I'm in the maintenance business, you'll have to forgive my enthusiasm."

"You're a car mechanic?"

"Planes. Less dirty. More money. At least in theory."

"Big planes?"

"Little ones. The fun ones. I'll take you up sometime."

"Oh, you fly them too. No thanks. Little planes scare the hell out of me."

"I don't think you could ever get me to swing on a pole in my underwear. So I guess we're both gutless."

She pulled the car out of the lot and shook her head. "Up on the pole is the safest place in the club. Up there, you're in control. Nobody can touch you unless you want them to."

"Just like in a flight deck."

"That where the pilots sit? Thought it was called a cockpit."

"We changed it. We're evolving as a culture. Generally putting fewer cocks in things."

She snorted. "Weirdo." But she had a smile on her face.

I checked the side view mirror to make sure Frank was behind us. She checked her mirror too.

"What's that guy do? He your bodyguard?"

"He just got out of prison for being a piece of shit."

She checked the mirror again, then looked at me. "Ah, damn. He's your dad, isn't he?"

"Dad is a word that means something. You have to earn that title."

"I used to think my dad was a piece of shit too. Till he died. Then I realized I had a lot of things I still wanted to say to him. You should feel lucky you still have yours to talk to, even if you're mad at him."

"Maybe. Right now I'm glad he's back there and not up here." I looked in the side view mirror again and checked on Frank. And the car behind him. I twisted in my seat to look out the back window.

"What?" Sapphire asked.

"You mind making a turn up here? Next left."

"Why?" She glanced in the mirror again too.

"The same car's been behind us since we left the lot. Just want to see if it's a coincidence."

"That black one?"

The SUV was generic, some form of Nissan crossover that

would blend right in at an elementary school car line, but the windows were tinted so dark it made it hard to see the driver or anyone else inside.

Sapphire made the turn, Frank staying behind us on the scooter, then a few moments later, the SUV turned as well, keeping its distance but following nonetheless.

"Who is that?" Sapphire said.

"Great question."

"You want me to lose them?" She up shifted the Firebird to third again.

"Not yet. Keep going."

She turned back on course toward wherever we were heading.

I ran through who might have an interest in following us. "You think that's someone your buddy Craig sent after us? Like to guard you?"

She checked the mirror again. "Craig's not really the 'guard me' type. And I don't think any of his friends would drive that car."

"How far to your boss's house?"

"It's close. Like three minutes."

My phone rang and I pulled it from my pocket. Cassidy was calling. Her picture popped up. Sapphire noted it too. Now wasn't the best time. I sent the call to voicemail. But a moment later the phone was buzzing again. Still Cassidy. We'd played this game before. She was going to keep trying till I picked up.

"Hey," I said, answering this time.

"You *are* alive."

"All's right with the world. What's up?"

"I got a call from Elsbeth. She was concerned about you."

"That's thoughtful of her. Tell her I'm fine."

"She mentioned you made a purchase on the company card at a gun store in the Keys."

I lowered the volume on the phone, then put it back to my ear. "Just had to pick up some supplies. Should be headed back tonight."

"That your wife?" Sapphire asked.

"Business partner," I clarified.

"Who are you with?" Cassidy asked.

"Uh, that was Sapphire. She's my ride at the moment."

"Sapphire? Why does she have a stripper name?"

"Pretty sure they call it 'exotic dancer' now." I looked at Sapphire. "Am I correct on that?"

She wagged a hand. "I've been liking 'burlesque queen,' lately. And you can tell her I'm not a hooker anymore if that's what she's worried about."

"Putting fewer cocks in things."

Sapphire laughed. "Yes. Evolving."

I twisted to look out the back window again.

"I can tell you are having a great time down there, Luke, but you do owe me an explanation at some point," Cassidy said. "I had to hear it from Reese that Earl died."

"He did. Yeah." I shifted my tone. "I promise I'll explain soon, hon. But I need to go right now. There's somebody following us and there's a lot going on. Good news is my father has agreed to sign over a bill of sale for the plane. I should have that in my hand by the end of the day. We'll have the business back on track."

"You talked to Frank? In prison?"

"He's out now. Reese didn't mention that?"

"Wait, is he with you?"

"Kind of a long story, but yeah. I promise I'll fill you in later. Don't worry about me."

"You can't go gun shopping as a business expense with your convict father you hate and then say 'don't worry about it.' And who is following you?"

"It's all going to work out. You'll just have to trust me."

"Luke."

"Gotta go." I hung up.

Sapphire raised an eyebrow. "You call your business partner 'hon?'"

"Old habit. We used to be married. It's complicated."

"Not that complicated. It's obvious you're still into her or you wouldn't be trying to make her jealous."

"You always this perceptive when you meet strangers or just with the handsome pilots who diagnose your car problems?"

"You're not that handsome. Though offering to fix my car is kinda hot. You want to clean my apartment and do my laundry later? That'd be sexy as hell."

"What about guys who cook? I look pretty good in an apron." I winked at her and she laughed.

"Now that's what I call a package."

Her phone buzzed while we were stuck at a stop light and her eyes alternated from the light to the screen, then she lost her smile and her jaw went tight.

"That text about me?" I asked. "You can say it."

She glanced over, her humor gone. "Your name really Ray?"

"Your name really Sapphire?"

She glared out the windshield as she accelerated the Firebird, some inner debate going on behind her dark eyes. "Look. I'm supposed to take you someplace else now. Craig says."

"Where?"

"Someplace his boys can talk to you."

"Pull over. I'll get out here."

"That's not what he wants."

"This come from Tony?"

She didn't say anything.

"How dangerous a dude is he?" I asked. "Scale of one to ten."

"Dangerous enough that I don't want to be on his bad side. Tony's a six. But he's connected to people that are a twelve."

"Craig too?"

"Craig's a pissant but he has a temper."

"You can leave me somewhere else. Tell them I had a gun."

Her grip tightened on the steering wheel, then she looked me over, checking for a bulge beneath my shirt. "Damned men are all the same. Even you, huh?"

"We're not all the same. Tony's part of something set in motion a long time ago, and whoever else is tied into it. It's not on you or me, it's on them."

"There's not a bad thing in the world a man can't find some way to blame on a woman if he feels like it." The next light turned green as we approached and she drove through that intersection but then pulled the Firebird into the parking lot of a mini-mart convenience store. Frank followed on the scooter. I watched the mirror as the black SUV behind him slowed but sped on. Still couldn't make out the driver.

Sapphire parked and turned off the ignition, then stared out the windshield at the jungle of palms that rimmed the lot. Her grip was still white-knuckled on the wheel. "Before you get out the car, you're gonna have to hit me. And make it convincing. 'Cause Craig's gonna be pissed."

"Tell him the gun convinced you."

"He'll knock me around worse than you will. Trust me. He'll hit me anyway, but maybe not so bad if I'm already banged up."

I stewed on that. "You're not giving me any good reasons to like your bosses."

"I go back there and say I just let you out, I won't work for a month, and I have bills," she said. "We have a deal?"

"Not yet. I need something first."

"Why? My end of this isn't bad enough already?"

"I need to know where Tony's place is. Where you were taking me before they texted you. An address."

"I don't have the address, I just know where it is. It's right down the street." She pointed.

"He lives here in the tourist district?"

"A couple years ago that house right next to the Southernmost Point came up for sale. They call it the Southernmost Southernmost House. Tony thought it would be funny to buy it. I heard it's worth twenty million in this market, though I'm sure he didn't pay that. Probably sweated someone for it."

"Busy spot. Explains why he's able to troll Duval Street so easily."

"Does that screw up your plans for him?"

"The less you know about it the better."

"What else do you need?"

"That'll do. Where do you need me to hit you? Somewhere in the face, presumably, to leave a mark?"

She gave me a resigned nod. "Thought you might be one of these guys who pretend they could never hit a woman because of chivalry or some shit."

"You spend any time in war, they tell you there's violence for the sake of violence, and violence for the sake of peace. My old sergeant once said 'God makes us capable of both, but it's where we draw the line that defines our character.'"

"How about when you cross the line?"

"The devil earns his due."

"Then the devil makes a fortune on this island." She straightened up and turned toward me. "Better not break my damn nose. I'll be pissed."

I sighed. "Look past my right shoulder." I raised my left fist.

She did.

"Count to three."

"One . . . Two . . . Three."

I'd intended to jab at two, but at three, my fist still hovered in midair.

Shit. I'd found my line.

She glared. "You're wimpin' out on me? What about our deal?"

"It's not as easy as it sounds."

"Sure is for the kinda guys I know."

I let my hand fall to my lap. "How many men have hit you over the course of your career? In your life?"

"Not sure I can count that high."

I sighed. "How about you hit me then. Hit me for them. Hit me for them. For all the times you wish you could've hit back."

Her eyes flashed. A spark.

"The place I'd need to hit you wouldn't work sitting down. You'd need to be outside standing up with your legs wide open."

"Fine." I opened my door and got out of the Firebird. I closed the door and walked around the back of the car. Once I reached the driver's side, I pulled her handle to open the door for her, but found it locked.

She rolled the window the rest of the way down.

"You getting out?" I asked. "I won't flinch away. Promise. Hit me anywhere you like. Use your knee if it makes you happy."

She looked up at me from the driver's seat, but the vengeance I'd seen flash in her eyes was gone. Instead she spoke softly. "You didn't even really have a gun on you, did you?"

"Sorry. You wanna get out and kick me?"

She gave me a resigned smile. "You seem like a guy that might someday figure out what a woman really wants. I hope you do. Maybe you'll find it with that business partner of yours. But you've still got a lot to learn."

Then she rolled the window up, put the Firebird in reverse,

and backed out of the parking space. She pulled out of the lot and onto the road, never once looking back.

Frank wandered his way over from where he'd parked the scooter. "What the hell was that all about?"

The sound of the Firebird's loud exhaust faded into the distance.

"I offered to let her hit me where it hurts," I said.

And she hadn't missed.

EIGHTEEN

FIGHT PLAN

A GUY WAS SELLING snow cones and fresh coconuts along
Whitehead Street, and I was vaguely tempted as we walked by in
the afternoon sun. We'd left the scooter a block north and
navigated the gauntlet of trolleys and sweaty tourists intent on an
Internet-worthy photo. The red concrete buoy that marked the
Southernmost Point in the Continental US was the sort of
roadside oddity good for postcard photographs, well-practiced
selfies, and not much else. But it attracted a crowd. It was easy
enough to blend in amongst the passersby and get a look at the
"Southernmost Southernmost House" as marked by a metal
plaque on the wall.

I trusted the duplication of emphasis on "Southernmost" was
to delineate it from the previous Southernmost House, now
turned into a hotel down the street.

This even more southerly house sat on the water, obscured by
a low stone wall and a dense barrier of palms and shrubbery. A
stone path ran from the locked iron gate back thirty yards to the
front door.

Frank fidgeted, crossed his arms, squinted at the horizon. No son of any parent grows up without learning their tells. Frank was in a mood.

"What do you want to say?" I asked.

"It's no good. This setup is garbage. There's no way we just stroll in the front door."

"The clock is ticking. You wanted me to help you find the guy. He's apparently in there." I held my arm out toward the house. "You're welcome."

"I knock on the door of that house, he sends a guy to throw me out on my ass. I never even look The Mooch in the eye. And I need to look him in the eyes to know if he's the one who sold me out or if I can still trust him."

"Sounds like a you problem."

He fixed me with a stare. "Is this how you work all the time? Doing a half-assed job?"

I bristled. "What the hell would you know about how I work? I came this close to punching a stripper for you today. You think that's a choice I'm faced with on a regular basis? No part of this plan of yours is my usual lifestyle."

A couple passing by looked over and then picked up the pace as they walked on.

"All I know is what I've seen so far," Frank said. "I see a guy who can't wait to be done with me and gone. So much so he's phoning it in when it counts. So are you going to bail off the board at the first sign of trouble, like a poser, or will you ride the wave all the way in?"

Suddenly I was ten again, standing on the shoreline in Costa Rica, Frank chastising me for not getting past the crashing breakers. It worked though. I got back on my board and paddled through the next set.

Now I was a grown man who didn't need his approval, yet here we were.

I glared back at him, then at the house. The wall was low

enough to hop. It also had water access. There were plenty of ways in for the dedicated. The only problem was the bevy of tourists and the likelihood that one called the police the moment we went over the wall. A place down the street looked more promising.

"Walk with me. We'll go around."

Frank followed me along South Street away from the tourists and past the next two residences. They looked like boarded-up rentals but had sturdy fences and PRIVATE PROPERTY signs on bold display. Fortunately, the next building was a boutique hotel called *The Mansion by the Sea*, and the place was doing a bustling business. It was the work of only a few minutes to enter the grounds, assume the casual we-belong-here posture of a guest, and stroll around to the rear pool area. We passed a front window that sported a bullet hole left there for nostalgia purposes. Rumor was someone had taken a shot at Al Capone while he was visiting once. I hoped we could avoid gunfire this trip.

The elegant pool out back was currently stuffed with cute-but-squealing children, bringing down the appeal. Beyond the pool was an inviting private beach with a bar to the left, and to the right, a pathway over a deteriorating seawall that looked just about right for us.

A brief check to make sure no one was paying close attention was good enough and we cut back across the grounds of the private property next door, picking our way carefully over the deteriorating seawall. We were exposed for fifty yards, but our only observers were a rooster and a pair of hens pecking around the yard.

It took less than a minute till we reached the perimeter of The Mooch's property and this corner of the lot featured heavy foliage. The privacy wall of plant life also served as a screen as we sank in between a pair of palms to observe the scene beyond.

The back of the Southernmost Southernmost House had a

broad patio pool deck, rectangular pool, and a two-tiered sea wall. The outer wall was crumbling in sections, battered by the Atlantic. A flagpole at the far corner of the outer sea wall was adorned with plaques denoting the joining point of the Atlantic and the Gulf of Mexico. The geographical significance of the place was dubious, but likely made for an easy conversation topic at dinner parties.

The pool area was occupied. Two pretty young women lounged on deck chairs, and the surface of the pool rippled with waves as a man churned around in the rectangle of blue. His head was bare, his hair thin, tan speckled scalp showing through strands of reddish gray. He wore a short beard over a spreading chin, and he stretched around in the water with broad shoulders and hairy arms. He swam width to width in what appeared to be around five feet of water. After splashing to and fro a bit, he lumbered toward the shallow end, rising by degrees then reaching the steps with the steady plodding of a sow. More of him emerged dripping from the water, his vast waist overflowing his swim trunks.

"Now I'm thinking I should've had you stop at a harpoon store," Frank said.

"That's Tony?" I parted the fronds ahead of me for a better view.

"In the flesh."

Tony's flesh was abundant but he was powerfully built. It didn't look as though he was going to be winning any sprints, but a hippopotamus can supposedly run nineteen miles an hour. Looks can be deceiving.

The two women were of the twiggy variety, owing largely to age. Neither looked to be over thirty and must have grown up in the era of self-deprivation for the sake of thigh gaps. Whatever skills they had beyond looking good in bikinis weren't currently on display. One was engaged with her phone, the other must have feared tan lines because she was lying topless on the chair for maximum sun absorption. Her eyes might have been closed, though it was impossible to tell with the oversized mirrored shades she wore.

"What's your play here?" I asked Frank, keeping my voice low. "If you're planning to rough this guy up, he's bound to have help inside. Could get nasty. Even if I can dissuade the help from tossing you out, the girl on the phone calls the cops, they'll be here in five minutes. They'd already have us on trespassing. You pull that gun on Fat Tony and they'll have you on brandishing, or assault with a deadly weapon. If things get rough, we've got no resources, not even a way out. Unless you plan to swim for Cuba."

Frank frowned down at me. "You always this worried about what-ifs?" He pulled the Sig from his waistband and handed it over. "If you're so scared of me brandishing a weapon, take it back. It was only for show anyway. I'll do this thing my old way." He straightened up and tightened his belt. "Just follow my lead and play along." Then he walked out of the bushes into the brilliant sunlight of the patio.

I swore. What kind of stupid plan was this?

But I tucked away the gun and followed.

NINETEEN

THE MOOCH

THE TOPLESS GIRL spotted us first. The one in the mirrored sunglasses. Her head turned and her posture tensed. Tony noted the reaction and turned too. His wide face and thick jowls quivered with an instant anger. "Who the hell do you think you are, walking—" but he cut himself off and narrowed his eyes. His gaze flashed to me for only an instant before refocusing entirely on Frank.

"Living the high life, Mooch," Frank said. "Not that I expected any less." He stopped at the edge of the pool and kept his voice casual, looking around the place like he'd been invited. "You always did know how to skim from the clients."

The stocky man on the pool steps weighed double what Frank did. He was hairy like a gorilla and possibly just as strong, but something went out of him at the sight of my father.

"Frank Angel? That you . . . buddy?"

Frank nodded to the women on the lounge chairs who were both staring. "You've moved up in the world," he said to Tony. "Used to be you only got the pretty girls by association."

"Surprised to see you out, Frank," Tony said. "Who's this guy you got here?"

"That's my boy, Luke. Keeping me company while I settle some old scores."

Tony's left cheek twitched at that, and he cast a quick glance at the house, then at the closest girl on a deck chair. "Samantha, honey, why don't you go see what's keeping José with those snacks. Tell him to get his ass back out here."

"She's Samantha," the young woman with the phone replied. "I'm Brittney."

"You know what I meant."

"I can text him," the girl said, not moving.

"You can go get him," Tony growled. "And make it fast."

The girl gave an exasperated sigh. "Fine. I needed another drink anyway." She climbed off the chair, ran her eyes over me again, then picked up an empty plastic tumbler and headed for the sliding door of the house, her thong bikini nearly invisible from this angle.

Tony's face had reddened. He seemed to notice he was still half in the water and climbed the rest of the steps to his full height which still wasn't tall. He dripped as he hiked his shorts back up. "You need a drink, Frank? Beer? Cocktail? What can I get you?"

"I think you know a thing or two about why I'm here, Mooch."

"Been a long time since we've worked together." Tony picked up a towel and began to dry himself off. "I'm retired now."

"That's not how I hear it."

I stayed vigilant, watching Tony. It didn't look like he had any place nearby to hide a gun, but he was shifting his feet, eyes roaming everywhere—antsy.

"When did you get out, buddy? If I'd have known, we could have put a little something together. Some of the old crew.

Made a real celebration out of it." He dabbed at his face and neck.

"I'll talk to some of them soon enough. But what I say depends a lot on whether you're willing to help me out with a business deal."

Tony stopped moving the towel, then started patting himself again slower. He chuckled. "You still have those damned diamonds. I wondered."

The topless girl on the chair lowered her sunglasses down her nose at the word diamonds, getting a better look at Frank, then Tony, watching both men with curiosity.

Diamonds. So that's what Frank had been hiding.

"You have them with you?" Tony asked.

"Not yet. Wanted to set a few things up first. Make sure you're still the right guy to deal with. But if you're retired . . ."

Tony gave another chuckle. "Samantha, baby, go check on your girlfriend. And get José, yeah?"

"You think your man José wants any part of this?" Frank said. "I think you want everything I have to say kept between us. Especially after what went down last time we worked together."

The girl on the chair froze halfway up.

"Keep on," Tony said. "You don't work for him."

She got up but didn't move much faster than her friend had. She picked up her bikini top and gave my father and me another long stare before walking away.

"Now what are you talking about, Frank?" Tony asked.

"You know damned well." Frank stared Tony down, waiting.

The Mooch put his palms up. "That crash. Your wife. The feds. That wasn't me, Frank, you gotta know I never would have done a thing like that."

"I want to believe you, Mooch. But I know it wasn't Ziggy or Barnes or Tito. They all died broke or in prison. Leaves a short list. Earl's dead now too in case you hadn't heard. I've had a lot of time to think about it, and the way I put it together, you had the best motive. Plenty of that crew had one, but now I get out and find you living in a twenty million dollar place with a big boat somewhere, soaking up the good life, and it makes a lot of sense it was you."

"Look, I took my cut of every deal we did back then. You knew that. And maybe I invested some of your old stuff too after the feds nabbed you. But you wanted that right? You been gone a long time. Money makes money. That's the game. The big nut. What you hid away? I never went after that. Not to say others didn't. But not me. I figured the feds got it. That's certainly not what this is." He spread his arms to encompass the house. "This was me. My retirement plan."

"Lucia is dead, Mooch. She didn't get to see her retirement plan. Because somebody turned on us and stabbed us in the back."

Some of the color drained from Tony's face. "I know it. And I know how it looked when that went down. But that wasn't me. I told you."

"Convince me."

"How am I supposed to do that?"

"Give me the name. So I can set things straight."

"You think I'd know that, Frank? I was torn up about what happened to you. And it was a real shitty accident, but I wasn't the only one in on that deal, you know it. There were a lot of players."

"I'm not the only one who doesn't think it was an accident," Frank said. "And it cost a lot of other people something on that deal. Big people. They'd also like to know for sure."

Tony bristled. "These are my people you're talking about. My customers. You've been gone a long time. Who do you even know anymore, Frank?"

"You ask the wrong question, Mooch. You don't ask me who I

still know. You ask who still knows me. And when they think about me, what do they know for certain? For one, they know I'm the kind of guy who doesn't fuck around. I'm the guy who did his bid with his mouth shut and never peeped a word about them. And they know the value of a guy with that reputation. So while you think about this situation, you think about that. Think about your reputation. Then you think about mine. And when you stack those two up next to each other you'll see what the kinds of people we deal with are going to see and who they're going to back if I find out you had anything to do with it."

"Frank. I swear on my mother's grave I had no part in what went down. You tell me what you need from me to prove it—anything within reason—I'll do it."

"Put me in touch with your guy," Frank said.

"My guy."

"Whatever this is," Frank said. "The guy who kept you out while I was in, because I know what the feds had on me and they could have knocked down your door any time and they didn't. So whoever that person is, I want to talk to them. Because if they know that much, they also know who took me down."

The sliding door opened and a guy with thick black hair and a bushy mustache came out. He wore a tight white polo shirt and khaki shorts and wore a gun openly at his hip. He came out with purpose and kept his eyes on us the whole time. He strode up beside Tony and flexed his neck muscles at us. "You need me, boss?"

Tony The Mooch stood a little straighter with his man next to him. But he watched Frank warily. His jaw worked, calculations in his mind showing as little twitches in his jowls.

"José, find me my phone, will you?"

José looked vaguely disappointed that's all he'd been summoned for, but he disappeared back into the house. He returned ten seconds later with the phone. Tony located a contact and put the phone to his ear. A moment later he said, "This is Tony. Frank Angel just showed up at my place, looking for some answers."

Someone on the other end spoke, but it was too low for me to make out.

"He wants to talk to you too," Tony said, and handed the phone to Frank.

Frank took it. "Yeah, this is Frank. You know who I am? Good. I've been away a long time but you'd better believe yours is a voice I remember too, so you probably know why I'm here."

He listened for a moment, then continued. "I'm willing to make you that deal too, but I need to know that in the end, you're going to do what's right. You know where I've been and for how long and you know why. So you know what else I need too."

Whatever the person on the other end said, it must have satisfied him. "Fine. I'll be in touch." He gave the phone back to Tony. "Here. He wants you again."

As he listened to whoever was on the other end, Tony's expression morphed from skepticism to attention and finally resignation.

He didn't speak until the end when he said, "I understand."

The phone went dead in his hand, and he stared at it a moment before passing it back to José. He turned to Frank and finally he said, "What else do you need?"

"I've got a buyer lined up. When I come back, you'll broker the deal, and you can double your usual cut. Then you get me out of here. Passport, travel, the works. Tomorrow."

"I don't know if I can line it up that fast."

"I know you can. We're going to settle this quietly and quickly. Because if you screw me over, or tip anyone else that I'm here, I'll start making calls. And if anything happens to me, stories are going to come out. And the business you've been doing and the people you've been doing it with are going to want answers. And they'll want their money. And they'll be very convincing, and they aren't going to ask so nicely. And then you're going to be retired for real. Maybe permanently."

"Relax. I'm on your side of this," Tony said.

"Then get me out clean this time, Mooch. And get me that name. I'm going to find out sooner or later and it would go better for you if it's sooner."

Tony stared at Frank a long time, licked his lips once, then turned to his security guy and said, "José, go get the car. We need to attend to some business for my old friend." Turning back to us he said, "How am I supposed to contact you?"

"I've got your private number," I said. "We'll call you."

Frank gave me a quizzical glance, but quickly put his game face back on. He pointed a finger at The Mooch. "We're going to settle this thing for good, Mooch. Don't disappoint me."

TWENTY

HEAD IN THE CLOUDS

WE WALKED out of Tony's place through the front door, Frank stuffing an extra wad of cash into his pocket that Tony had donated for "expenses."

I was nearly to where we parked the scooter before my heart rate started to come down.

"That was pretty slick back there," Frank said. "You really have Tony's cell number? It's a lousy thing to make up if you don't."

"I've got it. I snagged it at the strip club."

"That-a-boy." He rubbed his hands together. "Now we're getting somewhere, huh?"

"Two days out of prison and what, you're Walter White now?"

"Am I supposed to get that reference? He'd better be somebody cool, because what I did back there was legendary."

"Walter White was a TV high school chemistry teacher turned ruthless crime boss."

"That doesn't sound like me."

"Fat Tony was terrified of you. Why? You're a smuggler, not a drug kingpin."

"My reputation precedes me."

I scoffed.

"What?"

"If you're so tough, what the hell was that phone call about? Who else did you involve in this deal?"

"Don't worry about it. It worked, didn't it?"

"I worry, because so far, none of the people you know are the kind of people I want to know. If I'm about to meet more, I'd like a heads up."

"I simply set a few things in motion, and gave our boy The Mooch adequate motivation."

"Threatening him."

"That's in the subtext. You want to leave most of it to his imagination. He knows the score. Old boy's crooked as a fishhook. Right now he's thinking hard about how much I know about his business and how badly it goes for him if he doesn't do what I say."

"One reason I can think it's worse in his imagination is that you don't have any cards to play. You made that whole thing up. What happens when he calls your bluff?"

"Who says I'm bluffing? You don't think I have the rep I said I do?"

"You're a consummate bullshitter. That's your rep."

Frank waved me off. "Eh, what do you know about it." He kept walking till he reached the scooter.

"I'll be willing to suspend disbelief if this works," I said.

"It'll work. The Mooch is about to pony up what he knows and get me paid. He'll make out like a bandit, of course. His percentage cut is always sky-high, but that's all right. I'll pick up a few things I need, and once we get what we're after, you get to say sayonara to your jailbird dad and fly off into the sunset with your plane. That's what you wanted, right?"

"What will you do with this name he gives you? Assuming The Mooch drops the dime on whoever it is, and they're still breathing."

"That's my business. Who knows. Maybe I'll forget the whole thing and just let them sweat knowing I know. Hell, maybe I'll go back to Tulum. Back to where I met your mother. We loved it down there. I'll get drunk on the beach and sing sad songs and become a borracho. That okay with you?"

I rolled my shoulders. "Fine. I don't believe you, but whatever. What now? How long before this egg you laid hatches?"

"We'll deal with our end. Getting the stones. We should probably get a room for tonight, in case it goes late. I know a couple of places that might suit us if they're still around. You're the one who knows where we're going for the stones. That was your job, yeah?"

"I said I had the pieces of the puzzle. I haven't put it all together yet." I perched my hands on my hips and sighed. "Before we do anything, I need to get back to the plane. I left what we need there. And I'll need to make some calls. And if we get a place, it needs to be cheap. Otherwise I'm flying out of here without gas money."

"By the end of this, we'll both be flush. You'll take off with full tanks and pockets stuffed with cash."

"Excuse me if I don't hold my breath."

We climbed back aboard the scooter and zipped east and north, me checking the mirrors frequently for a tail. I weaved through a few parking lots to be sure but didn't spot the black SUV or anyone else taking a particular interest in us.

The spot Frank knew about was certainly cheap. A dingy motel tucked off Simonton Street called The Driftwood. It looked like it hadn't been updated since the 1960s. The dude at the desk had a cigarette dangling from his lips despite the no-smoking sign perched next to his ancient computer.

"This by the night or by the hour?" he asked, his eyes wandering to Frank.

"We're not a couple. He's my father," I said.

"I don't ask, so you don't gotta tell me." He tapped at his computer. "I have one with two queens. And I got one king. No. I got two kings in adjoining rooms. Uh . . . that's it." He raised his eyes and stared at me from beneath eyebrows left untrimmed since the Clinton administration.

"Give us the room with the two queens," I said.

"We're gonna want separate rooms," Frank said.

"On whose credit card? You don't have one."

"Put the card down for now and I'll settle up with cash later. This is a man who prefers cash. Look at him."

The guy behind the counter shrugged with his mouth. He didn't disagree.

"The two queens." I slapped my company credit card on the counter. "But don't run it yet. He's buying, apparently."

"It's only for the room charges," he said. "Pay-per-view movies. Whatever you like."

"Are the TVs in color?" I asked.

"Sure," he said, missing my sarcasm.

He put two room key cards on the counter. I half expected real keys with plastic room tags. I gave one to my father. He frowned.

"Cheer up, Frank. You should be used to having bunkmates," I said. "Or do you miss your buddy Deacon?"

He shrugged. "I guess we'll manage."

The path to the rooms involved a walk through an enclosed patio overgrown with palms, then up some stairs to a balcony rimmed by a three-bar metal railing. Old school Florida vibes. I swiped our key card and let the door swing open. I was greeted by a view of dated furniture, two hideous floral bedspreads, wicker headboards, and art that you'd have to pay to leave at Goodwill. The door hit a rubber stopper on the wall and swung back again. "It's a room."

Frank caught the door before it shut. "I'm going in to take a shower and freshen up."

"I'll head back to the plane," I said. "I've got a go-bag there with my stuff."

"Pick me up a toothbrush if you see one. Maybe some mouthwash. Sometimes the counter staff will hook you up with stuff like that. Especially if you say you're a pilot on a delay."

"You're going to stay put, right?"

"What kind of trouble do you think I'll get into?"

"I don't want to find out."

"I'm fine. I'm just going to relax. I know you've got higher standards, but after where I've been, this—" he gestured to the overgrown patio of palms, "this is paradise."

"I'll leave you to enjoy it then."

"Oh, I will." The door shut behind him and I stared at it for only a moment before making my way back downstairs to the scooter. It was significantly lighter and easier to maneuver without Frank on the back, so I zipped through traffic easily, the evening sun descending. I needed to check in with Reese and give her an update on my plans. She'd no doubt give me an "I told you so" when she heard I was getting stuck overnight, but that was her prerogative. Even being wrong could be fun if the needling came from a friend.

Reese had carried the load of the Archangel maintenance department on her shoulders a lot lately and I looked forward to repaying her efforts. Having *Tropic Angel* on the charter certificate would mean more trips down to the Keys and out to the Bahamas, hauling tourists to and fro and generally being a bus driver for customers on vacation mode, but that was fine by me. The Mallard was classic. Once I had it fixed up pretty, it would attract the right kinds of higher paying customers. Archangel would thrive. There would be pay raises for my crew, maybe enough cash to add extra hands. Elsbeth would be off my back and I could lean into the kind of flying I loved. And Cassidy ... Cassidy ...

Cassidy would still be up north. The thought dimmed my vision for the shining future. The thought of her still away, nothing bringing her back. I frowned at that. But at least the dream of a thriving Archangel Aviation gave me some hope. The partner meetings would no longer be her worrying over the state of our finances or what new trouble my family had dragged us into. Maybe St. Pete would be a place she wanted to spend more time. I wouldn't complain.

Frank could bug out to Mexico if he wanted. Out of sight, out of mind. As long as he stayed put somewhere and didn't drag me back into his nonsense, I could live with that.

My mind was still on my imaginings when I left the scooter in the Signature Flight Support parking lot and jogged up the stairs and through the doors. I was only seeing the months ahead, my mind not registering the world around me. But after I'd waved to the counter staff and the door buzzed open to the ramp, I had a nagging in the back of my consciousness. Something tugged at me. A warning. I trotted down the stairs but paused halfway across the ramp and turned around, taking in the planes around me, the fresh FBO building, line guys on golf carts. There was a crab on the tarmac, scuttling its way somewhere, but other than that, nothing out of the ordinary. What had I missed?

I shook it off. Maybe I was getting paranoid.

I continued to the Mallard. A lineman let me use his stepladder again to access the boarding door. I retrieved the boarding steps and climbed aboard, breathing in the comforting old scents of the plane. A history of water landings and skyfaring leaves a tangible residue. The smell of adventure. I opened the aft baggage compartment and fetched out the small army-green duffel I kept back there, then I stooped as I looked up the aisle toward the flight deck.

The sun hadn't set yet. I could still blast off into the late afternoon sky, engines thrumming. It was tempting.

Soon.

The magnetism of the idea drew me forward, through the passenger cabin, and I stepped through the keyhole to the flight deck. I settled into the pilot seat and exhaled.

I ran a hand over the yoke, letting the feeling of the space settle over me. My name finally being on the registration wouldn't change the nature of the plane, but it felt like it might change something about me. A silly thought. It was just a plane. I'd flown hundreds. Owned half a dozen over the years. But this plane. This plane was something else. The history. The memories. I reached into the side pocket of my seat and pulled out my flight log, then slipped the photo from inside the back cover. The photo was of my mother, smiling in a sundress on the shore of a lake, *Tropic Angel* in the background.

"She's almost home for keeps, Mom," I said out loud.

The word home felt intangible on my lips.

Home.

Home certainly wasn't a building. Not Hank's boat that I slept on. Not even Hangar 4, though Archangel was as close to a geographical location as I could pin it to. The people there were my family. My crew. But as for a physical place? I didn't have one. I looked around the flight deck of *Tropic Angel*. I reached up and rested my hand on the throttles. This plane was home.

I slipped the photo of my mother carefully back into the logbook, then tucked it away. I found the other items I needed, Earl's old sectional chart and the airport facilities directory and the kneeboard. I stuffed them into the canvas duffel. My next puzzle to solve. I took one last look around the flight deck, then looked out the window toward the terminal.

That's when I saw it. Through the chain link. An old chevy sedan in the lot on the other side of the fence. The mixed paint job and missing hubcaps. That's what I'd missed. It had failed to register in my consciousness on the walk in. But I knew that car.

Deacon.

Shit.

I took my duffel back through the plane to the rear boarding door. But before I stepped into the frame of the open doorway, I paused and pulled the 9mm Sig from my waistband and ejected the mag, checking the tips of the rounds inside. I switched mags to the one with live rounds, ramming it home and racking the slide, then put the gun away again under my shirt. I had no idea what Deacon was planning when I walked back through the FBO doors, but I was game to find out.

TWENTY-ONE

CATCH OF THE DAY

HE WAS SITTING in one of the plush armchairs in the lobby, a smug grin on his face.

He hadn't been there when I walked in. I was confident of that much. He must have followed me upstairs and kept an eye on me out the window. There was no sign of Lyla. He had different sneakers on this time, checkerboard hight-top Adidas with golden lightning bolts on the sides.

I walked over. There was no point trying to avoid him.

"They'll probably impound that piece of shit car of yours if you leave it in the lot much longer," I said. "This is a classy place."

"They can have it," Deacon replied. "Soon I'll be driving a big-ass truck. One of those hundred thousand dollar rides with the automatic lift gates and a sound system so good it shakes women's panties off."

"Didn't know you were a music lover. Where's your girl?"

"Crazy bitch thought we'd have better luck finding your ass in town. She out looking around. I told her, you want to catch a bird, you watch the nest. Looks like I was right."

"You're a real brainiac all right. But it's a long drive to the Keys just to be disappointed."

"Only thing disappointing me is I don't see Frank. Where my boy at? I know he dipped out with you, so you got him around here somewhere."

I sized Deacon up. Ex-con, out for a payday, that much was obvious. Didn't seem like there was much more to him, but I'd been wrong before.

"You were cellmates with Frank at Union?"

"Best cellie I ever had. Ol' Frank had that OG rep. I liked that. But there's always the occasional banger wanting to hassle him, didn't know the way of things, thought they could punk him. I had to set those fools straight."

"You were a bad dude inside."

"I was a shot caller. You know what that is?"

"Sure. You ran things. Told people how it was."

"That's right. That's why I'm gonna tell you what's what right now. Me and Frank have some business. Maybe you think you want in on it. Maybe you lookin' for a piece of that action. But I'm gonna tell you right now, this is my deal. You want in, you talk to me."

"What did Frank tell you he was up to down here?"

Deacon looked around, checking out the counter staff, seeing who was listening. The two women at the counter had watched when I first walked over to him, curious, but had shifted their attention to other duties. Deacon kept his voice low anyway. "Frank and me came to collect. You don't need to trouble yourself on what. But I'll give you one thing. That plane you got could come in useful. How far it go?"

"Where are you headed?"

"Out. Someplace they got bumpin' clubs and topless beaches. You play the game right, maybe we cut you in. Long as you know your place in the game."

"Seeing as Frank already tried to cut you out, what makes you think *you're* still in the game?"

"I'm gonna have some words with Frank about that. Remind him who his friends are. But we'll get to that. This game is mine to run. You remember that."

"Shot caller."

"Damned straight."

I stuck my hands in my pockets. "All right. I'll take you to Frank, I've got a scooter out front. You can follow me."

He stood. "Nah. How 'bout you ride with me?"

"Scared you can't keep up?"

He scoffed. "Where this place at?"

"A hotel. Coconut Beach Resort. Room 110."

"You give me any shit, I'll serve it back times ten. You got that?"

"Why would anyone give you shit? You're the shot caller." I walked out then, Deacon steaming on my heels. Once we were downstairs, he broke away at a jog to get to the Chevy Caprice while I mounted the scooter. I took it easy getting out of the parking lot, making a show of going slowly, ensuring he could follow.

I checked the mirror a few times, Deacon right on top of me, glaring out his windshield, hands tight on the wheel. There was no point trying to get distance on the straight stretch of South Roosevelt we were on anyway. There were no turns other than the Margaritaville Resort we passed along our way. But once we made the turn up Bertha Street I had more options. Traffic slowed, the streets became residential. I waited till a particularly busy intersection, then gunned it, turning across traffic and setting a horn blaring from a guy in the oncoming lane. But then I had the throttle pinned down, bobbing and weaving around slower cars and a golf cart while Deacon struggled to get the Caprice through the intersection. I heard him make the turn before I saw him, the engine revving and roaring as he raced to follow. But I made a breezy left turn, then a right, zigzagging from George to Johnson to Ashby and Laird streets in short order, then back to George again, circling the block and heading North once more. I'd lost sight of Deacon easily enough, though I could still hear the engine of the Caprice raging through the neighborhood. But he must have continued west. The sound grew fainter.

See ya, Deke.

I raced across Flagler and kept making turns, staying vigilant. I crept through quieter neighborhood intersections, alert for the Caprice, then rocketed on, making my way via a roundabout path toward The Driftwood Motel. The hotel I'd given Deacon was south, but I was under no illusions that he'd fall for it. He could actually check it out though eventually, and that might buy me some time.

For now the clock was ticking. He'd be pissed and wouldn't make the same mistake again.

I approached The Driftwood from the rear, and left the scooter in a spot partially obscured by a dumpster. I vaulted the stairs two at a time, traversing the second floor balcony at a trot, my duffel bag slung over one shoulder. I swiped the key card in a hurry, pushed the door open, and was rocked back on my heels by a jolt of feminine shrieking. Frank's bare ass greeted me from the far bed, a woman's leg wrapped over his. I caught a flash of pale breast and dark nipple.

"Oh geez," I blurted, averting my eyes and backpedalling to the patio railing. I let the door swing shut while I waited for the hubbub to die down on the other side. What a mess. Frank appeared at the door a few moments later, breathing hard and wrapped in a towel. He slipped outside and kept the door cracked behind him.

"Hey ... son. Didn't expect you back ... so soon."

"I gathered that."

"I've just got to . . . uh . . . finish up something. Did you see—"

"Nothing. I saw nothing." I put my hands up. "You go figure that out. Take your time or whatever, I'll wait downstairs, or at the bar on the corner . . . or something."

"Fine. Yeah. That's probably best." He tightened his towel. "Won't be long. I'll come find you. Over on Duval?" He jerked a thumb west.

"Sure."

He slipped back into the room with a sheepish grin, deadbolting the door this time.

I turned on my heel, blew the air out of my cheeks, and headed toward the front of the motel. Halfway down the stairs I realized I still had my duffel bag. But I wasn't willing to face that scene again to dump it. I hitched it farther up my shoulder and kept going.

Frank sure worked fast. Or maybe Sherri from the restaurant did. Either way, the sight of my father in flagrante with a woman was not something I wanted in my memory banks. Might be burned in there anyway. I did my best to expunge it and focus on the scenery as I made my way down Rose Lane.

The first bar I came to on Duval turned out to be an iteration of the ubiquitous Hard Rock Cafe, though there was nothing "hard rock" about the exterior of this location. Painted blue with bright white accents, it looked like a sweet grandmother from the Victorian era might live there with her cats. Historically speaking, a bar directly on Duval wasn't my ideal spot for a respite, but the adjacent outdoor bar area appeared to serve a few no-nonsense drinks. After the day I'd had, I was ready for a cold beer of any variety.

I found an open bar stool and slid onto it, ordered a Dos Equis with a lime, and yanked out the facilities directory from my bag. Might as well get working on it. I tried adjusting the pistol in my pants to a more comfortable position but couldn't find one where my shirt adequately covered it, so I stuck it in the duffel at my feet. Then I noticed the kids at a nearby table. A nagging at the back of my mind spoke of gun safety so inside the confines of the duffel, I ejected the mag, stuck it in my back pocket, then cleared the chamber, before tucking the gun away under my spare clothes. I tossed the mag with the blanks in the bag too and zipped the bag up.

I was partially in view of the street, so when I retook my seat on the stool, I angled myself to keep an eye out for the Caprice. At least the myriad of other pedestrians milling about gave some cover.

Deacon was probably still on the hunt. Our encounter with The Mooch was bound to have repercussions soon too, so I'd keep a wary eye out for trouble.

As I took my first sip of beer, my mind wound over the events of the day, but eventually the facilities directory on the bar enticed my interest. The first page I flipped to had one of Earl's purple Sharpie marks on it. The letter H in hazardous conditions was circled.

If Earl included seeing your father's bare ass as a hazard, then I agreed.

TWENTY-TWO
CARPE DIEM

"DID YOU MAKE A WORD BANK YET?"

I'd only lasted ten minutes into my search of the airport facilities directory before calling Reese.

"I'm getting there," I replied. "So far it seems like a jumbled mess."

"Your man Earl had a system, we just need to figure out what it was."

I sipped my dwindling beer. "Not sure why he couldn't have just said, 'Luke, it's on such and such island with a big X on it. Bring a shovel and dig it up.'"

"What fun would that be? Besides, he obviously thought you'd be smart enough to crack his code. That's a compliment."

"Then why do I feel so non-brilliant looking at this mess?"

"Run me through the words you have and I can check against what I have."

I read off the words and numbers I had circled from the book. Besides "unattended" and "hazardous conditions" he had also used the words island, numerous, traffic, birds, and a dozen others that didn't flow together into any comprehensible message. We compared notes and I gave her a few she'd missed when taking photos.

"He's only circling letters in words so I think we ignore the word and put the letters together," Reese said.

"I get X, L, I, H, M, E, Q, S, and a bunch more. They definitely aren't in order."

"Or they are and they're coded. Has your dad given you any ideas on what Earl even hid?"

"Turns out it's diamonds."

"Whoa. Nice. How many diamonds?"

"No idea."

"Have you asked him?" she said.

"Frank is busy at the moment. Getting busy at least. He found himself a friend. They're in his motel room."

"Oh, good for Frank. I love that for him."

"Do you? I sure don't."

"He's your dad. It would be weird if you were into it."

"More weird when I walked in on them."

"Ew, yeah. That I wouldn't love. Who's the woman? Not a hooker, I hope."

"Didn't get a good look but my money is on the waitress from lunch who was dripping all over him and gave him her number on the bill. Her intentions weren't subtle. I think he could have motorboated her chest at the table and she'd have just giggled."

"Love a slutty waitress. Good for her for working those job perks."

"What's got you in such a good mood? Did you get laid today too? Never mind. Don't answer that."

"What's the matter, Grumpy? You feeling left out?"

"I ran into Deacon. My trouble thermometer says things are about to heat up around here."

"He must have made short work of that drive. No one came by here today."

I checked the street. "He could have driven through the night for all I know. Somehow they knew we'd be down here. I get the feeling Deacon knows more about this setup than I do."

"He was Frank's cellmate for years. They had to talk about something."

The bartender offered to get me another Dos Equis and I nodded, taking down the dregs of mine and passing him the empty.

"Frank's using me as a pawn in this game of his. I don't like being kept in the dark."

"You need backup? I can find my way down there."

"I'll let you know if things escalate."

"By then I might be too late. You have your gun handy?"

"Picked one up down here."

"Good. When in doubt, shoot everybody."

I stared at the facilities directory some more and the scribble of letters and numbers I'd accumulated. "I'm not finding any diamonds if we don't figure this out."

"We'll crack it. I feel like we're close. You already know the island from the chart, right? How many ways can it be hidden on a little spit of a key?

"Yeah, I guess. Hey, I've got to go. Frank is walking up."

"Roger that. Keep me posted."

I hung up and closed the facilities directory as Frank came up from the sidewalk.

"Sorry about that," he said by way of greeting. "Didn't mean to run you off."

"Sherri sure made short work of meeting up. Really gives new meaning to the term service industry."

"What's that? Oh. Right. Gotta love a girl who can get off early. In more ways than one."

"Gross. I don't want details. Date's over already?"

"She had to run."

The guy beside me had an open stool vacate near him so he slid over one spot for Frank. Frank thanked him and then picked up the drink menu. "I feel refreshed," he said. "Might go for an Old Fashioned. That sounds decent."

"Your boy Deacon says hi."

Frank didn't look up from the menu. "Though this Hurricane might be fun too."

"You hear me?" I asked. "Deacon is in town. Ran into him at the airport."

"Took him long enough," Frank said and waved the menu at the bartender. "Going with the Smokey Old Fashioned."

The bartender nodded and moved off.

"You don't seem surprised," I added. "Or concerned."

"I'm not. Deacon is a pest. Screw him."

"The bonds of prison brotherhood run that deep, huh?"

"He went down for assault, more assault, burglary, plus some other nonsense. We got on all right at Union, but he's not the kind of guy you want around on the outside if you're making a fresh start. You're welcome to buddy up with him if you like, but I'll pass."

"Seems keen to stick to you. Has that bloodhound determination. I don't give it long till he finds us again."

"Once we gather my stash and The Mooch comes through for us, we're out of here. What's Deacon going to do about it?"

"How about beat you up and take your lunch money? Or The Mooch's guys could. Easy play would be to pay you off and then have someone jump you after. Thanks to you, we've got targets on our backs."

"They'll have to jump pretty high to catch *Tropic Angel*."

"This is a small island, but it's going to feel like a long way to the plane from wherever this drop goes down."

"That's easy. We have The Mooch do the meetup at an airport. Problem solved."

"That's actually a great idea."

"Don't sound so surprised. Your old man's head isn't just a hat rack." He tapped his skull. "Thinking smarter not harder."

"That's still not the phrase." I checked my watch, then pushed my beer away. "But if we're planning an exit tonight, we shouldn't have bothered with a hotel room, and I shouldn't be drinking."

"I used the hell out of that hotel room. And we used to bring an entire case of beer along for the flights up from Columbia."

"When you have a cargo of the cartel's finest cocaine, the 'eight hours bottle to throttle' rule understandably falls pretty far down on the list of flying violations. But I'd rather not get busted."

"Don't you ever get bored playing by the rules all the time?" he asked. "Life is short. You need to keep your heart pumping. Make sure you're still alive."

"Nearly two decades inside and you still subscribe to that philosophy?"

Frank shrugged. "I could have made a few better choices. But nobody is ever going to write 'boring' on my tombstone. You know I'm not the only one. I can see it in you. The coconut never falls that far from the palm tree."

I thought about the way I'd dive-bombed the pickup truck with the two drunks in it the morning before. Had I been convinced it was going to plow through those summer campers or had I been itching for a rush?

"At some point you have to grow up," I said. "Face reality."

"Reality is we're all headed for a dirt nap," Frank said, accepting his Old Fashioned from the bartender. He took a sip and smacked his lips. "So I'm going to have the good times while I can."

"Carpe diem till you run out of diems?"

"Exactly. This is already the best day I've had in decades. And I haven't even gotten paid yet."

I frowned at him. But as I reflected back on the day we'd shared, I had to admit that I'd enjoyed most of it too. Despite it being with him. What did that tell me?

"Cheers to never being boring," Frank said, holding up his drink.

I picked up my Dos Equis and begrudgingly clinked it against his glass, then took one final sip. It did taste damned good.

Carpe diem.

But finding more things in common with my father didn't give me any warm feelings about my future on this island.

"IT'S PROBABLY A SUBSTITUTION CIPHER," Frank said. "We used them all the time in prison."

I'd finally shown him the airport facilities directory and the circled letters in the various airport remarks sections that Earl had made.

"So far it's a word jumble," I said.

"Because you need the key."

I'd listed the first dozen or so circled letters in order on a bar napkin for us. XLIHMEQSRHWEI. Then started a new line for MRXLIXYVRGSSV. Currently nothing made sense, though there was one double set of the letter S that looked suspicious. "That could be an O," I said.

"Could be a lot of things," Frank said. "That's all the letters?"

"No. Not yet. But I figured we'd start with these."

"What exactly did Earl say was the key to cracking this?" He was on his second Old Fashioned already, and the condensation kept adhering his coaster to the bottom of his glass.

"He said the key was the purple Sharpie," I said, tapping the facilities directory and the purple circles on the page.

"Hmm," Frank muttered. "Nothing else?"

I told him about the chart and the kneeboard. "When you put the holes over the airports, it shows an island north of Sugarloaf."

"That's not surprising," Frank said. "Earl knew that area well. We all did. Which one?"

I got my phone out, pulled up the Foreflight app and expanded the map. I pointed out the island. "This one marked as a National White Heron Refuge, which may limit our flying options."

"Told you we'll need a boat," Frank said.

"Why hide this treasure of yours down here in the Keys at all?" I asked. "Seems like he could have stuck it in the barn with the rest of your junk, or under his mattress."

"He said he kept it close to home for a long time," Frank said. "At least at first. But he came to see me at Union right after he got his last cancer diagnosis. The bad one. Told me it was terminal and he was done fighting it. Said he was making a plan to move my stuff."

"Any particular reason?"

"Didn't think they were safe where they were anymore. Didn't say why but I got the impression someone had been asking questions that made him nervous. He thinks someone had been in the house and the barn too, searching. Margery kept mentioning things being out of place. Like maybe someone had been in the house more than once."

"They never told me about that. How long ago was this?"

"About a year and a half ago. Earl knew where I got the jewels from in the first place and knew I might have to go back to the source once I was out. I'm guessing that's why he brought them south. Make my exchange easier."

"With The Mooch."

"When I was planning to go on the run with your mother, trading our cash in for stones made sense. Easier to hide and carry. We would've found a way to sell them piecemeal in Central America. But after doing my time, I don't have to smuggle them anywhere anymore. I'm cashing in."

"How many diamonds are we talking about?"

"More than a thousand little ones. A few big ones."

I whistled. "Worth how much?"

"Now prices? I think they might fetch The Mooch close to ten million from my buyers. Though he'll take at least twenty percent on the deal."

"You expect to fly out of here with eight million in cash? Deacon might be the least of your problems. You don't think every prison buddy you ever knew isn't going to come out of the woodwork when they find out you have that kind of money? Not to mention the feds."

"Who's going to tell them? Not me. Deacon doesn't even know the real value. He's guessing."

"He knew enough to follow you here. Makes a poor choice of confidante by the way. What inspired that brilliant decision?"

"You think I spilled it to him on purpose? I was high on damned laughing gas at the time. I got dental work done and they put me back in my cell still loopy. I must have let something slip about my plans for when I got out. Stupid bad luck. Deacon's been on me about it ever since. Tried telling him I was in a drug-addled hallucination, but he wouldn't buy it. But so what? Once we bug out of here, what's he going to do?"

"Hound you relentlessly till you die is my guess. You'll probably have to pay him off. Him and his girlfriend."

"No way. That numbnuts will blow through any amount I give him and be back on my doorstep in a month." He held a hand out. "Let me use that pen. I'll start unscrambling numbers too. We need to get after this."

I handed over the pen, one I used for logging flight hours,

then I fished in my pocket and found the fine-tipped Sharpie Earl had given me. I'd pocketed it on the way down without a lot of thought. But now I took a closer look at the marker itself. It was just a standard-looking fine-tipped Sharpie. I tried pulling the end cap off to check if something was jammed inside but nothing came loose. The only thing out of the ordinary was that the back half was scratched up a bit. There was a logo with a large AP and below it some fine print that said it conformed to some standard. Except some of the letters and numbers had been scratched off. It was hard to tell if it was deliberate, but the only part remaining was the letter-number combo of D-4. The rest of the number had been obliterated.

It was innocuous. Anything could have scratched it. But it also could have been done with a razor or pocket knife. Now that I looked at it closer, I was nearly sure it had been deliberate. D-4. Out of curiosity, I wrote out the first few letters of the alphabet A through G, then backtracked from the D by four spaces. D minus four would be a Z? I jotted down the rest of the alphabet, then started again on a line just below it, shifting each letter 4 spaces. It couldn't be that simple, could it?

But as soon as I started decoding, XLIHMEQSRHEVI became THEDIAMONDSARE.

"You found it?" Frank asked, looking over my shoulder.

"You were right. It's just a basic substitution cipher. Shift everything left by four."

The next letter and number combos worked out to INTHETURNCOORDINATOROF then the combo R7598X. The letter and number combination resembled an aircraft registration number. That wasn't a number I knew, but once I did the minus four conversion, it read N3154T. The registration number of Earl's old Super Decathlon.

"That bugger had it hidden in his plane," Frank said.

"Close to home until it wasn't," I said.

Frank slapped me on the back.

I caught myself smiling. I was so pleased we'd figured out the solution that I almost missed the black SUV parked in the street. The same one that had been following us earlier leaving the strip club. Frank looked too. The SUV had pulled over to the side of Duval, in front of Caroline's Cafe. This time the dark driver's side window rolled down and the driver's face became visible. From a distance he looked Hispanic, around my age. Another big White guy in the passenger seat peered out past his buddy to glare at us. I nudged Frank. "More friends of yours?"

Frank gave the men a cursory glance, but then returned his attention to the decoded message in front of us. "Don't worry about them. This is what matters."

The guy in the passenger seat had a neck tattoo. Made me think they weren't cops.

"Think they work for The Mooch?" I asked.

"No. They're something else."

"More prison buddies? What the hell, Frank? You ever going to give me a heads up before walking me into a bullet?"

"I told you. You don't have to worry about those guys. They won't bother us."

"Until we have a bag of diamonds in our hands?" I stood up, pocketed the facilities directory, then marched down the steps from the bar and onto the sidewalk. When I made the street, the SUV rolled forward and the driver's window went back up. But a car in the road ahead was waiting for some pedestrians to cross so the SUV couldn't flee. The tint made it impossible to see what was going on inside, but the car was stuck.

"Hey!" I shouted and rapped my knuckles against the driver's side window. The driver could be pointing a pistol at my face for all I knew, but I didn't care. I wanted some answers. My own reflection shone back at me from the glass, haloed by the glow from the bar's cantina lights. But the window remained up. The street cleared ahead and the SUV surged forward, tires chirping on the asphalt as the vehicle shot down Duval.

I stood in the street and watched it go, then turned and looked back to the bar in exasperation.

But Frank Angel was gone.

TWENTY-FOUR

CANCELLATION

THE NAPKIN I'd been scribbling on at the bar was missing when I walked up. I had no doubt it was in Frank's pocket right now as he breezed toward whatever end he had in mind for his night. I fumbled through the recently unzipped duffel bag which I'd left at the foot of my stool and found that the Sig Sauer 9mm was gone too.

I swore.

But when I felt around in my front pants pocket and fished out the spare magazine, I noted I still had the one with live rounds in it. Hope Frank wasn't planning to shoot anyone. He was going to be in for a surprise. That gave me a glimmer of satisfaction.

Even so, I'd given him the island name. Now he had the gems' location too—inside Earl's old plane. The crazy old man must have sunk the damned thing out there. Or buried it?

Dying from cancer or not, Earl's devotion to my father was notable. And misplaced.

I swore some more.

I'd been stupid to believe this was going to go any other way. Frank had only needed me to give him the location of his treasure, and now he was close enough. Sayonara Frank, just like he'd said.

I paid our tab at the bar, tipped what I could afford, and shouldered my duffel bag again, making my way back toward the street, still chastising myself.

What had I expected? That he'd actually follow through on a promise?

The sun was headed for the horizon, so the general flow of tourists was toward Mallory Square. I turned right instead, cut back along Rose Lane, which resembled an alley more than a street, and gave me some respite from the crowds. At the corner, I turned down Simonton and made my way back to The Driftwood.

It was still early. I could return to the airport, fire up *Tropic Angel* and blast home. But I'd be damned if I wasn't at least going to get a shower first, get rid of the tacky stickiness of humidity and failure that clung to me, and make some use of the lousy hotel room that I was now going to have to justify to Elsbeth on our expense report.

"Thanks for nothing, Frank," I muttered as I walked.

But I had no one to blame but myself. I'd invested too much of myself into this.

He'd need a boat. That was certain. Maybe he was in Mallory Square right now hunting down his old buddy Jerome, AKA Big Tuna. That seemed probable. If not, he'd be sweet-talking some woman into a sunset boat ride at her expense.

But no. What if he had to dig and root around out there for a while? Even the prospect of a buried treasure might not keep a date around. He'd find Jerome. Or some other long lost underworld connection of his. Someone ready for a quick score.

I made it to my motel and trudged up the steps to the second floor. After getting the door open and stepping inside, I tried not to focus on whether the place smelled like someone just had sex in there. It did smell like that, but maybe it smelled that way all the time. More reason not to linger.

I dropped my duffel bag on the dresser, fished out a change of clothes and a Dopp kit and headed for the shower, ignoring the rumpled second bed I passed. Washing the funk of this day down the drain sounded like a wonderful idea. The water was hot and steaming by the time I'd stripped out of my clothes. But I was hot enough already, so after I stepped into the pounding spray, I turned the temp down by degrees till finally it was as cool as Florida tap water could get— which meant tepid at best. Even so, the rinse was rejuvenating. Like I could hose off the regret and let it swirl down the drain.

I wasn't angry. Not anymore. Frank had wasted my time and my money and left me high-and-dry, but getting mad at him was like blaming this shower nozzle for getting me wet. Once a con man, always a con man. I should only be angry at myself for believing he could change.

I stopped the shower and toweled off.

I'd pulled on a soft pair of worn-in khakis and was in the process of buttoning my shirt when I walked out of the bathroom and spotted the earring on the floor. It was under the rumpled bed, resting near a leg. A big golden hoop no doubt left behind in a hurried departure. I squatted to pick it up and turned it over in my hand. In a more forgiving mood I might have been bothered to walk the item back to the restaurant where we'd had lunch, and discreetly hand it back to our lush of a server. But I wasn't in that kind of a mood. I launched the earring into a neighboring trash can where it rattled once at the bottom and then fell silent.

Cost of doing business with Frank Angel.

I gathered up the remainder of my things, stuffed them all in my duffel, and departed. Grumpy cigarette guy wasn't at his post in the lobby, so I simply tossed my key cards on his desk and walked back out. Maybe he was busy enjoying the pay-per-view somewhere. I had only two items left on my agenda. Return the rental scooter, and get the hell out of here.

The scooter had remained unmolested where I'd parked it behind the hotel and it fired up like a champ when I started it. Any other time this could have had the makings of a fun evening. If I had Cassidy on the back? If I had brought her down instead of Frank. We'd zip off to dinner at Bagatelle or Milagro, enjoy a glass of wine or a cocktail and find our way back to a BnB with an ocean view and a king bed to have some fun in. In the old days we would've made love to the sound of palm trees waving in the breeze and kept at it till the moon went down.

The fantasy was still playing in my head as I turned east on Fleming. And it might have lasted all the way to the airport if I'd had an opportunity, but the Chevy Caprice that blindsided me took the thought right out of my mind. Rolling onto the hood of the car and smashing my head into the windshield didn't help either.

Everything went into slo-mo.

I felt myself being dragged off the car by strong muscled arms amid the scent of too much cologne that was also somehow not enough to disguise the body odor. I was shoved summarily and horizontally into the back seat of the Caprice. My body was limp and my head rang. When the stars in my vision stopped twinkling, I rolled over with a groan, looked up and found the shiny barrel of a snub nosed revolver pointed at my face, and Lyla-the-Looker peering around the front seat head rest.

"Hi there, sweetie. Miss us?"

I didn't. But since when did that ever seem to matter.

The Caprice sagged on its springs as Deacon climbed behind the wheel and slammed the door. The car started moving. The sky out the windshield had turned into a watercolor of sunset hues.

Somewhere over in Mallory Square people would be cheering as the sun went down.

But I just closed my eyes and let the world go dark.

TWENTY-FIVE
.38 SPECIAL

DEACON MUST HAVE OWNED bolt cutters.

It's the only way I thought it likely we'd be where we were when I opened my eyes again.

I was on the ground, lying near a broken gravestone. The white marble was difficult to read in the fading light but listed the name of the deceased as Thomas Romer, born 1783. He apparently died in Key West at the age of 108 and the gravestone noted him as being a "Good citizen for 65 years." It didn't go into great detail as to what he'd been up to the rest of the time. Maybe he'd beat people up in cemeteries like someone else I knew. Though the way Deacon loomed over me at the moment, I couldn't picture him living to 108.

My lifespan didn't seem especially promising at the moment either.

Lyla sat atop one of the neighboring crypts, admiring her pistol. Deacon's attention was on me. My focus was on the tire iron in Deacon's hand and what he intended to do with it.

"Where's Frank?" he growled.

"You ask great questions," I said.

He swung the tire iron. It connected with my shoulder.

"Ow. Geezus."

"You want to run your mouth, you get one of those every time. I warned you. I pay shit back times ten."

Deacon the shot caller.

"What do you think of your little zippin' away on a scooter trick now?"

"I hear you," I muttered and rubbed my shoulder.

I wasn't tied up. There was a chance I might be able to get my hands on that tire iron and turn the tables at some point, but lying prone on the ground wasn't the place to attempt it. I ached all over and my right leg was numb. "Frank ditched me," I said. "He's going to find his treasure on his own."

"Where?" He raised the tire iron, ready for my next word.

"Baby, he can't talk if you pulverize him," Lyla said.

"I'm not gonna be able to buy your fine ass those Jimmy Choos if he don't talk," Deacon added.

Lyla quirked her mouth. "All right. I guess you gotta hit him a little, then."

"It's fine. I'll tell you," I said. "You can buy whatever fancy shoes you want together." I put a hand up to block additional blows. "Frank screwed me over too. So you two can have him."

"The treasure then. Where's it at?"

I told them. I told them that the island was in the bird sanctuary north of Sugarloaf and that Earl had hidden the diamonds in the turn coordinator of the Decathlon. It was none of my concern now anyway.

"What the fuck is a turn coordinator?" Deacon asked.

"One of the instruments."

Lyla said, "It's like the dashboard, dummy. But of the plane."

"Shut up. Like you know anything about planes." To me he said, "How's he going to get it?"

"Beats me. But he'll need a boat."

"You know how to drive a boat, baby?" Lyla asked.

Deacon frowned. "I fuckin' hate boats."

"Maybe we should take him. Bet he knows how to drive one."

"You don't need a boat," I said. "You can just wait till he comes back ashore."

"See, that's right," Deacon said. "We'll jump his ass when he gets back."

"'Less he don't come back the same place," Lyla said. "Would you if you were him and you had a pocketful of diamonds?"

Deacon looked down at me again. "Where'd he get a boat?"

"I don't know."

He raised the tire iron. "Better think real hard."

I put my hands up. "There are a *thousand* boats around here. It's impossible to know, but I know where he's going after."

His brow furrowed. "Where?"

I told them how Frank planned to make a deal exchanging the diamonds for cash with The Mooch and whatever buyer he had set up. Both of their faces lit up at the mention of the cash.

"Holy shit, baby," Lyla said. "What if we got the diamonds *and* the cash?"

Deacon's wheels were turning too, but I imagined more slowly.

"Can I get up now?" I asked. "I kind of want to see if you broke my leg."

Deacon took a step back. "You try any shit, Lyla here gonna drop you."

Lyla leveled her pistol at me. "I was top shot at my gun safety class."

"Congratulations," I said.

"Shot a dude's toe off once," Deacon added.

"The littlest one," Lyla said. "And yes, I was aiming for it."

"You're serious?"

"He was being a real dick to me," Lyla explained. "Walks funny now. Fixed his manners though."

"Tell him how many dudes you took pieces off of so far," Deacon said.

"That you know about? Four."

Deacon grinned. "That's why you my girl."

Lyla blew him a kiss.

I used Thomas Romer's headstone as a crutch and got to my feet. My knee had swollen but it didn't buckle under my weight. It was vaguely numb from where they'd hit me with the Caprice. My hip and head throbbed too. Add in the recent thumping from the tire iron and I was a fairly balanced lump of pain, but if I had any broken bones, they didn't make themselves obvious.

"You done thrashing me? I think I'd like to visit a hospital."

"Fuck that. You're fine," Deacon said. "You standin' ain't cha? But we ain't done with you yet. You're gonna tell us how to find this here Mooch."

"I can show you where he lives."

"All right. That's a start. What time's this big deal going down?"

"I don't know. Frank ditched me before we could set it up."

"That's all right," Deacon said. "We gonna interrupt it early anyway. Way I see it, this here Mooch is the key. Like the nexus of events and shit. Long as we keep an eye on him, Frank won't be able to dodge us. We just gotta stick close and wait for our moment."

"Nexus of events?" I asked.

"You like that? One of them ten-dollar reading words your daddy likes to throw around. He used to always say to me, 'Deacon, If you want to elevate your situation, you gotta elevate your vocabulary.' I'm about to elevate the shit out of our situation right here."

"Do your thing, baby," Lyla said. "Your plans are always the best." But she kept her eyes on me, smirking.

If Frank had acquired a boat, he might have found his way out on the water toward Sugarloaf by now, but I had my doubts. The sky was darkening and it would be hard to see anything without spotlights. To do it right would take some setup. Dive gear possibly, depending on where Earl had ditched the Decathlon.

I was directed back to the car. But this time they made me sit in the front passenger seat, Lyla in the back with the gun.

"In case you try anything stupid," Deacon explained. "She'll blow your brains out that windshield."

"Would hate for her to dirty your car," I said.

"You already dented my damn hood," Deacon said. "Pisses me off."

"Let's exchange insurance information later," I said. "I'm hoping you sprang for comprehensive coverage."

"Nah. Insurance is a scam for suckers. Besides, that accident was *your* fault," Deacon said.

"You're giving me a better sense of why my rates are so high in Florida."

"Just shut up, wiseass. Where we going?"

"The Mooch's house is next to the Southernmost Point Buoy."

"Where's that?"

"South."

Deacon glared at me. "I know it's south, motherfucker, but where exactly?"

Lyla held up her phone. "I got it, baby. Don't worry. I Googled it."

The electronic voice from her phone was male with an Australian accent. But it gave accurate directions. It took us on a zigzagging route to Whitehead Street. The gaggle of passersby and selfie takers was keeping its distance from the buoy this time, as the tide was up and waves broke over the seawall, making a watery puddle around the colorful landmark.

Deacon showed no reticence about driving the Caprice through saltwater, however, and plowed around the corner through the standing water at a speed that sent a fountain of spray over a pair of unfortunate tourists with a stroller who had inaccurately assumed he'd slow down.

The young father glared and flipped us off as we maneuvered through the potholes. Deacon didn't bother with subtlety. He jammed the Caprice to a halt directly adjacent to the metal gate and the plaque that declared the home the Southernmost Southernmost House. He craned his neck and attempted to peer through the gate. "That's the place?"

Stopping in the road had given the drenched father of the equally drenched family a chance to catch up to the car. Suddenly he was at my window, banging and yelling. He was a good-sized guy, well on his way to a dad bod, rocking a full and recently dampened beard. I could imagine him waxing poetic on the hop content of his favorite craft beer while attending his local fantasy football draft party. But when Deacon opened the driver's side door and stood to confront him, the color went out of the guy's face. His chivalrous rage deflated like a balloon and he retreated to the sidewalk.

"That's right, run, you little pussy-assed bitch," Deacon shouted.

"Deke always gets angry when when people bang on his car," Lyla explained.

"A man's choice of vehicle says a lot about him," I replied.

Once Deacon was done shouting at the retreating figure of dwindling masculinity he'd offended, he settled back into the car. He frowned at the seawater he'd acquired on his sneakers, wiped at it futilely, then addressed me again."Ain't no lights on in this place. You sure this is right?"

"I never claimed to know if he was *at* home. I just said this happens to be his home. One of them at least."

"What good does that do us if the dude ain't here?"

"Maybe he's resting," Lyla offered.

"You should go ding the doorbell," I offered. "I'd go, but I'm currently being held hostage by Lyla."

Deacon glared at me. Then he turned and pointed at her. "Watch his ass like a hawk. I'm going up to have a look. You have to shoot him, I ain't even gonna be mad."

"I got you, baby." Lyla held up her little snub-nose.

Deacon got out and slammed the door, then stalked toward the metal gate. I hit the flashers button on the dashboard. When Deacon reached the locked gate he frowned. I pivoted in my seat to get a look at Lyla. "Five bucks says he's going to go over the wall. Unless your guy can pick a lock."

A moment later, Deacon vaulted over the cement wall, proving me right.

Lyla held her gun up. "You turn back around."

"That looks like a Smith and Wesson J-frame."

"Thirty-Eight Special, baby." She wagged it at me. "Got it off a—"

I snatched the pistol out of her hand so fast she didn't have time to finish the sentence.

"What the—?"

I fitted the pistol to my hand and pointed it at her. "You know the problem with these double-action revolvers? The trigger pull is heavy as hell. If you wanted to keep me on edge, you'd cock it first." I rocked the hammer back and demonstrated. "Like this."

Lyla's face paled.

"I was the best shot in my gun safety class too. But mine was in the Army. They didn't really call it 'gun safety' there."

"You aren't going to shoot me though, right? With all these people around." Without Deacon in the car, her "ain'ts" had disappeared.

I slowly uncocked the gun, opened the cylinder and dumped the rounds into my other hand. I pocketed them, flipped the cylinder closed, then tossed the pistol back to her. "This lesson was free. Let's not do it again."

I turned back around in my seat and stared out the windshield. I blew out a long breath.

"You aren't leaving," Lyla said softly from the back. "You aren't going to run?"

I should run. It would be the logical thing to do. But there I sat anyway. Not moving.

"You're worried about Frank," she said.

Deacon reappeared at the fence, gave a cursory look around, then leapt back to our side again. He strode into the street and came around the driver's side and got in.

He twisted to look at Lyla, then addressed me. "I see you decided to be smart, not mess around. Maybe you got some sense to you after all."

But as the car started up again, I couldn't agree less.

Whatever I was doing, the last thing I'd call it was smart.

TWENTY-SIX

CELLIES

DEACON DROVE with his nose over the steering wheel, peering at the sky and uttering swears using a lexicon of vulgarity I could barely decipher.

We'd circled the block a few times, taking two more passes in differing directions in front of The Mooch's residence but with the same results.

I didn't gather from the action that Deacon was much for stakeouts or patience.

"This old dude better be around here somewhere," he muttered. "And you'd better find his ass."

We were cruising back up Duval Street now as if that was the only place on the island he knew to look for The Mooch. Though to be fair, Frank and I had tried the same approach previously, so I couldn't climb too high on my horse to critique him.

"He has a boat here on the island. Also owns a strip club."

"He got himself a titty bar?" Deacon's interest piqued. "That wouldn't be such a bad place to look."

"Manager says he's never there till late though," I clarified.

"Good thing for you, Deke," Lyla said. "Tell him what happened to the last stripper I caught you with."

"You scared the living piss out of her." He checked the clock on the dash and frowned. It was off by an hour, not having been reset for Daylight Savings Time, but that didn't seem to phase him. Even if it had been correct, we still would've been too early for the strip club. "Where's he keep his boat?"

"Definitely not on this street."

"You're worse than a damned woman. How about instead of telling me what's not working, you come up with some answers, otherwise maybe we heading back to the graveyard for another tune-up of your attitude."

"Let me have my phone back. I can probably look up his boat name and figure out where it is."

"Hell no. I give you your phone, you're gone text the cops and blow this whole thing for us."

"Text the cops? And accuse you of what? I don't have any proof."

"Never stopped any cop I ever met from hassling my ass."

"I've got a phone," Lyla said from the back. "Soon as you two old ladies stop arguing, you can tell me what to search for."

I said, "If you put in the name of the strip club it'll probably be owned by an LLC or corporation. If you plug that name into some boat sales or realty websites we might get some hits on other properties he owns or where to find his boat."

"What's the name of the club?"

I told her.

After some scrolling she found something. "Says here it's owned by Sunset Properties LLC. And if I Google that I get some other hits."

"I've got the guy's personal phone number too. We can add that to the mix and see what comes up."

"You have this fool's phone number?" Deacon said. "Why didn't you start with that?"

"Why? You gonna call him? Say please can I have the address of where you keep all your cash so I can rob you?"

"Man, I'm 'bout to pop you soon if you keep up this lip."

He could try. But I was feeling more myself by the minute. Unless he found a way to hit me with a car again first, he was going to find our next confrontation would go differently.

Lyla interjected. "None of these real estate sites have anything about his boat. I even looked through some pictures. But I looked up some of these dancers from the club. Most of them have private fan pages."

"You about to show us some coochie shots or what?" Deacon said.

"A lot of these profile pics are on boats. Like this one." She held up a photo of three girls posing on the stern swim deck of a boat called *Sea Notes*.

"All right, now we gettin' somewhere, baby," Deacon said. He nodded while he drove. "You got some more?"

She did. No fewer than three of the dancers had photos of themselves aboard *Sea Notes* in their social media photos.

"I knew a guy once used a boat to shoot all kinds of porno and stuff," Deacon said. "Maybe this cat do that too. Ladies always be taking their clothes off once they on a boat."

"Too bad your broke ass never had a boat," Lyla said.

"About fixing to get me one now though, ain't I? Once we get this cash we be rollin' in boats. Gonna hafta get me some new Jordans too since home boy back there made me get puddle water on these." He flexed his left foot and shook his head. What else you gonna buy, baby?"

But Lyla didn't reply.

Deacon gave me a look. "She actin' mad on account of she thinks I screwed some of them chicks on the porno boat."

"Not something you should bring up while I'm carrying this gun," Lyla said.

"You already work out a split with Frank?" I asked, eager to change the subject. "Or are you planning to take it all from him?"

"We'll give ol' Frank his cut if he play this cool. Old boy's my cellie. But he's gonna need to make amends. Gonna hafta straighten up. He don't? Then I guess we'll have to see. Sometimes even cellies gotta get cut out."

We reached the north side of the island and I directed him along the harbor. Dozens of boats were stored all over the marina.

"How the hell we supposed to find this one boat in all these boats?" Deacon complained. "Like tryna find a clean needle in a junkie's trash can."

"Won't be that hard," Lyla contested. "They put the names right on them."

From the photos, *Sea Notes* looked to be a good size. Lyla searched the Internet and came up with a few more hits on the name. The only *Sea Notes* based in Key West was a Horizon 88 motor yacht. Ten years old it was still easily a five million dollar boat. I didn't want to burst Deacon's bubble, but even if he took all of Frank's score, he wasn't getting his hands on more than one of these. But that didn't seem to be discouraging him.

"Maybe once we get this Mooch's money, we borrow his boat too," Deacon mused. "Then we won't even need dumbass flyboy here."

"Thought you said you hated boats," I said.

"But I like the ladies takin' they clothes off all over the place don't I. Lyla, baby, you know you'd look good stretched out nekked on the front of one of these here." He pointed. "Picture us all up in the Caribbean rolling up to the beach in one of these shiny-ass yachts."

The particular boat he was pointing to would have had a hard time with more than four feet of swell, let alone sailing the island chain, but enlightening him was going to take more time than we had.

"We going to walk around or not?" I asked. "We should probably split up. We're definitely not going to find it from the car."

"Nah, you know I can't trust you walking around by yourself."

"You might have to. Unless you just want to sit here and stare at each other. Frank could be motoring up to make the deal anytime for all we know. Plus you banged up my knee. I'm not going to be running any wind sprints."

"We're gonna walk around, but we gonna stick together. You try to bust loose, Lyla gonna drop you with her .38 and then I'll kick your ass into the water for the fish. Get me?"

"I get you just fine."

We climbed out. I'd been exaggerating some about my knee but it did hurt. The swelling made it stiff and hard to bend. I didn't need to fake a limp. I was mobile though. Lyla met my eye when she got out of the car. She kept her hand in her purse.

My line about Frank was a lie. I doubted he was even to Sugarloaf by now let alone on his way back. But a fuzzy timeline worked to my benefit. I wasn't sure what would happen when Deacon and The Mooch crossed paths, but I was curious to see it. Because if anything can spark a fire, it's a couple of hotheads and money.

THE MARINA at the city harbor was well-lit. Music drifted across the docks from the Half-Shell Raw Bar. The place had a live band tonight and had gathered a bustling dinner crowd. The smell of fried conch fritters hung about the place, mingled with the brine of seawater lapping against the pilings. We walked the docks, reading names on sterns. When we finally spotted *Sea Notes*, it was on a private dock across from the public access one we were on. I pointed to it. "There you go."

Lights were on aboard the boat. At nearly ninety feet, it was a good size without being monstrous. There were other larger boats in the vicinity but not many. Several souls were aboard. I spotted one of the young women from the house, clothed now in a stewardess uniform and helping set a table on the stern deck.

"How the hell we supposed to get over there?" Deacon complained, noting the locked gate that barred access to the private dock. "Let's go see if somebody else gonna let us in."

But by the time we made it back to the walkway near the restaurant, he changed his mind. A pair of uniformed officers were making their way down the boardwalk in our direction, one of them a Key West city patrol officer, the other was Gail Warner in her county sheriff's department uniform. They were still forty yards away, but Gail pointed directly at us. The city cop pulled his mic for his radio and spoke into it.

Deacon took one look at me, then at Lyla, swore, and took off running in the opposite direction.

"Deke, what are you—" Lyla put her palms up in exasperation. Then she backed away too. But before she turned tail, she pointed a finger gun at me, mouthed the word "pow," then blew the imaginary smoke from her finger before hiking up her purse and following Deacon into the crowded sprawl of the restaurant.

The uniformed city cop with Gail put away his radio and cut diagonally through the Raw Bar in pursuit of Deacon and Lyla, one hand planted on his gun.

I stayed put and waited till Gail reached me.

"Seems like you've got a story to tell," Gail said, looking me over as she walked up. "You okay?"

"You have impeccable timing."

She smiled. "I spotted you out there on the dock with those two and tried calling to see if you were okay. When you didn't pick up, I figured you were in trouble."

"They left my phone in their car. How'd you find me?"

"Took some doing. But local PD had several frantic calls by tourists earlier about a guy on a scooter getting knocked down and dragged off in an old Chevy. City cops found the scooter and tracked down the rental company. Your name was on the rental agreement. They put out a county-wide alert, so when I saw it, it obviously got my attention. Lucky for you, I happen to be friends with a judge who was willing to give me a warrant to track your phone—given the circumstances. Found Deacon's Caprice in the lot out there. Bingo bango bongo. Here we are."

"That's some expedient police work."

She shrugged. "Where's Frank?" Her eyes traced the docks.

"Frank's busy being Frank."

"EJ called and told me you two were down here," she said. "Don't tell me Frank has you mixed up in one of his bad ideas."

"The guy attracts more trouble than anyone I know." I eased myself along the dock at a limp.

"He's two days out of prison and you already look banged up from it. You need a doctor?"

"I think I'll be okay. Thanks though."

The uniformed city police officer returned. He and Gail conferred briefly. Evidently Deacon and Lyla had been able to elude him. She wasn't happy about it, but didn't seem surprised. She turned to me. "Come on. I'll buy you a cup of coffee."

We walked into the raw bar and found the hostess. She took one look at Gail's uniform and sat us at a four-top ahead of several other waiting patrons. Gail didn't object. She simply adjusted her gun belt and slid onto a stool, keeping her back to the wall and eyes toward the doors like most cops did.

Gail ordered a coffee from the server. My stomach was growling so I ordered a basket of Buffalo shrimp and an iced tea.

"What's Frank up to?" Gail asked.

I rubbed a hand over my stubbled jaw and considered how much to tell her. Warners were practically family so she warranted more than most cops could have wrung from me. "Frank has old grudges," I said. "And he's here to settle them."

"Sounds too cliché for Frank. Revenge is one of the reasons so many ex-cons end up reincarcerated within a few years. He ought to know better. How exactly does he mean to do it?"

"Unclear. I just know he's gathering a list of names. Righting wrongs. In his mind anyway."

"He's been incarcerated a long time. Is anyone from his day even still around?"

"Apparently a few."

She harrumphed. "And Deacon? Why'd he bring you to the harbor?"

"Turns out he has a newfound affinity for boats."

"Any boat in particular?" Gail asked, her eyes roaming out the window to the marina. From our vantage point *Sea Notes* was plainly visible.

"Deacon and Lyla are here for a score. They know Frank has business down here with a guy named The Mooch." I pointed to *Sea Notes*. "Guy who owns that boat. They're planning to interfere."

Gail didn't look pleased. "Some trio these three make. Frank sure knows how to pick 'em."

"Frank called Deacon and Lyla 'barnacles,'" I said. "I don't think they're in this together by his choice. But if you find Frank, I'm sure Deacon and Lyla will be hovering around like stink on shit."

Gail thanked the server when the girl delivered her coffee and took a tentative sip.

"You know this guy, The Mooch?" I asked.

"Tony Brewer. Yeah. He's been a point of conversation around the station plenty of times. Donates heavily to all the city and county department fundraisers and the sheriff's political campaigns."

"He's done well for himself."

"Better than most. He's about as connected as his type can get. Frank thinks Brewer is going to help him out in some way?"

"Frank hopes The Mooch knows who set him up and got my mother killed."

Gail paused her coffee cup halfway to her mouth. "Christ." She stared out the window at the boat, then set her coffee back down. "What makes him think Brewer knows that? He say he did?"

I shrugged.

She palmed the mug of coffee with both hands and turned it slowly. "Whatever Frank's doing, you've still got a chance to get out of it. I know what Margery said. But him being out of prison isn't your responsibility. Frank's not worth it."

"Your brother sure loved him."

Gail leaned back in her chair. "Earl thought Frank was as slick as Steve McQueen. Or maybe Paul Newman. They thought of themselves as Butch and Sundance flying around evading the law. Last of the flying cowboys. But that's what all the desperados think till they're caught. That movie ends badly for a reason."

"At least Earl was lucky enough to keep himself out of prison."

"A feat that took more work than you know. He's lucky the cartel guys never came calling. But look where his luck got him. Nowhere. He hid out in Central Florida the rest of his life, quiet as a Key deer. Smartest thing he ever did. But there were plenty who didn't have that kind of luck. When the cartel makes people disappear from these islands, it doesn't make the papers, because we never find the bodies. They just vanish."

"Like Bum Farto?"

She shook her head. "People like to fantasize that that guy lived large in South America somewhere after he disappeared. I promise you he died bloody."

"Frank seems to think he's got one last ride in him."

"And what do you think?"

The server interrupted us with my shrimp and ice tea and when she was gone, Gail had another question for me. "Rumor was, back in the day, that Frank had stashed away a lot of money the feds never found. He say anything to you about that?"

"You heard this rumor when?"

"Around the time he went away. A few people from his old crew even went looking for it."

"You were around then?" I eyed the two gold captain's bars on her collar and took a bite of a shrimp.

"I was just a green deputy. Road patrol. Our chief deputy that recently retired—Harlan Mercer—he was my sergeant when I started. He knew Frank well. Made some of the case against him."

"So everyone knew Frank was flying for the cartels at the time."

"Him and a hundred others. Was worse back in the seventies and eighties but even later the drugs weren't exactly a secret. But Frank always operated in a cloud of rumor you couldn't quite pin down. The story of his stash was one of many urban legends around the department for a while. But nothing ever came of them. You ask any of the new deputies and they'll have never heard of Frank Angel."

"Except he's out now. New rep to earn."

"So my question is, do you really think he's going after whoever set him up, or you think he's just back in town for that stash so he can fly off into the sunset? Only reason I ask is, the longer he's in town, the more sharks are going to show up."

"Plenty of those already," I said. I thought about the guys in the black SUV. "Is the cartel still active here?"

Gail gave a derisive snort. "What do you think?"

I wiped Buffalo sauce off my lips with a napkin after I finished my last shrimp. "Frank is up to his neck in this either way. I don't know where he'll go next. I know he ditched me and is off on his own. But he's got other people tied up in this too and if I know him, it's all going to end badly."

Gail reached over and rested a hand on my shoulder. "Let us handle this from here. You've done enough. What else do you need?"

"I could use a ride."

"I'll get you sorted."

Gail paid the bill and we headed back to the parking lot to where her truck was parked.

"You have a place to stay tonight?" she asked.

"Sadly, yes. But I have a bag in that car I need first." I pointed to where Deacon's Caprice was still parked. A city police cruiser sat nearby, lights flashing. We walked over to the Caprice and I opened the back door. My duffel was still on the floor behind the driver's seat where it had been tossed during my hasty abduction. I rooted around and also found my phone on the floorboards under one of the seats. Deacon and Lyla being forced to flee on foot had worked in my favor. "Deacon loves this car. If you leave it alone, there's a chance he might come back for it."

"I'll advise the city guys on that. This is their jurisdiction."

I climbed into her truck with my bag and she gave me a lift back to The Driftwood Motel. "You're staying in this roach fest?" she asked as we pulled up.

"This trip was over-budget when we took off. You're looking at the results."

"Right." She gave a supportive nod. "I'll advise the local PD where you are in case they have more questions for you. What's your room number?"

I told her.

I was about to get out of the truck when Gail put her hand on my arm. "One more thing."

I waited.

"That scooter the local PD found smashed tonight? The one that started all this?"

"Yeah?"

"They said it had a couple of boxes of Speer 9mm in the storage compartment and a receipt from a gun store on Stock island that says you bought a handgun."

I frowned.

"You still have that pistol on you?"

"Not at the moment."

She released her grip on my arm. "I'll keep that between us for the time being. But stay put tonight. I'll check back in the morning. You hear anything from Frank, do me a favor and give me a call on my cell first, okay?"

"Roger that." I climbed out of the truck.

"Hey, Luke?"

"Yeah."

"You did all you could for him. His fate is his to own now."

I let that settle into my brain while her truck pulled away.

The results of this trip were out of my hands.

I wasn't sure why I didn't feel relieved.

There was a different attendant at the counter of the hotel lobby when I limped in, and my request for a new room key card went without comment. So much for my grand plans to get home tonight.

Back in the room I settled onto the bed with a groan and checked my phone.

I had three texts, two missed calls, and a voicemail, all from Cassidy.

She picked up on the first ring when I called her back.

"Hi, Cass," I said. "I've got some disappointing news."

I SLEPT BADLY. A fistful of Tylenol had done little to abate the soreness in my joints and hip from my collision with the Caprice. I was up twice to piss as well, but at least there was no blood in it.

At 3 a.m. I awoke to the sound of the room telephone ringing.

I fumbled in the darkness and found the handset, then groggily held it to my ear.

"What?"

"Hello, son."

Frank sounded calm. Decidedly alert and awake for that hour, but calm.

"What the hell, Frank," I muttered.

"I need your help."

"Fat chance." I rubbed my eyes.

He was quiet for a long moment then said, "There's a cop watching your hotel. Out front in an unmarked car. You think you can slip away from him?"

I got myself upright and my feet hit the floor. "What's this about, Frank? Where did you disappear to tonight?" I reached for the knob for the lamp, but paused with my hand over it. Turning it on would alert anyone watching my room that I was awake. I let my hand fall back to my lap.

"I don't know if they're listening in on this phone, but if they are, I don't want to say too much. You remember the bird from yesterday? The one who swore at us? Let's meet there, soon as you're able. We can talk more then."

"You found what you're looking for?" I asked.

"Not yet. That's why I still need your help."

"What's that phrase? Fool me once, shame on you. Fool me twice?"

"I didn't abandon you."

"Current circumstances suggest otherwise."

"I had to take care of a few things and I needed to keep you out of it. For your safety. You still have The Mooch's number? I've been trying to reach him with a number I got off our bird friend and nobody is answering. Can't raise him. Thought maybe you could try."

"It's the middle of the night, Frank. And I'm tired of your bullshit. I'm going back to sleep."

"If you could talk to him for me as soon as—"

"I won't."

"Well, when you do, tell him I'll bring him what we discussed later today. By noon."

"I'm going home, Frank. Early as I can get out in the morning. Sorry, but you're on your own."

"Luke."

But I hung up.

Fool me twice, shame on me.

I laid back down and pulled the second flimsy hotel pillow over my head. Screw you, Frank. This whole trip has been a waste of my time.

My call with Cassidy ran through my head then. "He's still your dad, Luke," she'd said. "At some point you're going to need to fix things between you two."

"Not how it goes in my family," I'd said. "In my family, he does what's in his interest at everyone else's expense. The rest of us pay the price."

"But that's not what *you* do, Luke."

I probably should have. If I'd never agreed to take him down here in the first place I'd have been better off. All teaming up with Frank had done so far was get me beat me up and waste my money.

I laid there for half an hour before giving up on sleep. There was no more to be had. I dressed in the dark, gathered my things and peered out the hotel blinds. There was no one visible in the interior courtyard. I slipped out the door and down the stairs to a spot behind the shrubbery where I could peer out the entryway to the street. It took a minute till I spotted the car with the figure in it. The dull glow of a phone screen partly illuminated a man's face. My chaperone from the local PD checking his text messages.

Sorry buddy. Frank's not coming.

I recalled what Gail had said about them tracking my phone to find me after the scooter accident. If I used it to send a message to The Mooch, would that be visible to the police as well? I wasn't sure. I pulled my phone from my pocket and turned it off.

I backed away, working my way to the rear of the hotel, then slipped out the alley near the dumpsters. I stayed vigilant as I walked, curious if the job of surveilling the hotel had warranted a second car. Evidently it hadn't, because I was able to get clear of the hotel and into the side streets without being accosted.

I headed north for reasons confusing even to myself. I should be heading to the airport. Frank's problem shouldn't be mine to worry about. And at 4 a.m. there was little chance The Mooch was even awake. Would he even still be at the marina, or back at his Southernmost Southernmost House? I had no idea. But if I couldn't find him, I could still leave a note, pass on the message and be done with it. Then my mind would feel unburdened.

I did every damned thing you wanted, Frank. What's your justification for stiffing me now?

My leg was still sore, but it loosened some as I walked. I even broke into a slow jog for a block before reverting to a walk once I reached the harbor.

Fishermen would be awake, but not many others. Key West lay still, the nightlife come and gone, evidenced now only by trash cans overfilled with drink cups and a smell of stale beer.

I preferred Key West in the morning. The quiet and the calm. It was an island with a breathing soul that could be felt in the stillness. Or maybe that was just the sea breeze and my imagination.

The docks were still lit, though not as brightly as the night before. I found the private pier where *Sea Notes* was docked. A gate blocked my path. But as I walked up to it, I saw it now stood ajar. I pushed on it and it swung open. A brief look at the lock showed it had been deliberately jammed open by use of a stainless steel screw wedged into the mechanism.

So much for security.

But when I reached *Sea Notes*, my experience at the gate gave me pause. There was a window on the starboard side of the boat with a bullet hole in it. Unlike the pane of glass at the Mansion by the Sea, I doubted this one had been left there for nostalgia purposes.

Vague noises drifted from on board. A low drone of television conversation.

I stared at the boat for several seconds and checked the area. There were no doubt people staying aboard other boats in this marina but none on this dock appeared to be occupied. And *Sea Notes* likewise lay mostly dark, except for the flickering on the main deck from the TV. It might have been left on. But the burbling of the boat's air conditioning system water pumps kept up a steady noise at the stern. Someone had certainly been aboard earlier. I recalled the girl from the house setting the table this evening. A pair of half-filled wine glasses were still in view on the stern deck dining table.

A bullet hole.

No sirens. No movement on the neighboring docks.

"Frank?" I called to the darkness.

Silence.

There was no reason he could be here, was there?

Damn it. I eyed the stern entryway and the small gap between the boat and the dock, then leapt aboard.

The swim platform had four steps that led up to the stern dining deck. The glass door to the main living area was there, the room dimly lit by the TV. The door was unlocked and opened a crack, venting cooler air through the inch-wide slit. I used the edge of my shirt and slid the door open enough to admit myself.

The salon was broad and deep, a couch on one side, sitting area with chairs, then a dining table. Beyond that was the galley kitchen and a second less formal dining table tucked into a booth. The TV was playing a replay of a soccer game. This salon was the room with the bullet hole in the starboard window. The bullet had penetrated at an angle, and as I walked through the room I found the origin of the shot. Beyond the kitchen countertop, sprawled out in the galley on the floor, lay José, The Mooch's mustachioed security guy. He'd been shot twice in the chest. The man's blood had pooled on the floor behind and beneath him, then spread toward the entryway of the galley. I was careful not to step in it as I leaned forward to have a better look at him. His pistol was still in his hand. Whomever he'd fired at must have been a better shot.

That he was dead seemed obvious, but I pressed two fingers

to his neck to be certain. His skin was still warm, but if he had a pulse, I couldn't feel it.

To the right of the galley was a set of stairs that descended to the lowest deck. I took the steps down. LED lights illuminated the edges of the stairs and I found the ship's control console in the wall midway down. I pressed a knuckle to the control panel and it illuminated, offering options. One was cabin lighting. The hallway lit up at the command, and after a brief pause to listen for any results, I was able to peer around the corner to see forward or aft. No sounds. No one objecting to the sudden light. I moved forward toward the bow, fairly sure of what I was going to find.

The Mooch was in the master bedroom, sat up in the center of the king sized bed. A dark hole stared at me from the center of his forehead, leering like a third eye. A stream of blood had tipped from the hole in his skull and run down his nose and chin painting him crimson.

The stewardess girl I'd spotted setting the table earlier was there too. Sprawled out partially nude on the floor, eyes wide, her hair fanned out around her as she stared blankly at my feet. Two holes in her chest.

Two in José. One in Fat Tony's forehead. Two in the girl. Five bullets.

The girl's eyes were a brilliant blue. I stooped to look at them. Her young face held the kind of beauty that opens doors and grants opportunities. But whatever life she'd been angling toward, she wasn't going to make it now.

A boat this size typically employed a captain and at least one mate while en route anywhere, so it was with some trepidation that I crossed the boat again and descended to the crew quarters at the stern. But I found the captain's quarters and the second crew room vacant, the beds neatly made, toiletries absent. The crew had evidently slept ashore and missed the violence.

A mercy.

Killing five people at two different ends of the boat would have been a noisy and complicated affair. Three was less complicated. José caught unaware on the way in. A quick trip down the steps to the master bedroom.

The girl had tried to run. Maybe she'd heard the shots upstairs—José being killed. But she hadn't had time to get far. The killer might have shot Tony first. Hard to say. The big man hadn't even made it out of the bed to retrieve his pants. Or they'd shot the girl first when she'd attempted to flee and kept Tony there through fear.

Five bullets. The same number I'd dumped from Lyla's J-frame .38 special.

Did she have it in her to do this?

Was it two shooters or one? Were all the shots fired from the same weapon? Those and a half dozen other questions floated through my mind.

The police would eventually have to find those answers. Not me.

I exited the boat from the stern deck, a clock ticking in the back of my mind.

I didn't know who the killer was, but I had an idea about who they were after next.

TWENTY-NINE
DECODED

THE STREETS no longer felt peaceful.

Lights were on at Harpoon Harry's diner, someone on the kitchen staff already doing food prep for the morning breakfast rush. I jogged past, my footfalls echoing loudly in the quiet of Margaret Street. It was five blocks to the cemetery and Angela Street. As I ran, my duffel bag flapped up and down against my back. I played the scene over again in my mind.

Three dead bodies.

Killings like that didn't happen in Key West. Murder was rare here. A robbery or drug deal gone bad, a drunken fight, those happened on occasion. But three people executed on a boat? Never.

I didn't stop running till I hit Angela Street, then walked while catching my breath, trying to locate the house we'd stopped at the day before.

I passed the spot where I'd shoved Frank to the ground.

Just one meal, he'd said. If you'd let me tell you the story, you'd be on my side.

I was on your side, Frank. Look where it got me.

The moon was still bright on the horizon while I banged on the door of the little bungalow. A lamp was on inside and the little dog erupted into fits again. It took longer for the ancient woman in the muumuu to arrive this time—her hair in curlers–but the door finally opened. No bird on her shoulder yet. She peered at me through her thick lenses again.

"Frank Angel," I said. "Is he here?"

"Who?"

"Guy who was here with me yesterday."

"That utility man?"

"Same guy. Is he here?"

"No. You missed him. He went out with Jerome."

"Where did they go?"

"How am I supposed to know? Nobody ever tells me nothin'.'"

"Does Jerome have a boat, ma'am? Where does he keep it?"

"Sure he has a boat. They took it out last night. Probably where they goin' again."

"Where, ma'am? Where's the boat?"

But she didn't know. Nor did she have a phone number for Jerome. The African gray parrot squawked from somewhere inside, "Go home, motherfuckers."

I hung my head.

Damn it, Frank.

I found her eyes through her thick foggy lenses. "Ma'am, I think your son Jerome might be in some danger. Do you own a car?"

When I pulled the dust cover off the old woman's vehicle in the detached garage, it turned out to be a sun-faded AMC Gremlin hatchback from circa 1977. The original chrome hubcaps were rusted, and both bumpers were dented, but the old woman had kept the interior upholstery in an admirable condition, considering it hailed from more than half a century in the past, and specifically an era of rampant cigarette burns. Even better, it started. It filled the garage with an oily exhaust cloud, but it stayed running. I thanked the woman profusely and took the Gremlin onto the road with promises to return it safely, but knowing full well that my track record with borrowed vehicles wasn't stellar at the moment.

Right now, I suspected I didn't need a car as much as I needed a boat. And the only boat I had was a plane.

The marina along the Palm Avenue Causeway housed a flotilla of charter boats. Tourists eager for the experience of hauling in sailfish or tarpon could meet their captains here and set out for high-priced adventure. But as I cruised the row of boats, there was no sign of Frank.

I found an early riser boat captain along the row and asked him if he knew a Jerome AKA "Big Tuna."

"I steer clear of that guy," he replied. "Bad for our rep."

"But have you seen him?"

He hadn't.

But another young guy along the row had. "I ran into him last night," the guy said. "On my way back from Marvin Key."

"Did they have dive gear aboard?"

"No tanks that I saw. But I think I spotted a hookah."

The air compressor system was a way to dive short distances without air tanks. I'd used one myself before when salvaging unfortunate aircraft from the bottom of Tampa Bay.

If they were on the water already, I knew only one way to catch them.

I parked the Gremlin in the parking lot of the airport FBO and this time I did a sweep of the lot first before walking in. No sign of the Caprice, or Deacon and Lyla. There was a police cruiser in the lot but it was vacant.

I was early. The Signature FBO wasn't open yet. I hung around the gate and tried a few different routes but the airport security fence was impenetrable to pedestrians. I was forced to turn on my phone and call the after-hours FBO number and got the call service. They informed me that if I wanted to have someone let me in early, I should have set it up in advance.

Silly me. Why didn't I know I would be racing a killer at this hour? I hung up, frustrated. But around 6 a.m. a mechanic appeared at the nearby seaplane tours hangar. When he found out I was there with the Mallard on the ramp he had no qualms about letting me through the maintenance entrance.

"That's one hell of a plane," he said. "It's yours?"

"Sort of," I said. "Barring further catastrophe."

He didn't pry further which I appreciated.

I got *Tropic Angel* untied and pulled the chocks. I still owed the FBO money for services but they had my credit card number. I was confident they'd have no trouble billing me. No one else seemed to have problems taking my money on this trip.

I pulled each of the propellers through a few times, did a quick walkaround, then climbed into the flight deck and continued my pre-flight checklist. By the time I had both engines running, the sun was nearly up. I checked my phone as I was moving down the taxiway. The newest text was from Reese.

>>> I solved the code. Find your treasure yet?

I texted back. <<< On my way there now.

She's evidently managed to figure it out even without Earl's Sharpie. Clever.

I finished my run up and prop checks on the big radial engines and taxied out to the runway. The tower wasn't open yet so I made my own radio calls.

"November one eight eight tango alpha is taking the active for departure on Runway two seven."

My phone buzzed in my lap. I looked down at the new text from Reese.

>>> Where did the flip move the destination? South?

I was in the middle of rolling out on centerline so I had my hands full, but my mind stumbled over the question. Move the destination? What was she talking about? The engines roared on either side of me as I throttled up. The big bird at my fingertips picked up speed. *Tropic Angel* thundered down the runway with the vibrations from the props pulsing through me. After rotating off the runway, I waited till most of the asphalt had vanished beneath me and put the landing gear up. I kept my right hand on the overhead throttles until I reached three hundred feet, then trimmed the elevator for a gentler rate of climb. I cleared the area around me, scanning for traffic and turned northeast to dodge the Naval Air Station's airspace. I adjusted the manifold pressures and once I was stabilized, I finally had a chance to pick up my phone and reread the message.

>>>Where did it move the destination?

My headset had bluetooth capability and Reese was obviously available so I simply hit the call button. She picked up immediately.

"Morning. You must be flying."

"What did you mean?" I asked, speaking loudly over the noise of the engines. "Move the destination?"

"What?"

"Your text. Flip the destination. Why would it move?"

"The kneeboard? The code? I was talking about the message. You decoded it, right?"

"Yeah. The Decathlon part. Which part are you talking about?"

"The end. You didn't decode the whole message?"

I fumbled around and searched for the airport facilities directory but I didn't have it. It was still in my duffel bag and I'd left it out of reach on one of the passenger seats on my way to the flight deck. I recalled the napkin I'd scribbled out the code on.

"I made it as far as the turn coordinator part," I said. "But I guess I got distracted. What did the rest say?"

"It said to flip the kneeboard over."

Flip it over? I recalled the three holes in the board. One over Key West. One over Marathon. The third hole had shown the island north of Sugarloaf. But if I flipped it over? Where would it go then? I checked the iPad in front of me and tried to estimate it. The hole to the north would now be the same distance south. There was nothing down that way. Was there?

"I tried checking it on a sectional chart. Just guessing where it would be," Reese said. "On Google maps, the only thing down that way is an abandoned lighthouse. You think Earl could have hid it there?"

"Beats me," I said. "All I know is Frank's currently on a boat, somebody is out to kill him, and he's searching in the wrong place."

THE TOWER CONTROLLERS at Naval Air Station Key West were pleasantly chill when I called and asked to transition their airspace. It must have been a quiet morning for air traffic around the Keys because other than a verbal reminder about Fat Albert, their tethered radar balloon, they left me alone to buzz along over the northern islands en route to Sugarloaf. It was a short flight in a Grumman Mallard and I never climbed above a thousand feet. When I overflew Frank Angel and what appeared to be a center-console Contender anchored near the island, I had descended to two hundred feet. Close enough to recognize the look of surprise on his face.

It was also close enough for me to recognize two other people aboard the Contender—Deacon and Lyla.

"You have got to be kidding me," I muttered into my headset microphone.

I circled the boat while shaking my head. Would these two never let up?

The idea of just flying on and going home crossed my mind—leave this doomed crew to their fate. The island below, for all its beauty, showed no sign of a Decathlon, sunken or otherwise. Thanks to Reese, now I knew why. They could search all they wanted and they'd never find it.

But then I recalled the bodies aboard *Sea Notes*.

Cassidy's voice was in my head. "He's still your dad, Luke."

As much as I'd learned to hate Frank Angel over the past two decades, no part of me believed he was capable of murdering The Mooch. Which meant someone else had. Was it someone on that island?

The captain of the Contender had it anchored in two feet of water along the northern edge of Great White Heron National Wildlife Refuge. He and Frank stood in the sand on the shoreline watching me fly circles. I gave the south side of the island a wide berth to keep from disturbing the birds roosting there, then circled out and back in a teardrop turn. There was a channel northeast of the island with deeper water that made for a good landing site. I angled into the wind as much as possible to still make the cut, then eased back on the throttles and descended toward the tranquil turquoise water.

Tropic Angel kissed the surface with a pleasant shushing sound that was audible through the hull, and the channels in the keel sent arcs of spray into the morning sunlight, creating a prismatic cascade of color on the aircraft's nose. By the time I slowed to a plow and turned toward Frank and the Contender, the effect of the sunlight had lessened, but the Mallard was in her element. I used differential thrust to turn the aircraft toward shore and kept the power up till I was confident the drift would carry me close to my target. Then I cut the engines.

This was where having a second crew mate aboard would be handy. The anchor was in the bow compartment and the only way to get there was a tunnel beneath the copilot side of the instrument panel. The rudder pedals on that side stowed away and revealed the passage. As tall as I was, it was a flexibility test every time I needed to bend my long frame and get under there. Then followed a cramped and claustrophobic crawl to the bow hatch. Once I had it open, the smell of sea air flooded the compartment. I rose, hauling the anchor chain up with me. I'd drifted into the shallows and I only needed a short length of line when I tossed the anchor out. I tied it off to a cleat at the bow and waited as the anchor caught and the seaplane weathervaned into the wind and current.

Frank and his crew on the Contender motored over, the three 400hp Mercs trimmed up to run shallow. It was a hell of a boat. The guy steering it was a jolly-looking black dude in a vented Bahamian-blue fishing shirt. Lyla was in the bow of the boat dressed in a bright bikini top and cutoff jean shorts. The handle of her Smith and Wesson peeked from inside the waistband in front of her hip. She waved.

Deacon looked less pleased to see me. He was in black jeans, a black T-shirt and his expensive-looking basketball sneakers, not an outfit one associates with comfort aboard a boat.

"I see you brought your crack squad of salvage experts," I said to Frank when they drew close.

"You remember Deacon and Lyla," he replied. "They were nice enough to look me up last night. Turns out they're in town for a visit."

"Friends till the end, huh?"

"Frank missed us," Lyla said. "We didn't want him to be lonely." She was chomping bubble gum and it showed when she grinned at me.

"And you must be Big Tuna," I said to the captain.

"Ain't nobody calls me Big Tuna that wants to keep their face unpunched," the big man said. Turned out he wasn't as jolly as he looked.

"This is Jerome," Frank said. "Signed on to help me find my good friend Earl's plane. For sentimental reasons."

"Ain't nothing sentimental about the five grand you said I'd get when we find it," Jerome said. "But you gonna have to pay up either way soon cause we ain't finding shit. Ain't no sunk plane out here that I seen."

"People sure do some crazy things for their lost loved ones," I said.

"Frank's sweet like that," Lyla said. "He'd do anything for his friends. Us too. Ain't that right, Dekey, baby?"

Deacon was sitting in the bow with a miserable expression on his face and his hand on his belly. Clearly seasick. "Let's get on with it already. We gonna find this damned plane or not?"

I sized up Frank and nodded toward the others. "This the problem you said you were having last night?"

"Among others. You just flew over the island. You see anything from up there that looked like the Decathlon?"

"Nope. And I know why too. It's not here."

"The hell you mean it ain't here?" Deacon said. "Frank cracked a code."

"Is that how he told it?"

"How do you know it's not here?" Frank said. "You said this was the island."

"I was wrong."

"Then where the hell it at?" Deacon shouted.

"Mind if we have a word privately?" I said to Frank.

"Anything you say to him you can say to us," Lyla said. "We're like family now. Aren't we, Frank?"

Frank had salt in his hair. He stood barefoot on the bow with sand on his legs from having walked the shoreline of the island. Reminded me of the version of him I recalled from Costa Rica. Or the night before we flew down, when he'd swum out to the buoys and just kept doing laps.

"If you know something we don't, I'm all ears," he said.

"I'm sure you are. Considering I'm currently the only one who knows where your treasure is."

"Treasure? What treasure?" Jerome said.

"A family treasure," Frank said without looking his way. "That plane means a lot to our family."

"You holding out on me, Frank? That what I'm hearing? I thought maybe this plane of yours was some rare antique, but if you got something else going on, you know I'm gonna need a cut."

"You want a cut?" Deacon said. "How 'bout I get my girl Lyla to shoot your damned dick off and then I shove it in your mouth. How'd that be for a cut?"

Jerome glared at his passenger, and almost said something else, but the eager look on Lyla's face shut him up. She blew a pink bubble and it popped audibly. Jerome retreated a few feet.

"Is that hookah portable?" I asked, pointing to the air compressor and lines jumbled at the rear of the boat.

"We rented it," Frank replied. "You want to know if it will fit aboard *Tropic Angel*?"

"It's a short flight," I said. "Longer boat ride. If you want to go, I'm going."

"Hey, you're going where now?" Jerome spouted.

"Come on, Deke baby. Sounds like we're going for a plane ride," Lyla said.

Deacon groaned.

And just like that I had three new passengers.

"YOU KNOW the deposit cost more than the rental on this damned thing," Jerome said as he helped me manhandle the compressor for the hookah aboard *Tropic Angel*. "Now you guys are leaving me high and dry out here on my own? That ain't right."

The hookah looked worse for wear. No doubt it had taken a beating during year after year of lobster mini-seasons, but I empathized with the boat captain. Dive gear was expensive.

"You know your way through Niles Channel?" I asked.

"I'd be a damned fool charter boss if I didn't."

"You run back through there and cut southeast to the edge of the reef. Run the edge of the reef awhile and you'll find us."

"Edge of the reef is six miles offshore. What you gonna be doing all the way out there?"

"Minding our own business."

"I can't run wide open under that bridge, but I guess that's all right. You sure you're still gonna be there when I hit the edge of the reef? You lose that hookah, they're gonna charge me three grand."

"Get out there fast then."

He swore and handed the rest of the hookah gear in from the bow of the Contender. I pushed his bow away from my aircraft the moment we were done and he hustled to the controls to reverse his props to get clear. I cringed as he came close to bashing the bow of the Contender off the Mallard's horizontal stabilizer, but he squeaked out without making contact.

My passengers were aboard, the three of them milling about the forward cabin where I'd installed several forward-facing seats and a couch.

"I'm going to need you in the flight deck this time," I said to Frank.

His face lit up.

"What the hell is that about?" Deacon asked.

"Someone's gotta help prime the muffler bearings," I said.

Frank kept his smirk contained, but just barely. I had him do the bow tunnel crawl and he managed it with a lot more ease than I had. Maybe because no one had hit him with a car lately. Once the anchor was aboard, I got the engines started right away to correct for our drift in the current, then nosed us back into the wind. Frank climbed back through to the flight deck and donned a headset. I switched the intercom to "crew only" mode so the rear passengers wouldn't be able to listen in.

"Feels damned good to be back up here," Frank said, fingers grazing the yoke.

"Don't get too comfortable. I just sat you up here to talk." I kept the RPMs of the engines unnecessarily high for the taxi, just to drown out any chance of being heard by Deacon and Lyla. "Where's your gun?" I asked.

Frank gave me a quizzical look, then fished around behind his hip and pulled out the Sig Sauer P365 still in the appendix holster I'd purchased at the gun store. "This?" He handed the gun across to me. "I figured you wouldn't mind if I borrowed it again."

I pulled the pistol loose from the holster and ejected the magazine. It was still full and still loaded with blanks. I rammed the magazine home again, peeked in the chamber, then put it back in the holster and handed it back. "Okay."

"The hell are you doing up there?" Deacon shouted from the back, evidently having witnessed the handoff. I twisted to look back down the aisle to where he was sitting and saw him unbuckle himself to come forward. The second he was on his feet, I bumped the throttles and the engines surged, tipping him off balance and back into his seat again.

"The captain has turned on the fasten seatbelt sign," I shouted back to him. "Please remain seated for the duration of the flight!"

He glowered at me, but as the hull of the Mallard plowed through some chop, he wisely re-buckled his seatbelt.

I readjusted my headset mic and took on the tasks I needed for takeoff. Frank helped, lowering the flaps to ten degrees.

"Where were you last night, Frank? Before you called me?"

"Out here with Jerome," he replied. "Until I got back ashore and that chucklehead found me." He jerked his thumb rearward to where Deacon was sitting.

"Was Lyla with you?"

"When I was with Deacon? Yeah. Why?"

"What time did they find you?"

"Around . . . two. A little before I called you."

"Any idea what they were up to before they found you?"

"None. Why?"

His expression seemed sincere. As was the tiredness in his face. He looked like a guy who'd been up most of the night on a boat, and if I had to hazard a guess whether he was telling the truth, I would have said yes. But I'd been fooled before.

"The Mooch is dead," I said, watching his reaction.

The surprise on his face would have been hard to fake. "What? When? Last night?"

"Found him early this morning after I talked to you on the phone. His bodyguard and one of those girls we met too."

While Frank ruminated on that, I applied more power and got the seaplane up on plane, then lifted off cleanly from the surface in a roar of raw power from the Pratt and Whitney engines. All other thoughts waited while I took us airborne up and away from the surface of the turquoise water. As I banked right, I caught sight of Jerome in the Contender already streaking toward Niles Channel.

"How the hell did a scammer like Jerome get his hands on a boat that nice?" I asked. "That belong to The Mooch too?"

Frank shook his head. "He manages it for a guy from up in New York. Sold him on a service where he 'exercises' the boat for him regularly for maintenance purposes. Apparently exercises the guy's wife for him too when she's down here."

"That sounds more like the character you described."

"He's a greedy old salt, but at least he's consistent. You're sure The Mooch is dead?"

"Unless he can breathe through a hole in his forehead."

"Goddammit," he muttered.

"Screw up your plans?"

"Who do you think did it?"

"Someone who knows how to shoot."

He frowned at the horizon. "Where are we going now?"

I'd retrieved Earl's old Miami sectional chart from the duffel bag on my way back through the cabin. I unfolded it to the spot that showed the Keys. "On Foreflight or any of the latest sectional charts, it looks like there's nothing out there," I said. "But this chart's from before it was deactivated." I pointed to the symbol for a light.

"A lighthouse."

"American Shoal Lighthouse," I said. "Sits right at the edge of the reef in about four feet of water. But then it drops off." I pointed out the window to where the color of the water changed from light to dark. "I think Earl must have used the lighthouse as a visual reference for a place to ditch."

Frank leaned forward in his seat and pointed. "I'll be damned."

The lighthouse was a skeletal rust-red metallic tower, helpfully designed to keep ships from plowing into the reef, but no longer in service.

I made the turn to put the lighthouse off our nose but then cut wide and banked *Tropic Angel*'s left wing high so we could look almost straight down at the abandoned structure. It sat in a pool of light green and turquoise, but just south of it, the hue of the water changed to royal blue, then navy. I kept the turn around the lighthouse going, doing a full three-sixty as we widened out, searching the water. The water north of the lighthouse was shallow, transparent, and vacant. But on the second turn around, overflying just at the edge of the royal blue, before the shelf plunged into darkness, was the clearly discernible shape of an airplane. It was deep enough that passing boats or the average weekend snorkeler or fisherman might never have known it was there, but Earl must have known it would still be visible from the sky. The Super Decathlon.

"Earl sure was a sneaky son of a bitch," Frank said. He turned to look at me with a grin on his face.

I smiled back. "X marks the spot."

THIRTY-TWO

HOOKAH

I LANDED in deep blue water.

Waves rolled with us as I water-taxied *Tropic Angel* toward the lighthouse. The tower had looked small from the air, but from the water's surface, the skeletal old structure now loomed overhead, stretching up a hundred feet. I kept it abeam my right wing as I taxied toward the spot along the reef where we'd seen the sunken plane. Even though we'd located it from the air, finding it again from the water wasn't as easy as it seemed. But I knew I could get *Tropic Angel* to the near proximity of where we'd spotted it. Prior to landing, I'd done one extra pass over the wreck from the air with the specific purpose of dropping a pin for my GPS location. Now it was time to see how accurate a phone map could be.

"This is the spot," I said into my headset.

Frank had entered the bow via the tunnel and was wearing a headset plugged into jacks near the bow hatch.

"Looks like maybe twelve feet of water here if I had to guess," he replied. "Deeper to the south. Any farther north and you might run aground."

"Go ahead and toss out the anchor."

This time I waited till the anchor caught and we'd weathervaned into the wind before shutting down the engines.

I pulled my headset from my ears and had just flipped the master switch off for the electrical system when Deacon stuck his head through the narrow doorway to the flight deck.

"Can't you make this thing stop rocking? Your damned plane's just as bad as the boat."

"It's the ocean, Deacon. It moves. Now get out of my way."

"Ocean or not, you best watch your mouth. Else I gonna shut it for you."

I pivoted in my seat and faced him. "You an open-water distance swimmer, Deacon? Or maybe you have a seaplane pilot's license you failed to mention? No? Then your time as "shot-caller" has come to an end."

His chest swelled, anger flared in his eyes, and if the keyhole entryway to the flight deck had been wider, he might have taken a swing at me. But as it was, his shoulders were too broad, the space too narrow and his balance was questionable. He teetered on shaky legs and took a hard grip on the bulkhead to steady himself.

"Six miles to shore," I said. "You want to see land again, you'd best let me get to work."

He clenched his jaw but gave way. I climbed through and shoved past him to the aft cabin, passing Lyla in the process. She gave me a wary look, one hand conspicuously on the handle of the Smith and Wesson, like she was worried I might snatch it out of her shorts.

"I had more bullets in my purse, you know."

"Happy for you. Be a good girl and help Frank when he gets out of the bow."

I worked my way to the aft baggage hold and located my

toolbox. Thanks to Earl, I knew where we'd be looking and which tools would be required. A turn coordinator is one of the easier instruments to remove from an instrument panel—just four screws and a cannon plug—but being underwater can complicate things, so in addition to the screwdriver, I also brought a pair of Channel Locks and a submersible headlamp.

I stripped out of my clothes next, undressing down to my boxers, then slung a mesh bag over my head to carry what I needed. Jerome had procured masks for the hookah rig that were scratched and worse for wear, but I fitted one to my face. Better than nothing.

Frank joined me as I was getting ready to hoist the inner tube for the hookah out the door.

"Get the ladder out first, then I'll hand it to you," he said.

I hooked the ladder to the lip of the boarding door and climbed out, descending to the bottom rung, waist deep into the cool tropical water. I tied off the float to the ladder and Frank and I worked together to get the heavy pump out the door and situated it in its raft. The hookah was, at its core, just a gas-powered air compressor, but specifically regulated to deliver air at a breathable pressure via lines to the divers in the water. Simple in design, and relatively easy to use, it still took a little practice getting used to, and I did a thorough check of the apparatus before intending to breathe from it. It was possible to suffer carbon monoxide poisoning from exhaust getting into the intake, or lose your air when something mechanical went south, so we'd need someone up top to keep an eye on things.

"You going to watch this rig?" I asked Frank.

"I was planning to go into the water with you." He already had his shirt off.

"Then which of these two yahoos do you trust to keep this thing running right while we're down there?"

"Neither, but I imagine they'll figure it out."

I stuck my face under water and started looking for the wreck. When I came back up I said, "I'm going to try a couple free dives first. See if I can spot it. Then we'll belt up and go after it."

He handed me out a pair of fins. "I'll be out in a few to help."

After hanging my mesh tool bag on the raft, I slipped my feet into the fins, took a few long breaths to steady my diaphragm, then dove.

Keys water is a joy, especially on the reef. Clear, clean, teeming with life. This section of reef was home to plentiful brain coral, sea fans, and mustard hill coral, plus schools of colorful fish that darted in and around them. With my first dive, I did a half circle aft of *Tropic Angel,* judging the terrain and trying to spot the Decathlon around the depth we'd estimated it. I surfaced after an unsuccessful search, took several deep breaths and tried again, swimming a wider arc back toward the seaplane. A splash and an eruption of bubbles alerted me to when Frank was in the water. He had likewise stripped to his shorts and donned a mask and fins. I gestured to him underwater, signaling where he should search and he nodded, swimming off with strong kicks forward of the Mallard.

It only took another two attempts till I spotted it. The Super Decathlon sat tail low and belly up, nosed against the reef almost as though it had landed there inverted after one of Earl's upside down stunts. My brief survey of the plane from above showed minimal damage to the structure. Earl had evidently done a nice job ditching it and other than the battering it had taken from the current, and subsequently flipping over, the structure of the aircraft remained intact.

I surfaced and waited for Frank to do the same. Then when he spotted me, I pointed. "Found it! Come check it out."

Deacon and Lyla were both in the doorway of the Mallard. I swam back over to the raft with the hookah on it. It took two tries to get it started, but eventually it coughed to life, spewing a cloud of exhaust. I frowned at the cloud it was putting out, then gestured to Deacon. "Hand me out those weight belts." He located them and I added them to the gear on the raft. "One of you needs to climb out here and watch this thing," I said. "We need to drag it out that way and run it so Frank and I can dive. You can man the hookah while we're down."

"I ain't going out there," Deacon said. "I'm no SCUBA diver."

"You know how a small motor works though, right? I assume you've mowed a lawn or run a weed whacker? I just need you to keep this exhaust outlet pointed downwind. If it spins around and starts ingesting its own exhaust into the intake, the air lines will get contaminated. We could pass out."

"Ain't it got a filter or something?"

"Filters don't stop carbon monoxide. So just keep it pointed downwind and don't let any boats come chop our lines with their props. That's all you need to manage."

"Yeah, alright. Fine."

He ditched his shoes but kept his jeans on, which was an interesting choice, but I didn't comment. I towed the hookah rig away a few yards, trailing a tether line to the plane, and waited for Deacon to get in the water. He swam toward me, not looking especially confident.

"You need a life vest?" I shouted.

"Nah. I'm good."

But when he reached the hookah raft he held on like a koala. I hoped he wouldn't accidentally capsize the thing while we were down. Luckily he seemed to get more comfortable as we swam together, all the way to where Frank had surfaced above the wreck. I retrieved my tool bag, handed Frank a weight belt, and we took turns belting them on one another to make the process move quicker. After a final check of the rig, we put our regulator mouthpieces in, let go of the raft, and submerged ourselves.

The end of our journey now lay a dozen feet straight down.

THIRTY-THREE
COORDINATED

AN AIRPLANE WRECK would no doubt have delighted any divers or snorkelers who stumbled upon it since its arrival. Perhaps a few even poked around inside for trinkets. If anyone had found it and had gone ashore with a mind to come back later and salvage the plane, even cursory research would have concluded that the market for ocean-soaked airplane equipment is practically nil.

Saltwater devalues plane parts faster than nearly anything, barring fire.

So here it had sat. A colorful but seemingly worthless decoration on the reef.

When we reached the fuselage, the door to the cabin was bobbing open and closed in the current. Some sunlight penetrated to the wreck, but dimly. My headlamp helped.

Upside down was a strange angle to attempt to enter a plane, though part of me appreciated the aerobatic nature of the Decathlon's final resting place.

The door, normally on the right, was now on the left. Frank joined me at the landing gear and held on to the brake assembly, both of us bobbing in the water and attempting to avoid the cuts and abrasions from coral and oysters on the ocean floor. I gestured to Frank and signaled for him to guard the air lines. There was a threat of them getting tangled down here. He recognized the danger and gathered the lines for safekeeping.

When I sank lower and entered the cabin, I found the primary benefit to the aircraft being upside down was that the instrument panel—usually a pain in the neck to get under—was now in an attitude where I could slide up into the footwell and look down into the cluster of instruments instead of up. When I poked my head into the space, a speckled crab greeted me and scurried deeper into the wiring harnesses.

The turn coordinator was one of six primary instruments common in small aircraft panels, serving a dual function of measuring standard rate turns and also coordinating rudder movements via a ball in a glass tube called an inclinometer that somewhat resembled a bubble level. Like many Decathlons, Earl's instrument panel setup omitted two of the primary six instruments—the attitude indicator—because when you spend as much time inverted as a Decathlon does, the instrument quickly tumbles and loses its usefulness anyway—and the heading indicator, relying instead on a fluid compass for heading information. Of the remaining four: airspeed, vertical speed, altimeter, and turn coordinator, the turn coordinator was arguably the least critical. It made sense why Earl had chosen that one to disable.

Another nice thing about it being less critical was that it sat lower in the panel, farther from the pilot's eye line, and was therefore easier for me to remove.

I reached into the mesh bag slung around my neck and fished out the Channel Locks. As I did so, I caught movement behind me and spotted a five-foot nurse shark nosing past. It did one turn amid a patch of loose sand, then swam off again in a flurry. I also had a few visitors in the form of yellowtail snappers browsing the wreck and warily eyeing my activity. Refocusing my attention, I got the cannon plug loose on the back of the turn coordinator and twisted it free, then got to work on the four screws in the front of the panel. I'd just freed the second of the four when something poked me in the back. I jolted, but turned and found it was just Frank hovering overhead from his post atop the fuselage. He signaled for me to look aft, so I stuck my head out of the plane and followed the angle of his pointer finger. Perhaps twenty-five yards away, a Goliath grouper bobbed in the current. The massive fish was harmless but struck an impressive pose due to its tremendous size. As I watched, the giant drifted south, then vanished amid the watery haze. Frank pulled the air regulator from his mouth and gave me a grinning thumbs up.

Good to see he was having a great time. I returned his thumbs up and got back to work.

The remaining two screws only took a minute to remove. Then the turn coordinator fell away from the panel. I removed it from amid the tangle of other wiring behind the dash and held it in my hands. A turn coordinator weighs around two pounds usually. This one felt lighter. If there were diamonds inside, it meant Earl had gutted the interior of the instrument case to make room.

I wriggled my way back out of the cabin and bobbed near Frank. His eyes were on my face. A vague sense of finality lingered in the water. Then I handed him the instrument.

There was no opening it down here. That would require more care. And other tools. But we'd done it. The diamonds were back where they'd started.

Frank did something that surprised me. He extended his hand. A handshake.

Deal done.

His hand lingered there in front of me and I hesitated, but finally shook it. His eyes were smiling.

He looked upward to the light. The hookah and Deacon's legs bobbed in the waves above. The hull of *Tropic Angel* floated in the near distance. But Frank waited. It seemed like he had something else he wanted to say, but submerged twelve feet with mouthpieces and regulators in wasn't any kind of place for a conversation. Instead, he gave me a nod.

Sure, Frank. You're welcome.

Then together, we rose.

Frank and I surfaced on either side of Deacon, startling him. But the thug had managed to keep the hookah working and properly oriented. "You get it?" he asked.

Frank held up the turn coordinator and grinned. "Success."

Then even Deacon smiled. "Hell, yeah, brother!" The two clasped hands.

"Look at you three treasure hunters!" Lyla shouted from the plane. We'd drifted nearly to the end of the tether line length, but were still near enough to *Tropic Angel* for it to be an easy swim.

"You sure they in there?" Deacon asked.

"Let's get aboard and see," Frank said. He swam ahead, kicking powerfully and reaching the seaplane first. Deacon and I trailed behind towing the hookah rig. I shut the motor down and gathered our trailing regulator lines.

Frank dripped his way up the ladder and was met by a smiling Lyla. She threw her arms around his shoulders and squeezed him, the infectious mood of success on her face too. She whooped. The fact that Frank was soaking wet did nothing to deter her affection. She turned to us after, saltwater running down her bare abdomen.

"Reel us in, yo," Deacon said. Lyla's fingers found the end of the tether, working on the knot tying it to the ladder. "You boys did so great! You too, Deke. I'm real proud of you, baby." She gave him a big smile. The ex-con made big arm motions to help get us closer to the ladder. Then Lyla tossed her end of the tether into the water. The gesture registered belatedly in my mind. But when she pulled the little Smith and Wesson from her shorts, the action was hard to miss. She still had the same pleased look on her face when she pointed the snub nose directly at me.

Shit.

She gave me a wink.

Then she swung the gun left, pointed it at Deacon, and squeezed the trigger.

THIRTY-FOUR

BLOOD IN THE WATER

THE GUNSHOT ECHOED in my ears as it reverberated across the water.

Deacon had jolted, and now stared down at a hole in his upper chest. "Goddamn it, woman. What the fuck was that for?" He'd managed to keep a grip on the float for the hookah, but now fumbled at the area below his collarbone with his other hand.

Lyla stood in the boarding door of *Tropic Angel*, the gun still pointed at him. "Word of advice for you, Deke. You tell a girl about a guy you know with a load of shiny diamonds? You should maybe make sure he's not also charming, smart, and a better lover than you."

"What?" Deke fumed. "My boy Frank's out two days and you already jumpin' him?"

"Oh, you sweet dummy. I've been visiting Frank at Union for six months now. Ever since you told me about him. I just didn't want to tell you." She brushed a strand of her dark hair behind her right ear. An ear with a notably empty earring hole in it. The image of her arriving at Earl and Margery's house with two big gold hoops registered belatedly in my mind.

"But you probably should have known better," she said, angling the pistol toward me again. "Considering you barged right in on us."

I was treading water but was ready to dive if she showed any inclination to shoot. Not that it was easy to tell with her.

"You knew?" Deacon asked, still not appropriately respectful of the danger we both were in.

"Frank says I can't shoot you as a goodbye, though." Lyla's lip pouted.

Then Frank reappeared at the doorway, his face serious. He took in the scene, then looked directly at me. "Sorry, son. I'm going to have to borrow *Tropic Angel* a little longer. I hope you understand, given the circumstances." He pulled the swim ladder up from the entryway and dragged it aboard, stranding us in the water. "Shallower over on the reef if you swim that way. I figure someone will be by before long. If Earl could do it, then you two sure can, huh?"

"This isn't like swimming the buoys for ice cream, Frank," I said. "Lyla just shot a man."

He rested a hand on the lip of the door and sighed. "I'd hoped this was going to shake out without anyone getting hurt. But things have gotten a little complicated."

Lyla brushed a hand over his stubbled jaw and beamed at him. "All the best ones are complicated, lover."

Deacon coughed. There was blood in the water around him. His anger had faded. Reality setting in.

"You're a real piece of shit, Frank," I said. But the words felt empty.

Frank took a long look at Deacon. "I thought she was joking about shooting you, Deacon. I only planned to strand you. But I guess you never know the true workings of a woman's heart."

Lyla nodded and waved her gun some more. "Deke knows I

don't play. Consider this payback for you romping around on that porno boat."

Deacon opened his mouth to object but then had the sense to shut it again.

Finally Frank said to me, "I know you won't see it this way, Luke, but it's probably best you're out of this now. Besides, you never wanted me to stick around anyway, right?"

There was no opportunity to respond because he closed the boarding door.

I clenched my jaw and could only watch as Deacon and I drifted farther from the big seaplane. By the time Frank cranked the first of the engines we were thirty yards away, me holding Deacon up and trying to keep him above water. I didn't know how Lyla and Frank managed to get the anchor up and get moving, I was too busy kicking, propelling Deacon and the hookah rig toward shallower water. I swam for the lighthouse, the only good landmark. My fins touched the reef here and there and I got us far enough into the shallows that Deacon could touch too. And none-too-soon because he lost his grip on the hookah float and fell into the water.

I dove after him and pulled him up sputtering.

"Hold onto me," I said. "We've got to stop your bleeding."

In the distance, *Tropic Angel* plowed through the water, got up on plane, then broke the surface tension and took to the sky. I paused only long enough to watch it get clear of ground effect and begin a turn shoreward. It banked left, swooping low and diminishing toward the horizon.

Frank obviously remembered how to fly it just fine.

Deacon coughed again and brought my attention back to our circumstances. The big man had left a trail of red behind us that clouded the water. We weren't far from the lighthouse, but that wasn't much help. The supports were encrusted with barnacles, and there was no way up it. Some desperate Cubans had managed to scale it from a boat a while back. I'd followed the news story, but it had taken them some doing. Even if I could climb it, there was no guarantee that there would be anything in the interior of any use to us. Deacon could bleed out by then.

We'd reached a section of the reef where we could stand and have the water only chest high. It was the best we were going to do. Deacon's chest wound glared at me.

"I need your jeans," I told him. "We're going to take off your belt and pants and I'll use them to stop your bleeding."

He swore something inaudible at me but worked his belt buckle with his one good hand. He only got them down to about his knees before I had to help yank them loose from his legs. I didn't have a dive knife. I did have the screwdriver though, so I punctured the jeans in one of the legs, enlarged the hole and started ripping. The Channel Locks came in handy for getting a better grip. Soaking wet denim made for a shitty bandage material. I had my doubts about its effectiveness. But the uneven strips I managed to rip away from the pants were the only option I had. I attempted to wring them out, then used them to stem the flow of blood from the holes in Deacon, one under his collarbone, another at the exit wound out his back. I belted some of the fabric to him, then used some of the tether line from the hookah rig to complete the job.

"We're shark bait, man," Deacon moaned, trying to keep his balance on the jagged uneven rocks. "Damned fish gonna eat me out here."

"Don't worry. Frank says sharks are just the dogs of the ocean, and most of them are friendly."

"I'm supposed to take his word on that? I seen Shark Week, man. They don't look friendly to me."

"Just hang tight. Somebody's gonna find us out here."

"Damn, I think I just seen a fin too. Right out that way. Big black one."

I turned and looked. Sure enough, a fin broke the surface and cruised in a wide arc with us at its center.

"Gonna be a dolphin though, right?" Deacon asked. "Like in the movies? Stars always gettin' freaked out by fins and then turns out it's Flipper there to save them."

"Sure," I lied. The shark fin looked big enough to belong to a bull shark, one of the Keys' more aggressive species. It certainly was no dolphin, but I didn't think he needed to hear that right now. I still had a mask on my head. When the shark angled closer, I squatted and stuck my head under the water and had a look. The shark saw me too, its angular head and long snout jerking away before its torpedo-like body shot off with a rapid flick of its tail.

I surfaced again and pushed my mask up. "Good news. Just a blacktip," I said.

"That mean it gonna take smaller bites of us?" Deacon asked.

"They're typically not aggressive. Probably just curious why you're bleeding all over the place."

Deacon swore some more. "How 'bout that one?" He pointed. "That a blacktip too?"

But the slow muscled movements of the approaching shark he'd spotted had me doubting it. This shark circled us from the other direction and I pivoted to keep it in view. I submerged myself again as it neared and had a good look. The tips of this shark's fins were a uniform grey. Its snout was broad and it swam with an easy, deliberate confidence. It was also large, at least seven-and-a-half feet. A grown adult bull shark. It passed within a few yards of us and seemed enlivened by the proximity. It shook its head back and forth and began moving erratically. It no doubt smelled a bounty of blood in the water. It swam away again but didn't go far.

Shit.

When I surfaced, Deacon was shivering. "This water getting colder?"

"Hang in there, man. We'll get out of this." Though I was starting to have my doubts. One shark was one thing, but if more showed up? Then we'd have a competition setting. I didn't like our odds in a game of "Who can chomp the most human?"

I kept my screwdriver in hand and tried to locate the bull shark again. It was out there somewhere, but its fin was under water. "Hold this," I said to Deacon. "It gets close, jab it in the nose or something. I'm going to restart the motor on the hookah and see if the noise keeps the sharks away."

When I attempted to start the motor on the hookah, it coughed twice, sputtered and died. I swore and tried again. It caught for a moment, burbled, then stumbled over itself and quit.

"They's two fins now, man," Deacon said. "Or maybe I'm seeing double. I can't tell."

But he wasn't wrong. Out of my peripheral vision, I spotted the movement of another big shark circling, opposite the one he was referencing. I couldn't tell which animal was the first one and which was the new arrival. I swore, then gave another shot at the hookah, this time pulling the start cord with violence. The engine sputtered, but it sounded flooded. It gurgled a few times and went silent.

Shit. Shit. Shit.

But the air wasn't totally silent. A steady buzzing continued well after the hookah motor quit. I turned and spotted the boat, bouncing over waves in the distance. The Contender. And gracias a Dios, it was headed our way.

JEROME TRIED to get me to hoist the hookah aboard before letting Deacon and me up the swim ladder. But I wasn't idiot enough to get stranded twice in the same day.

The sight of Deacon's bloodless face and the ill-fitting bandage I'd rigged on his chest seemed almost enough to make Jerome abandon his deposit on the hookah just to stay clear of whatever mess we'd incurred. Thankfully, his humanity prevailed. That or his morbid curiosity. He helped me get Deacon up the ladder and comfortable on one of the forward sun chairs of the Contender while I searched the various compartments of the boat for a First-Aid kit.

I'd found one by the time Jerome had us underway.

Deacon groaned with each bump and wave we plowed through, but remained conscious.

"Try not to let him bleed all over those cushions up there, man!" Jerome shouted from the controls.

"The blood will wash off. Just get us to shore!" I shouted back.

I focused on the task of getting Deacon's wound re-bandaged.

The clean exit wound above his shoulder blade gave me some hope he hadn't suffered catastrophic internal damage from the bullet bouncing around inside him.

"At least the sharks didn't get us," Deacon said. "But you think I'm going to make it?"

"Just stay awake. I think if you were going to die, there's a good chance you would have done it by now." I handed him a bottle of water with the cap off and he choked some down.

"That bitch sure knows how to get even, huh?"

"Sounds like you had some fidelity problems. How many times did you cheat on her?"

"I'm supposed to keep a count?"

"Maybe you should be grateful she didn't shoot you more than once. Seems like she lumped all of your offenses into one bullet."

"She always been into shootin' dudes who piss her off. Guess I shouldn't be surprised. Can't believe she pulled that two-timin' shit on me, though."

"Blame Frank. He's the bastard who no-doubt talked her into it."

Deacon leaned his head back against the cushion. "Nah, I don't blame Frank. Do eighteen years and you always gonna come out blinded by some cooch. Hell, I hit the first thing I saw when I got out too. 'Sides, I was planning to play him dirty anyway."

"No offense, but that may have been obvious." I finished getting the bandage on Deacon's back securely, then settled him and began a rewrap of the front wound. "If it makes you feel any better, Frank and Lyla won't get far in that plane without being spotted. The cops are already looking for him. I'll tell them what he did, and they won't have much trouble running him down. He and Lyla are going to have a short honeymoon."

"You be underestimating Frank again. My money's on those

OG skills getting him away. But Lyla gonna be on her ass any way it play out. She just don't know it yet."

"Why's that?"

"Cause she don't realize I was the only one doing this for Frank's own good," Deacon explained. "Frank's fixing to waste all his opportunities. I was tryna save Frank from Frank."

"How so?"

"He didn't tell you? He ain't even planning to keep those jewels. He's cashing them in just to give 'em to the Mexicans."

"What Mexicans?"

"I told him he's a dumbass. I was him, I'd say to hell with them narco bastards and go spend that cheddar on himself. The man already did eighteen years in the cooler on account of them. Wasn't no Club Fed time neither. Hasn't he earned his retirement?"

I tried to piece together what he was saying. "Frank told me he was going to jet out and go live on a beach in Mexico somewhere."

"Maybe so. But he ain't taking the money with him. Old boy set up a drop here in the Keys. Giving all that shit away."

"For what? Are they trying to get him to pay off the drugs he lost in the crash?"

Deacon canted his head and stared at me. His eyelids were drooping. "You mean to tell me. . . he ain't told you none of this?"

"Why would he tell me?"

"'Cause you're . . . the one he been doin' it for."

"What are you talking about?" I asked.

But Deacon's eyes closed. I nudged him, but he'd lapsed into unconsciousness.

Shit.

I checked his throat for a pulse and found it, but it was weak.

"You call the EMTs to meet us at the dock?" I shouted to Jerome.

"Against my better judgement!"

An ambulance was waiting when we arrived. Along with two sheriff's department deputies in SUVs. I helped lift Deacon ashore and onto a gurney. He groaned during the process but never woke. The EMTs got to work on him straight away and told me they'd be transporting him to the Lower Keys Medical Center on Stock Island. They wasted no time in getting him transported.

The presence of the two sheriff's department deputies wasn't merely an act of service. And Jerome, despite his obvious discomfort, struck a far more presentable pose than I did since he was fully clothed and wearing topsiders. I was barefoot and standing on the dock in my damp boxer shorts—and those had Deacon's blood on them. It was no surprise that I was asked to take a ride to the Monroe County Sheriff's Office in Stock Island. Jerome vehemently objected that he was only the transportation, hadn't seen anything, and couldn't leave a customer's Contender unattended on a random dock. After I backed up his story, the two officers questioned him out of earshot for a few minutes, while I swatted at the mosquitos determined to capitalize on my bare skin. Five minutes later, Jerome was allowed to return to the boat, no doubt with instructions to not go far. I got the impression he was a known entity for the two deputies and they could find him later if they needed him.

I was escorted to the rear of one of the SUVs and invited inside. They did it without cuffing or Mirandizing me, so I was grateful for that. I also appreciated the respite from the mosquitos. But other than the change of scenery, my current prospects were poor.

I had no diamonds, no airplane, and currently no way home.

The fact that I'd lost Frank again registered more in the pros column.

The deputy that drove me was a young guy, late twenties, professional about his work. If he felt I was the shooter in the incident, it didn't show. He didn't question me in the car. He left me in peace and cranked up the A/C.

The back of the cruiser smelled like 2 a.m. drunks, but for fifteen minutes I was able to simply stare out the window at the passing Keys. Deacon's words about Frank rattled around in my head.

"You're the one he doin' it for."

In what world did that make any kind of sense?

The sheriff's department compound was a no-nonsense facility with a big block detention center and several mobile trailers. I was escorted into one of the double wide trailers under the watchful gaze of several deputies outside. Once indoors, they led me to a small office that might have served mixed use as a conference room. I was told to wait and someone would be in to get my statement.

Ten minutes later, Gail Wagner was the one to open the door. She leaned against the doorpost and gave me a once over.

"Let me guess. Frank?"

I didn't have to answer.

"Sit tight. I'll find you some clothes. Then we'll sort this mess out."

She shut the door again.

Fool me twice. Shame on me. Fool me three times? Everyone could spot the dumbass.

THIRTY-SIX
WASHED UP

I SAT in a cheap plastic chair facing a cheap plastic table, wearing a faded black T-shirt that read "Bike Week Poker Run 1998." The shirt had a pair of wings fanned out from a pair of Harley Davidson motorcycle cylinders. The pants I'd been given were loose in the waist by at least a size but I was clothed. They'd even found me a pair of brand new plastic flip-flops left over from a sheriff's department community engagement event. Evidently, besides being an ugly color, the flip-flops were also uncomfortable so no one had wanted them. I could verify the complaint.

The overworked A/C wall unit struggled to keep up with the humidity assaulting the outside of the trailer and its drone sounded like a duck gargling Pop Rocks.

Gail had an iPad in front of her and had taken a few notes. But after the first few minutes of my statement, she'd dismissed the deputy who had been lingering nearby and studied me quietly.

Finally she slid her tablet aside and gave me a sympathetic pat on the hand.

"Frank being out of prison has really done a number on you this week, hasn't it?"

"If you want to take him back to Union just to give me a break, you won't get any objections from me," I replied.

"You didn't call me."

"Things got busy."

I told her the basic facts of the shooting. That we'd gone looking for Earl's old plane in the Mallard and that Lyla had been the one to shoot Deacon. I hadn't mentioned the diamonds, but Gail also hadn't asked.

It didn't mean she didn't already know.

"I don't want you to have to go through more than you have already," Gail explained. "But if there is a case to be made that Frank is involved in illicit activity in Monroe County, I'd like to know where you stand and how you can help."

"Are you asking if I'll rat on my father for him stealing my plane? I'd love to but I'd have a hard time with that since he's technically still the owner. The feds might be able to bust him for operating a plane without a license. That's probably the most obvious crime. Is that something to start with?"

"Unfortunately, after a cursory look into that, we'd actually have a difficult time making that case too. I had one of my staff dig into Frank's flying history, and according to the current FAA registry, Frank's pilot license hasn't been officially revoked. Whatever case they had against him at the time, he must have had a stupendous lawyer, because the revocation case was dropped and he only received a suspension—which has since been lifted. That was years ago. Only things standing in the way of him flying now would be a currency requirement and a medical check. Hardly something we can nail him to the wall with. But if you and your boy Deacon want to tie him into the shooting, maybe we get something worth sending him back to Raiford."

"How is Deacon?"

"I'm keeping tabs on the situation. Last word was that they considered him stable. I'll go by there after this and check on him."

"You plan on arresting me for something?" I asked. "Otherwise, I think I'd like to get out of here."

"Do you intend to go after Frank on your own? If so, how do you mean to do it?"

"He won't have gone far yet. He's still arranging his meet-up."

"With who? Tony Brewer?" Her eyes narrowed as she studied me.

The visual of The Mooch sitting up in his bed with a bullet hole in his forehead appeared in my mind. But placing myself at that scene didn't seem the wisest move.

"Frank isn't done in the Keys just yet," I said. "But I don't know how much longer he needs. My guess is he'll be in the wind by nightfall. If you and your deputies plan to find him, I recommend you get on it."

"Been a busy day around here already. Some parent assaulted a teacher over in Marathon. A bicyclist got clipped in a hit and run. Four fishermen claim they weren't drunk when they rammed their boat into a bait shop on Cudjoe Key. Add in the cases of norovirus that have been ripping through the department this week, and we find ourselves somewhat short on personnel to be running down ex-drug runners in stolen-but-technically-not-stolen airplanes. But don't worry. I'll stick with you."

It was obvious the Key West police had yet to discover The Mooch or his dead crew in the city marina, otherwise I had a feeling there would be county deputies aplenty on Frank's case.

"If you aren't allocating any resources to find Frank, that's more reason to let me get after him," I said.

"How about you ride over to the medical center with me, and

we'll see what other useful information we can get out of Mr. Deacon Johnson," Gail said. "Maybe he knows where Frank is headed."

"I doubt he likes me much better than you."

She shrugged. "Let's go see."

Her eagerness to visit Deacon made me think she might have more on her mind than she was letting on, though I didn't know what other use the ex-con could be to her. But it beat sitting in the trailer waiting for the overworked wall unit to shake itself to pieces. Plus, I had no other ride.

The medical facility staff took issue with my lack of ID when we showed up. Without Gail I never would have made it past security. But her credentials proved sufficient to the task. We were signed into the visitor log and directed down a long hallway toward the post-op recovery rooms. Like most hospitals, the place was over-air conditioned and gooseflesh prickled on my arms as I trod past room after room of weary patients. My borrowed flip-flops squeaked on the linoleum while I walked, but if it bothered Gail, she didn't show it. Deacon's recovery room was dim when we found it, a nurse finishing some charting in the better light near the doorway.

Gail smiled at the woman. "How's our patient?"

The nurse glanced at our visitor ID stickers, then at Gail's badge.

"Just got him moved in. He was lucky," she said. "Bullet only grazed the clavicle. Some muscle and small vein damage but no major fractures or lung involvement. They cleaned the wound and controlled the bleeding and closed him up. I just checked his vitals and he is stable. He's awake but take it easy, he's still coming around from the anesthesia."

"Roger dodger," Gail said. "Just saying hi."

The nurse kept an eye on us while we entered.

Deacon was at the far side of the room, propped up at a forty-five degree angle, an IV in his arm and heart monitor taped under his gown. He also had a tube I recognized as a drain coming from the area of his shoulder. His coloring was still off but his eyes widened as we walked in.

"What the fuck?" he muttered as we approached. "The hell do you two want? Ain't I been hassled enough for one day?"

"Just checking in on you, Mr. Johnson. Making sure you're still with us."

"Like you give a rat's ass."

"Is everything okay?" The nurse was back. "You need me to clear the room?"

Deacon looked us over but finally laid his head back. "Nah, they can stay."

The nurse gave Gail and me both what I took to be a warning look and walked out again.

"Sorry to hear your relationship went south," Gail said. "That Lyla was a pretty lady."

"Pretty like a snake."

"Sounds like you'll recover, though. Maybe you'll even reconcile. I've seen crazier things. Though I hear she has a new boyfriend now."

Deacon scowled at that.

"Where do you think Frank and Lyla will be headed next, Mr. Johnson?" she pressed.

Deacon ignored her question, looked at me and frowned. "The hell you doing bringing her here, man?"

"Technically, she brought me," I said.

"You her badge bunny now? Thought you'd be smarter than to hang with this county clown."

"Calm down, Mr. Johnson. We're just being friendly."

"Get friendly with this, law dog." Deacon used his good hand to grab his crotch and gave it a squeeze.

Gail sighed. Deacon might have been medicated, but it hadn't helped his manners any.

"Why don't you give me a few minutes alone with him," I said.

Gail looked Deacon over one more time and nodded. "Sure. He's all yours. See if you can get him to say something useful, huh?"

I waited while she walked back to the hall. The nurse was gone too. When we were finally alone I turned back to Deacon. "Get all your anger out?"

"Fuck that mall cop."

"And me too while we're at it, huh?"

His expression softened some. "Nah. I ain't mean that. You been cool, not lettin' me die out there with the sharks and the barracudas or whatever. But you ought to know better than to ride around with that tin star. Bad for your rep."

"Afraid my rep is taking a hit anyway. I used to be a cool guy with a plane business. Gonna be hard to run it without a plane."

Deacon leaned his head back against the pillow again. "You still complaining about that? No offense, but for a smart guy, you dumb as shit. If you were as clever as your daddy, you'd have it figured out by now."

"As smart as Frank. The con-man who left us to die."

"That old cat's the sharpest dude I ever met."

"You must not have met many winners."

"Played you didn't he? And he ain't done yet. Just watch."

THIRTY-SEVEN
GARDE

I'D OPENED the blinds at Deacon's request so he could look out the window at the cumulus clouds clipping along in the easterly breeze. After his eyes adjusted to the light, he turned his attention back to me and brushed one hand over his forehead. His eyelids drooped, maybe from the painkillers.

"On the boat coming back, just before you passed out, you said Frank was doing all this for me. What did you mean by that?" I asked.

He shifted in the bed and winced. It was evident he was uncomfortable, but he replied anyway.

"First time I ever met Frank, I'd come up from county after my trial. I got assigned as his cellmate day one. Frank knew I was coming. He'd never met me, but the day I walked into the cell he had a couple things for me on the bunk. Stuff from commissary, peanut butter, a few of those mackerel packets that get passed around. Said protein was hard to come by at Union, and he figured a big guy like me might want some extra to hold me over on days they underfed us. I'd been up a couple times on shorter stretches before and nobody ever done nothing like that for me.

"Come to find out, it wasn't just me. Frank was always doing shit like that for people. Guy need a stamp for a letter, extra pair of socks, batteries, whatever. Frank had your back. But he didn't just dole out stuff at random. He was always the guy with just the right thing for the right guy at the right time, you know what I'm saying? Commissary always running out of shit back then. Shipping problems. Frank seemed to know who was gonna run dry on what even before they did. He'd parley stuff around like he was his own micro-economy. People paid him too, and he made his percentage, but it was how he knew that was the magic. I asked him why he always seemed to be Johnny-on-the-spot like that and he shrugged it off. Said he just 'paid attention to people.'"

Deacon tried to rotate his left shoulder and winced again. "Never could tell how he did it. But I figured he was always running a tally up here." He tapped his forehead with his good hand. "He was reading people, finding out what made them tick, storing it away for later. Everybody in there playing checkers while Frank's playing chess, you know what I'm saying? Wasn't always commissary shit neither. Sometimes a guy need a referral to a good lawyer or a way to get out of trouble with a gang, they always come to Frank. Not that he could help everybody. He was too smart to miss getting his benefit, and man, he'd tell people straight up when they crossed a line. Sometimes being useful is a curse. All the hopeless slackasses want you to do their dirty work for 'em. Remember how I told you I watched Frank's back, kept him safe in there?"

I nodded.

"That only sorta true. Coupla new punks needed straightening out now and then but nobody with any sense ever messed with Frank. That'd be like shooting your own self in the ass. Too many people liked Frank. Too many people owed him."

"He controlled people that way?"

"Controlled? Nah. Wasn't like that. His shit ran on respect. Told you, in prison you get a rep. And his rep was gold bullion, baby. Lots a fellas woulda loved to be respected like Frank. He inspired the masses. He just kinda did it one dude at a time."

I ruminated on that.

"You had a rep too."

"Me?"

"Everybody knew Frank had two boys. He told me he had one son wanted to be just like him and one who wanted nothing to do with him. I liked Frank so I figured any guy who couldn't see what a legit dude he was wasn't no kinda son I woulda wanted. But he said funny enough he was proudest of the one wanted nothing to do with him." Deacon met my eye. "Talkin' about you, by the way."

"I gathered that."

I wasn't sure where Deacon's musings on the past were headed but I waited anyway. After a minute he continued.

"People that owed Frank favors used to ask what they could do for him in return. But he always kept his shit tight and never let on much what he was up to. When he did call in a favor, it was for extra phone time or maybe books. My boy loved to read. But you could tell he was always workin' and making plans in his head, steps ahead of everybody else. One long chess game. Everybody knew when he finally got out, he'd be doing something big. But I'm the only one knew about his treasure."

"Frank said you pried it out of him after dental surgery."

"That laughing gas had him loopy, boy. Got all funny and chatty. Told me that when he got out he was gonna make things right with his boy. The one that hated him. Said he had this treasure stashed away worth millions and it was gonna be his ticket back. He wouldn't tell me where it was. Even loopy. Said he wasn't sure. But when he got it, he said he was gonna make his biggest play yet. I asked what he was talkin' about and he said there was only one thing in the world he figured might level the scales. Said he was gonna get his hands on the most important thing he ever owned. The right thing. Then he was gonna give it to you. Said it was the only thing that might come close to patching the hole he left when he went away."

I sat back in my chair, my mind working. "I never wanted a thing of his, especially not his dirty drug money. Even if it was in the form of diamonds."

"No shit. Why else do you think he's trading those diamonds for the thing you do want. That damned plane."

Tropic Angel.

Frank had been working to give it to me all along?

"Frank crash-landed the Mallard in Mexico before he even went to prison," I said.

Deacon nodded. "Feds closing in on him. Needed a place to stash it where he could get it later."

"You're saying he did that on purpose to preserve it?"

"Of course he did. But keeping an old drug plane safe and secret in Mexico come with a hefty price tag."

"My brother, Landon, is the one who got the plane out of the Yucatan."

"And who you think told him where to find it?"

"So Frank made a deal with the cartel down there long before that," I said, piecing it together. "Made them promises."

"Must have been one hell of a plane because cartel promises come with interest. Almost twenty years of interest. Shit ain't cheap."

I looked out the window. "So now Frank's got what he wants. He has the diamonds. He can pay off the cartel, and keep the plane. He's free."

"He ain't keeping the plane. Told you, he's giving it to you."

"You see me in a plane right now? He's obviously changed his mind and run off with Lyla instead. What did you call it? Blinded by cooch?"

"I'm telling you. For a smart pilot dude, you're one of the dumbest suckers I know. Told you already that Frank ain't done."

I crossed my arms and tried not to bristle at the insult. But he had a point. I hadn't thought much about what Frank pulling the strings on the *Tropic Angel* deal with Landon would have cost him. But it was obvious in hindsight. Landon was a piece in Frank's chess game. So was I. Only he was keeping me out of play.

"If he was planning to give the cartel the diamonds the whole time anyway, why did he need The Mooch?" I asked.

"A fence is a fence. Maybe the local cartel thugs only accept cash."

"The Mooch is dead," I said. "Frank won't be able to fence his diamonds in the Keys unless he goes direct to his seller now."

"When this happen?" Deacon said, blinking fast to stay awake. The meds were working on him.

"Last night. I thought it might have been you and Lyla, making your move for his cash."

"Damn, man. If he dead, it wasn't us. Lyla's actin' a trigger-happy two-faced ho but she ain't no killer. That shit was all for show. She actually a pretty good girl if you get to know her."

"She shot you, didn't she?"

"But *I* deserved it. She just leveling the scales like she do."

"She's in this deep now, either way," I said.

"You better get out there and watch her ass for me then. Keep her safe. Somebody snuffing The Mooch means it was the other player makin' moves. The one Frank's up against."

I recalled what my father had told The Mooch.

"Frank said he wanted a big bag of money and a name. You think whoever he's after got wind of it?" The request was personal. But it could also have been part of the game. "Or he could have included The Mooch in the deal because he knew he was connected," I added. "It wasn't ever about the deal. He was trying to draw someone out and knew including The Mooch would get their attention."

"I ain't much for chess," Deacon said. "But I do know when you get near the end, it's only the pieces that really matter still left on the board." His eyes drooped again as he said it. "Frank always said this shit gonna end where it started, and with the same players. That's how come I know he ain't done."

A knock came on the door and Gail Warner stuck her head back into the room. "The nurse out here is about to come in again for rounds. You get what you needed?"

I stood and pushed back my chair. "Yeah. Maybe."

"Hey, Angel," Deacon said, though his eyes stayed closed. "When you find Frank, tell him I ain't mad. He's still the best cellie I ever had."

I FOLLOWED Gail out of the medical center without much in the way of conversation, but when we reached her truck in the parking lot, she rested an arm on the hood and addressed me.

"Well? What did you get from our contrary convict friend? Tell me he knew something worth sharing."

I squinted in the sunlight and wished I still had my shades. "He gave me a lot to think about."

"How about what his ex-girl and your flown-away father are planning?"

"Don't think he was included in all of their schemes." I crossed my arms and looked skyward. A small plane departing Key West International buzzed northeast, skirting the Naval Station airspace.

"Looks like a Mooney," I said.

Gail gave the plane only a fleeting glance. "Who gives a shit?"

But I watched the plane a few moments longer. It reminded me of what Frank had said at the restaurant. "Frank's going to make his deal happen at an airfield," I said. "Somewhere low-key, but easy to depart from."

Gail mused on that. "Key West would be too well monitored. Next closest would be—"

"Sugar Loaf Shores," I said. The same airport where Frank's plane had been sabotaged when he went down. 'Shit gonna end where it started,' Deacon had said.

"Come on, it's hot out here." Gail climbed into the truck, then reached across the cab to pop the passenger side door loose. "You coming?"

I walked around to the passenger side of the truck and climbed in. Gail fired off a text to someone, then she shifted into drive and worked her way out of the parking lot. I studied her weathered face. A lot of years of sunshine had done its work on her skin, leaving it browned and taut—a tax the Florida Keys extracts from all long-term residents. She had even longer history here than Frank.

"You said you were a young deputy when Frank went away. Must have been eager to make a name for yourself back then."

"Same as most," she replied. "Not that it was easy to gain headway in a boy's club like the sheriff's department."

"You said your chief that recently retired was your mentor. Did he work the case they made against Frank?"

"Mercer? Made his career on it. Would have got there sooner if Frank hadn't dodged longer than most."

"Mercer must have appreciated your help on it."

"Green deputies aren't regarded as much help to senior officers. Not that they should be. You should see some of the fresh recruits we get from the academy these days. Think they can solve every case by browsing the Internet. You tell them to go knock on doors and they look at you like you asked them to churn butter. And don't get me started on their conflict resolution skills."

"Frank said half the cops in the Keys were in on the smuggling deals back in his time."

"And you've said your old man was known for his tall tales."

"Kept your nose clean then?"

She made a left turn then straightened out the wheel. "You come to the Keys, you find all kinds of different attitudes on drugs. Most long-term residents just want to be left alone. If your neighbor wanted to puff some reefer or do a few lines of coke, nobody much cared. I never touched the stuff myself."

"Frank said he never did either."

"That's probably true. He and Earl were always high on airplanes."

She mused out the window for a bit. "When I got down here I didn't know anyone," she continued. "But Earl would always be buzzing around on account of Frank. He followed your dad like he was God's gift. Those two were in and out of airports all up and down the Keys." She pointed to a crab shack we passed. "Earl and I used to meet right there sometimes. He'd visit and make sure I was getting on all right."

"I had the impression from Margery that you and Earl didn't talk much."

"Later years we didn't." Her jaw set and she glared at the road.

"Must have been tough. I have a memory from when I was young. You and Earl having it out on the phone over something. Don't think I'd ever seen Earl that mad before. He never told me what it was about though."

"You were a kid. You were Frank's kid. My brother was always going to keep you away from trouble."

I dwelled on that for a bit, imagining a younger Gail, new to the Keys, working to make a name for herself, her brother the one person she was close to. Then to lose that connection. A hard loss. One that had to come from a significant trauma.

She'd pulled the truck onto Highway 1 and headed north. We passed the Naval Air Station and kept going. She had a lead foot, passing cars wherever she could, but doing it with a relaxed ease, used to other vehicles yielding the road to her. We made it as far as Lower Sugarloaf Key before she slowed down.

Sugar Loaf Shores airfield wasn't much to look at. A small sandy ramp for parking, at max, a dozen small planes, and a shack of a building with some potted palms in front that was the office of the local skydiving club. Tourists wanting an adventurous view of the Keys could pile into a doorless Cessna and fall out at thirteen thousand feet for a thrilling free fall followed by the relief of a canopy opening so they could drift back down in the humid sea breeze.

Today only a trio of planes sat on tie-down and not a soul was in sight at the skydiving building. I rolled my window down, getting a clearer look at the airplanes.

But Gail didn't stop at the shack or the parking lot. She turned right on the dusty asphalt ramp and toward a collection of boats and RVs stashed in the back corner of the property. One ratty old Winnebago in particular caught my eye, because standing atop it was a skinny man with a pair of binoculars. He was studying something in the distance to the east. His thin lanky frame and slightly lopsided stance was distinctive and when he turned around to peer at us driving up, my suspicions were confirmed. It was EJ Warner.

He waved to the truck, let his binoculars dangle on their lanyard at his chest, then proceeded to climb down the ladder at the back of the Winnebago. The action of him leaning over to step down the ladder is what revealed the presence of a pistol on his hip.

When he reached the bottom of the ladder he spun to face us again and limped over to my side of the truck. He paused parallel to where I sat and seemed unsure of how to address me. "Hey there. Luke," he finally managed.

"EJ."

He then approached the back passenger door and yanked it open. He climbed in, slamming the door behind him. Gail had said nothing for the last ten minutes, but she now turned in her seat. "He's there?"

"Yep," EJ confirmed. "Just floating out in the water. You called it. You talk to him yet?"

"Not yet," Gail said. Then she turned to me, handing me her phone. "Call your dad. He's evidently out in that lagoon, and it seems we have some business to work out."

I stared at the phone, then at her, and finally turned to look at EJ in the back. "There's only one reason I can think of why you're here, EJ. Is it the one I'm thinking of?"

He reached behind him then and removed the pistol from the waistband of his pants. "Way I hear it, ain't one reason. It's millions."

I took the phone from Gail.

There's nothing like a treasure hunt to bring a family together.

THIRTY-NINE
NOW BOARDING

"HE OBVIOUSLY KNEW you'd find him," Gail said. "So call him."

She had driven to the back of the property where a makeshift boat ramp met the shoreline. A flats boat was tied up to the mangroves there and beyond it stretched an open section of blue-green channel. In the distance was Upper Sugarloaf Key and about mid-distance was an unmistakable silhouette. *Tropic Angel* was anchored around a half mile out. The tide was high, otherwise I might have wondered how he even got the plane there, but as it was, it bobbed lazily in the sunlight.

"What exactly is your play here?" I asked.

The pistol in EJ's lap wasn't pointed at me, but I had to wonder when it might be. Gail was of course armed, and my inclusion in this party now bordered on involuntary. Her tongue brushed over her dry lips and she squinted toward the old seaplane. "Frank has some decisions to make," she said. "It's my hope that he's going to make the easy one."

There were no other cop cars. She hadn't called this in. Gail was flying solo other than the cooperation of EJ. Made me wonder what else she kept private from her law-and-order brethren.

It was certainly going to stay private if she shot Frank.

"How'd she talk you into this?" I asked EJ.

"What's not to get?" he asked. "Frank coming into a windfall shoulda been a happy occasion for the whole family, don't you think? Dad sure treated you like family. Told me to think of you like a brother back when you stayed with us. Big brother Luke. But it looks like you two were more than happy to cut us out. Hell, even Dad cut me out at the end, didn't he? 'Shut the door, EJ.' Gonna say my last words on this earth to Luke fuckin' Angel, not to you."

I thought about Earl's final conversation with me. His death was a raw wound that I hadn't even had time to process. But it sounded like EJ was well into the raw now. Anger was a big part of grief and this was his first time losing a parent. I remembered that anger.

"I'm sorry his last words weren't to you, EJ. Or your sister, or Margery. I can see why that might sting. But what Frank has out there? It's just a big bag of trouble. Your dad knew that as much as anyone. And if he wanted you kept out of it, then I imagine he was trying to keep that trouble off your head."

"I hear he even sank his damned Decathlon for Frank," EJ said. "Lied to me. Said he sold it. Didn't think I might like an airplane? Hell, I don't fly but I coulda sold that shit for good money, got something nice for the boys. But no. He took the one damned thing on that farm still worth a damn and plunked it out here in the ocean just to hide Frank's stash for him. You think that's right?"

I brushed my fingertips over my brow and sighed. "It's not right, EJ. But it was Earl's choice. The man made his own decisions. He made promises to Frank out of friendship and he was always good to his word."

"Good to his word for a guy who ain't never gave it back."

"You want to complain about Frank, you're not going to get any argument from me. He's made shitty decisions and hurt people. You've got every right to be mad. I've been furious with him for decades."

"Then what are we all waiting for? Call his ass up and get him to come ashore."

Gail was studying me. Waiting.

I typed my own phone number into the phone and hit the call button.

"Hello?"

"It's me," I said. "On Gail's phone. Looks like you found a quiet spot for the Mallard."

"Are you in that truck over there? Tell dear Gail I said hello. Bet she wants to meet up. How many of her county friends did she bring along?"

"None. But EJ is here. He's none-too-pleased with you either."

"EJ? What the hell has he got to gripe about?"

"Not sure which is worse, Frank. That you're an asshole or that you can never tell why."

"I've made my share of mistakes, son. That's never been in question. But we're nearing the end of this situation now. You ready to hear the plan?"

"Tell him to come ashore," Gail said.

"Gail wants you to come in," I relayed.

"I'll bet she does. But that's not how this is going to go. Tell her if she wants to talk, she comes out here. All three of you. I see a boat right there you can use. A sheriff's deputy shouldn't have much trouble commandeering it. Motor on out. We'll talk."

He hung up.

"You hear that?" I asked Gail.

She nodded.

"What the hell is he doing?" EJ said. "He say why he's just sitting out there?"

"Gail didn't tell you?" I asked. "Frank's settling old scores."

"With who? The fish?"

"Let's go," Gail said.

She evidently hadn't shared the entirety of the situation with her nephew.

We climbed out of the truck. EJ was obligated to tuck his pistol away again to help untie the flats boat.

"You get to drive," Gail said, gesturing to the console.

"Lucky me," I said. She climbed in with me. A brief search revealed that the owner had left keys stashed in the live well. Saved us from having to hot wire it. I got the motor started. Then EJ pushed us free of shore and splashed his way aboard. I turned us into the current and kept the boat at idle speed for the first fifty yards, then trimmed the motor down and sped up once we had some depth. The flats boat skipped over the smooth turquoise water, scattering droplets of spray. By the time we neared *Tropic Angel*, the water's depth gave it a darker hue, but we were still relatively sheltered amid the various Keys.

The boarding door on the Mallard was open and the ladder was out. I dropped back to low idle and maneuvered up slowly.

"Show yourself, Frank!" Gail called across the water.

"Come aboard," he shouted back from somewhere in the interior. "Guns holstered, if you don't mind." I looked back and found EJ had his pistol out and wasn't doing a great job of pointing it in safe directions.

"You mind not flagging me with that barrel?" I said. "I'm on your side, remember?"

EJ looked to Gail, and she gave him a nod, so he slid the pistol back into his waistband. "Sorry," he muttered.

It was a relief to have the pistol away, though Gail kept a

hand lingering on her gun belt while I put the boat alongside *Tropic Angel*.

"Does Frank have a weapon?" she asked me quietly.

"He does," I said. Though what good it would do him was questionable.

"EJ will go up first," Gail said. "Stay with me."

"We sure about this?" EJ asked.

"You're the one all fired up to talk to him," I replied.

He touched the pistol at his waist again, making sure it was secure, then climbed the ladder. When he was aboard without incident, Gail gave me a nod. "All right. You're next."

She scanned the area for boat traffic.

Weekday activity here was light. Our only observers would be distant cars on the A1A. Whatever was about to go down, we had the water to ourselves. I took a firm grip on the ladder for *Tropic Angel*, said a silent prayer to whoever might be listening, and climbed aboard.

FORTY
GUNS BLAZING

A GRUMMAN MALLARD is a good sized plane. Some commercial turbine versions stuff as many as seventeen people aboard, but I don't know how. *Tropic Angel* was from the old school of plane interiors, when flying meant a luxury experience complete with cocktail glasses and cushy sofas. The maintenance manual referred to the sofas as divans. There was one installed in the port side of the forward cabin. Another in the aft cabin and several recliners of a more standard variety to make up the remainder of the seating options. Two of the optional seats in the rear cabin of *Tropic Angel* had been removed entirely at some point in its life. Probably to make room for kilos of cocaine. Though Frank had tried to preserve the character of the old bird even in that hard-working era of his ownership.

Right now the missing seats provided space for me and EJ to stand in the rear cabin stooped like hunchbacks.

The main spars of the wing passed through the top of the cabin amidships which naturally lent a division to the space. The passage was narrow, however, and meant no one was getting toward the bow in a hurry. It also forced passengers to travel forward in a straight line. EJ appeared unenthusiastic about moving at all. Probably because Frank sat on the divan nearest us with the Sig Sauer pistol I'd bought him resting casually on the knee of his crossed leg.

"Go right on through, EJ," Frank said, gesturing with the gun. "Plenty of seats up front."

EJ continued forward.

Gail climbed aboard behind me, her expression a mask I couldn't decipher. "Hello, Frank."

"Come on in," Frank said. He looked to me. "Good to see you too, son."

"Some situation you've got us into," I muttered.

"I always said *Tropic Angel* was built for adventure."

"Oversized for a casket, though." I moved forward and slid into one of the seats on the starboard side. I used just the edge of the cushion so I could keep my eyes on Gail and EJ. EJ took the divan on the port side.

"Where's your new girlfriend, Frank?" Gail walked all the way forward, peeking through the keyhole entryway to the empty flight deck seats.

"We'll get to Lyla in a minute."

"She's ashore, isn't she?" Gail said. "That's irritating."

"Why? Wanted us both in one place?" Frank asked. "Didn't think I was going to make things that easy for you, did you? Take a seat." He'd stood, but lingered near the midship's bulkhead, the pistol hanging at his thigh, finger on the trigger guard.

"Where are the diamonds?" Gail settled onto the divan and adjusted her gun belt. "We know you found them."

"They're in a turn coordinator Luke and I pulled out of Earl's Super Decathlon. Isn't that fun? Your brother hid them so well even you couldn't find them. Though I bet you tried plenty of times over the years, huh?"

The space was muggy. Frank had the flight deck side windows rolled down, but minimal air flowed through the cabin while sitting still. My shirt was already sticking to me. Maybe Frank meant to cook us all to death.

Gail sized my father up from where she sat and despite the heat, her expression was ice. "You should have flown away when you had the chance," she said.

"Where would I go? You think I was just going to let it all slide, what you did?" He smiled at her, but it was a sad smile that never reached his eyes. "The Mooch call you last night? After Luke and I stopped by? He told you what I was up to down here in the Keys?"

"Actually, Luke here was the one who filled me in on your plans. Enough that I knew what you had in mind. But Tony wasn't ever going to make your deal."

"You made sure of that, huh?"

"What's he talking about?" EJ said from beside her. "Who's Tony?"

"Nobody," Gail declared.

I found it interesting that she hadn't filled EJ in on the shooting aboard *Sea Notes*. And if he didn't know, it meant he wasn't involved in the killings. Made me wonder what else he didn't know.

What *I* didn't know was what Gail might do once it came out that she was the one who'd shot three people in cold blood aboard that boat.

Then it dawned on me. She'd simply blame it on Frank. Ex-con recently released and settling old grudges? You couldn't ask for a better fall guy.

She had a hardness in her eyes and her right hand lingered close to her gun. Would she draw down on Frank, hoping she could get a shot off first? It was tight quarters for a gunfight, but she'd had no trouble gunning down The Mooch's bodyguard. I had a feeling she wouldn't balk at this. This whole situation was teetering on a knife's edge and I couldn't tell which way it would fall.

"You should give her the turn coordinator, Frank," I said. "Salvage this so no one else gets hurt."

"Can't," he replied. "It's not here."

"Don't tell me you gave the jewels to that bimbette?" Gail said. "Are you stupid? She's probably halfway to Miami with them by now."

"Maybe. But I told you this was never about the jewels anyway. This is about justice for Lucia."

"Wait, who?" EJ asked. He looked lost.

"EJ, you should get back to the airport," Gail said. "Make sure that idiot girlfriend of Deacon's is still there."

"You're still not ready to own up to what you did, Gail?" Frank said. "I know it was you. I've always suspected it, but I wanted to hear you admit it. EJ should hear it too."

"You don't know what you're talking about," Gail retorted.

"There were only a few people there the day Lucia and I landed and switched planes on that last job. Most of them are dead now. But none of the dead ones ever knew I had the diamonds. The Mooch knew. One other person who always knew was Earl. I have to admit, there was even a time when I wondered if it could've been him that set me up that day."

"If you suspected my brother of betraying you, why the hell would you trust him to hide the jewels?" Gail said. "That makes no sense."

"Only to you. Because you've been after those diamonds ever since he let something slip about them, so long you can't see anything more important than having them. A concept like justice for someone you loved would be beyond your capacity. You want those jewels so badly, nothing is off limits for you. Even betraying your own family."

"You aren't my family. You only ever played at it."

"But EJ is your family. You've dragged him into this now too. You going to make the poor man an accessory to murder?" He met EJ's eye. "Twenty to life in the federal pen is no joke, son. Trust me. Your daddy wouldn't want that for you."

"What's he talking about, Gail?" EJ said. "What's this about Aunt Lucia?"

"Go get in the boat, EJ," Gail said. "Take it back to the airport. Find Lyla. See if she has the diamonds."

"Your dad always knew she did it, EJ," Frank said. "Knew Gail was the one that set me up and got my wife killed. He trusted the wrong person with the secret. He wouldn't ever tell me outright because I suspect he knew what I'd do if I found out for sure. That was a line he couldn't cross even for our friendship. But you should know why they never spoke after I went away."

I groaned. He wasn't leaving Gail any way out. He was going to force her to pull on him. He'd shoot first most likely, but with a gun I'd only loaded with blanks. Now seemed a bad time to tell everyone I hadn't trusted him with live rounds. Especially since that pistol might be the only thing keeping the two of us alive at the moment.

But I'd set him up to fail.

Gail had fire in her eyes while glaring at Frank. A hate I recognized. I'd felt it myself enough times thinking about my father. Frank was just waiting, goading her into it. She'd pull, he'd try to shoot and fail to stop her and die in a blaze of gunfire hell-bent on a revenge he could never win.

A day ago, I don't know that I'd have much cared.

Today I did.

Not to mention, once Frank was dead, I'd be next.

In the narrow pressure cooker that was the front of that airplane cabin, I probably could have gone for Gail's gun. But EJ would have drawn on me then too. So when I saw Gail's hand touch the handle of her service pistol, it was Frank I went for.

I caught him by surprise and shoved him bodily through the narrow passage between the fore and aft cabin with a yell of fury erupting from my lips. I shoved him hard enough to keep him backpedaling all the way to the entryway, slamming him into the bulkhead adjacent to the seat that doubled as a lavatory.

"You never could take one second of responsibility, could you?" I shouted. "You want to know who's to blame for Mom's death? How about you look in the mirror for once." I reached down and stripped the Sig from his hands, his eyes wide and mouth hanging open. I shoved him toward the boarding door. "I'm sick and goddamn tired of listening to you blame every soul on earth but yourself." While I said it I ejected the mag from the Sig, checked the load, and rammed it back home again. I racked the slide. Then I aimed it at his chest.

He put his hands up. "Luke, now wait a minute. I'm handling this."

"You think you are, but you're wrong. There's only ever been one way out of this situation. And this is it."

His eyes narrowed. "You can't really mean that."

"*Don't let this be for nothing, Dad.*"

Then I squeezed the trigger.

Gunpowder exploded from the barrel and Frank jolted as it impacted his chest at close range. I fired twice more and he reeled backward, tumbling out the boarding door into the water with a splash. I stepped to the door and fired down into the water two more times for good measure. Then I tossed the gun, untied the line from the flats boat that had drifted aft, tossed that too, and dragged the boarding ladder back aboard. Then I slammed the boarding door shut and jammed the latch closed.

When I turned to face Gail and EJ, still standing amidships, they both had stunned expressions on their faces.

"Good thing I can fly this bird, huh? Cause we're down a pilot." I brushed past them and headed for the flight deck, not slowing down.

No one stopped me.

FORTY-ONE

TOUCHDOWN

IT WAS ONLY when I was under the dash and through the tunnel to the bow that I caught my breath.

I popped the hatch and took in several lungfuls of tangy salt air as I stood, the shifting breeze cooling my clammy skin. I reeled in the anchor, casting my view aft along the port side of *Tropic Angel*. There was no sign of Frank. The boat we'd used to get aboard was drifting away toward shore.

We'd be drifting that way ourselves soon if I didn't move quickly.

What now?

I had to think.

Climbing back through the tunnel under the copilot side instrument panel something glanced off my head. I reached up and found it was a loose cannon plug. Had I dislodged that during my crawl through? When I reached up to feel where it came from, a fleck of something dripped on me. I wiped the droplet from my face with my fingertips, then sniffed. It was seawater. From one of the instruments.

I squeezed out of the narrow space and rearranged myself

into the pilot seat, quickly beginning the engine starting checklist before the current had time to drift us into trouble.

Gail appeared in the doorway.

"That was an unexpected turn of events."

"Hang on. I need to get these engines running. Otherwise we'll drift and run aground."

She waited while I got one engine started, then the other, then used differential thrust from the right engine to steer the big seaplane on course for open water.

Gail leaned low and peered out one of the port windows as we came around. I knew what she was looking for. A body.

"I've seen some things in my time here in the Keys, but today might beat all." She still had her hand on her gun belt. "That was some cold-blooded shit. Shooting your own father?"

"Frank had what was coming to him," I said. "This was always going to end badly. And I told you I was on your side."

"I guess you proved it. Just didn't expect you to make your point so . . . vividly."

I glanced aft past Gail. EJ was in one of the starboard seats, his arms wrapped across his chest, fingers clamped on his elbows. He watched us with his brow furrowed.

"Your nephew has had a rough week," I said. "You might have overdone it."

"He'll manage. Tell me, how do you see this playing out?"

"You're after Frank's diamonds. Lyla's got the turn coordinator that Earl hid them in. If she's back on the airfield, we find her and you take them from her. It's not complicated."

"And what cut are you expecting?"

I met her eye. "I don't want the diamonds, Gail. They're all yours."

"Bullshit. You'd walk away from all of Frank's millions just like that?"

"I only ever wanted one thing, and now I have it." I patted

the yoke. "If we're together on this, there's no reason for you to tell your cop buddies any more details than they need about what went down today. I noticed you haven't included them so far. How about we keep it that way."

"Covering up a murder is a big ask."

"I just did your dirty work for you. Don't pretend you weren't going to be finding a shallow grave for Frank anyway." I located my shades in the side pocket of the seat and slipped them on. "Might want to get yourself buckled in."

I'd reached the open channel and had enough room to get *Tropic Angel* up to speed. I pushed the throttles forward, got the big bird up on plane with some pressure on the yoke, then increased the throttle some more. The twin Pratt and Whitney radial engines drowned any possibility of more conversation. Gail settled back to a passenger seat amid the roar. I exhaled, eased back on the yoke, and broke the water's grip on the hull. At a hundred feet I started a turn.

Up and away.

Airborne was the safest place for me to be right now, and I rolled my shoulders to unbunch them once we hit three hundred feet. The likelihood that Gail might put a bullet in the back of my head was low while I was in control of the airplane and she needed me to land it. But I was already within the bounds of the traffic pattern for the runway at Sugar Loaf Shores. It was nearly time to descend again.

I climbed just enough to give myself some assurance of making the field in an emergency and then actuated the landing gear. The hydraulics moved the main wheels out from the sides of the hull and the nose wheel extended from the bow. I only cast one glance back at the cove we'd departed from as we came around. The flats boat was still adrift.

"Know when to stay down, Frank," I muttered.

When I was abeam the touchdown point for the runway I

reduced throttle and deployed the flaps. I was low, but this was an uncontrolled field. I made a radio call, but there was no one around to complain about a big seaplane buzzing the A1A.

Back on the ground again was where things were going to get dicey. I felt around in the seat pocket of my chair and discovered my phone was still in there along with the flight logbook for the plane. My phone was still on, though low on battery. I had about a zillion notifications. Most from texts or voicemails from Cassidy but several from Reese too. The initial where-the-hell-are-yous had escalated to worry. And the final message from Cassidy said they were flying down. Cassidy and I still shared locations as emergency contacts so I tapped the photo by her name and waited while her location popped up. It said unavailable. Either she'd turned it off, or maybe she was airborne too, somewhere the service was poor. Like over the Gulf of Mexico on the way down here.

Shit. I'd gotten Frank out of danger. But who else was I dragging in?

I needed to end this quickly.

But as I lined up on final for the runway, my sense of impending danger only worsened. At the end of the airfield, near where Gail had parked her Sheriff's department truck, there was another vehicle I recognized. The black SUV that had been following Frank and me around Key West. Who the hell were those guys? Two men climbed out of the vehicle and watched as we descended. I blasted overhead, and flared for the runway, the tires of the Mallard kissing the asphalt on touchdown with a chirp.

It was a long roll out and a hard turn. Sugar Loaf Shores was designed primarily for single-engine Cessnas and Pipers and didn't have the requisite taxiways for big aircraft like mine. I was forced to use both shoulders of the runway and lots of braking and differential thrust to get the huge seaplane turned around.

Then I back-taxied for the only buildings on the field and the two guys waiting in the parking area.

"Who are these idiots?" Gail asked. She'd reappeared in the doorway without me noticing. She peered out the windscreen at the newcomers as I pulled *Tropic Angel* onto the ramp.

"Maybe they're here to ask if you've accepted Jesus as your personal savior," I said, and started shutting down the engines.

"One time I'd welcome that." She grunted and turned to EJ. "Head on a swivel when we get out of here. I need you watching my back with that piece of yours."

"You told me no one was going to get hurt," EJ said.

"Did I?" Gail replied. "We're going to amend that. Some people are probably getting hurt."

I caught EJ's eye, but he regarded me warily, like I was part of the danger. I didn't blame him. From his point of view I'd just murdered my own father. Whatever he'd signed up for, he was in well over his head now.

As I headed for the boarding door, I considered that I probably was too.

I was about to find out.

FORTY-TWO
STANDOFF

I CLIMBED down the ladder from *Tropic Angel* first, feeling the stares of the two dudes from the SUV. The bald white guy with the neck tattoos easily weighed two-sixty. His companion was trimmer, a well-dressed Latin man who would have looked at home on the Miami strip. He was overdressed for the heat, sweat showing on his silk shirt, but he didn't seem to mind.

The big guy had a gun in his waistband. He straightened up when Gail climbed out of the plane in her Sheriff's uniform.

EJ was the last out. He lingered warily behind Gail till she dragged him forward to stand next to her. "Show some backbone, will you," she said. We walked around to the other side of the bow to meet the two guys closer to the building.

"What's your business here, gentlemen?" I asked.

"We're waiting for Frank," the Latin guy said. "Told us to meet him here." The SUV was still running, the A/C condenser making a puddle beneath the engine.

"Frank won't be making your meeting," Gail said. "So I recommend you take off."

"Our business is with Frank," the man explained. "The kind

of business I get paid well to handle. So we'll wait for him to tell us if the meeting is off."

"Going to be waiting a long time then," Gail said. She turned to EJ. "Go find the girl. She's around here somewhere."

But he didn't have to look far. Lyla stepped out from behind the skydiving office looking well-sunned. The humidity hadn't done her hair any favors but she'd found a colorful top to cover her bikini and cradled a turn coordinator in one arm like a football. In her other hand was the little .38 special, extended at arms length. She wasn't pointing it at anyone specific at the moment, but more in the direction of Gail and EJ than at the newcomers.

"Frank, you in that plane, baby? Better come on out before I shoot all these friends of yours!"

"He missed his flight," Gail said. "Gonna miss the next one too. That the instrument you pulled from my brother's plane?"

Lyla pointed the pistol at Gail then. "Frank told me that if he didn't get off that plane, it's because you killed him. That what happened out there?"

"You need me to arrest you right here?" Gail said. "Put that thing down before someone gets hurt."

"If you were here as a real cop you woulda called in more by now and we both know it."

EJ had his hand on his gun too and seemed unsure as to whether he should use it. He was sweating enough that dark patches had appeared on his chest and abdomen.

"Gail?" he said. "What are we doing?"

Lyla moved the barrel of her revolver and pointed it at him next. "No sudden moves from you either, slim. You look hard to hit but I'm game to try. Now which one of you assholes killed my Frank?"

"Lyla, if I have to pull my weapon, you're going to regret it," Gail said, one hand on her gun.

The Latin guy muttered something to his buddy and both he and the big guy drew their pistols too.

"Hey hey hey!" EJ shouted, pulling and aiming his gun toward the Miami guys.

"Fuck," Gail muttered and drew too. She aimed her gun at Lyla and backed away a step toward the plane. But no one fired. "What is this, the goddamn movies?" she shouted.

"Luke, what do we do?" EJ said in a panic.

I put my hands up. By some miracle, no one had actually squeezed a trigger yet so there was a chance cooler heads might yet prevail. But I didn't love our odds, especially as the only guy in the circle without a gun. "Let's take a breath, guys. There's still a way out of this."

"If Frank gave the girl the diamonds, then we deal with her," the Latin guy said. "Put your weapons down."

"Bullet holes are a real pain to patch on planes," I said. "How about everybody lowers their guns."

"Them first," EJ said. Nobody budged.

I sighed. I squeezed my eyes shut, pressed my fingers to my temples, then released them again. "Okay. There's one thing you all should get straight before blasting holes in each other. One pesky fact we're all going to have to agree on. It's not going to make everyone happy, but it's hard to argue with at this point." I had their attention. "The fact is—Frank Angel is a damned good liar."

I took two steps into the middle of the circle. "He's lied to every one of us over the last few days. Well, he's been lying to me since I was a kid actually, telling me he flew 'medicine for doctors' and that's why he went to Mexico and Colombia so much. He lied about everything. How fast his planes were, how many flight hours he had. Hell, he lied about where he got his hair cut. But then he lied to the police when the plane he was flying went down and took the life of my mother. Said he wasn't even there. I hated him for a long time for that one. But more recently he lied about why he was back in the Keys." I turned to Lyla. "I bet he promised that you two were going to cash in his diamonds and fly away together. Life on a beach somewhere living like millionaires, drinking Mai Tais?" Lyla's jaw set but she didn't argue. I pointed to the two Miami types. "I'm betting he told you guys he was going to sell his diamonds to you. At a steep discount no doubt, to pay off whatever he owes your bosses." The Miami guys glared. The big guy looked unsure where he should keep aiming his gun, but it wasn't at me so I kept talking. "Those promises kept you guys off his back long enough to make his real play."

I looked at EJ. "That was the big trick. One he couldn't pull off on his own. So he told your dad to make up a treasure hunt. A good enough reason to get us all down here. Make a fuss. Because he wanted to get everyone believing he had a plan. Believing the feds didn't take it all when he went away, that a few of the old legends were true. Some of us even swallowed the lies so well we've been willing to kill for it." I turned to Gail. "But the whole time this was really all about you. About how you set him up that day, sabotaged his plane so it would go down. This trip was Frank's revenge tour to draw you out."

"Bullshit," Gail said. "There's no way he made the whole thing up."

"The diamonds may have been real once, but if they were, the feds took them. Have any of you ever seen the diamonds since?" I asked. I turned back to Lyla. "You get that thing open and actually look at them yet?"

"It won't open," she said. "Trust me, I tried, but I couldn't get it apart."

"Takes a wrench," I said. "Or at least a good pair of pliers. Anyone have those on them?"

No one looked in danger of offering.

"Hang tight. Nobody shoot anybody," I said. Then I walked back around to the boarding ladder on the other side of the Mallard, climbed up to retrieve a couple of wrenches from my tool kit, then trekked back around again. I went to Lyla and held out my hand. "Let me take a look?"

She hesitated, her grip still tight on the turn coordinator. "You give anything to them and I shoot you right in the ass," she said. "Swear to God."

"I believe you."

She handed the turn coordinator to me at arm's length, then switched to a two-handed grip on her pistol. Despite the guns, everyone took a few steps closer to watch.

I adjusted my grip on the turn coordinator so the instrument faced the ground and exposed the back of the case. The cannon plug protruded through the case, as well as three small studs with nuts on the end that didn't look like they could hold the whole thing together but they did. I loosened all three nuts, spun them off and pocketed them. Then I tucked my wrenches away. I lifted the turn coordinator back to level, held it up so everyone could see it, and applied some pressure on the back. The rear of the case popped loose, revealing the frame for the gyro gimbal and the gyro inside.

No diamonds.

I showed the empty casing, then dropped it.

Then I shook the turn coordinator assembly just to be sure.

"See? Lies."

Lyla's face looked liked someone had kicked a puppy. The Miami guys lowered their guns. They looked more annoyed than disappointed. EJ lowered his weapon and seemed vaguely relieved. But Gail turned chartreuse. "There's no way in hell. No fucking way."

I held the turn coordinator out to her. "See for yourself."

She walked over and snatched it from me.

It was heavy and she was forced to holster her pistol to inspect it with both hands.

"This thing in the middle. Does that open? They could be inside."

"Try."

She pried at the gyro to no avail, then swore and flung the instrument to the ground.

I turned to the Miami guys. "If you had a deal with Frank, then you'll need to do it with his ghost."

The well-dressed guy turned and looked toward the SUV, then took out his phone and made a call. Or maybe someone was calling him. His buddy put his gun down.

After a brief conversation with someone, the well-dressed guy jerked his head back toward the SUV. He and his companion retreated to the vehicle and climbed in. They didn't go anywhere. They just sat there, talking and occasionally glaring at us.

Gail's gun came back out. Pointed at Lyla. "You hid them, didn't you? You give off this 'nobody suspects me of anything' image, but I know your type, conniving little backstabber. Your boyfriend in the hospital is living proof."

"What do you know?" Lyla spat back. "Deacon's a better man than I'd bet you've ever had, you ugly old crone."

"That why you shot him?'

"I shot him to teach him a lesson. Doesn't mean I don't love him. Men are stupid. Sometimes you need to straighten their asses out to make them respect you."

Gail scoffed and turned to me. "Twenty years I've dealt with shit-for-brains criminals like her and like your father and at the end of the road there's nothing to show for it. Nothing!" She let the gun sag and swore again.

"There really aren't any diamonds?" EJ asked.

"This was all your doing, wasn't it?" Gail turned on me. "Acting like you've been on our side. Did you take the diamonds?

You hid them somewhere? You did, didn't you?" Her gun came back up. "Like father, like lying son."

"Gail," EJ said. "What are you doing?"

But she paid him no attention. She advanced on me.

"How'd you do it? That why you shot Frank? Because you already knew where he put the diamonds and now you have them?"

"Him?" Lyla said. "Shoot Frank? Bullshit."

"Three shots in the chest," Gail replied. "Maybe you don't know men as well as you think."

Lyla stared at me, met my eye. "Him? No. Not buying it."

"Believe what you want," Gail said. "What I see here is a cold-blooded murderer trying to put one over on us. And if he doesn't start talking right now about where those goddamned diamonds are—"

"Frank told you. This wasn't ever about diamonds," I said. "It was about justice."

Gail narrowed her eyes at me.

"You tell him?" I asked, nodding toward her nephew. "You tell EJ why your brother stopped talking to you all those years ago? Earl figured out that you set up Frank and caused the crash, didn't he? He was mad enough that you got my mother killed that he even helped set all this up while dying of cancer. Why'd you set my parents up? Was it because you thought you'd get your hands on that rumored retirement fund back then, or did you just hate Frank that much?"

She glared at me. "You don't have any idea what you're talking about."

"Sure I do. Earl treated Frank like a brother. Like family. He trusted Frank. Even more than he trusted you. Must have been hard to be the one on the outside. Did you think if you got Frank out of the way you'd get Earl back? Or was it just about the money? Did you tell EJ how you searched Earl's house for the diamonds?"

"That was you?" EJ asked. "Dad told me someone had been in the house."

"Frank Angel was a menace," Gail spat. "He was going to drag the whole family down with him. I did what I did because I had to. And I didn't know Lucia was going to be aboard that day till it was already done."

"You were a cop. You could have arrested them."

"It didn't work that way. Frank was too well established. Too connected."

"So you tried to kill him. Why kill The Mooch and his crew? To keep them quiet? Was he going to out you? Who else died keeping your secrets over the years?"

"Killed who?" EJ asked.

"Your aunt shot three people last night," I said. "One of them an innocent boat stewardess who was just in her way."

"Is that true?" he asked.

"How did you bring the plane down?" I pressed. "The one my mother was on."

"That was easier than it sounds, actually," Gail said with a shrug. "Balloons. I dropped the great Frank Angel right out of the sky with a couple of water balloons. Took a few tries to get the material right. Something Avgas wouldn't eat through straight away. But after I solved that problem it was easy. Take off and fly fly fly, then pop. There go the engines. Even slippery Frank couldn't dodge that."

EJ was staring now. Mouth open. His gun hung loosely at his side.

"You're the cold-blooded killer," I said.

"That's rich. Guy who shoots his own father wants to cast stones."

"Rumors of my death have been greatly exaggerated, Gail," Frank said.

We looked up to find him standing atop *Tropic Angel* dripping wet, but alive and well.

Gail's eyes widened. But then her jaw clenched and gun hand swung up. I moved into action to stop her, but I was too late. EJ barreled into her first with a shout of "No!" He knocked her off her feet and sent them both sprawling, the gun flying out of Gail's hand and clattering away across the ramp.

"Enough!" EJ shouted at her as he held his aunt down. "Angels are family!"

Gail collapsed back on the ground and glared.

EJ stood over her, red in the face but steady, more conviction in his face than I'd seen in years. I nodded to him, then turned my eyes up into the sunlight, shielding my eyes with my hand.

"How long have you been up there, Dad?" I asked.

"I think I heard most of the important parts," he said.

I checked my watch. "That couldn't have been more than a half mile swim. Sure took you long enough."

"Told you I'm not back to full form yet." He grinned. "But I'm getting close."

FORTY-THREE
OLD SCHOOL

"THIS DOESN'T MAKE a bit of goddamn difference," Gail shouted at us. "You're all a bunch of crooks. No one is going to believe you!"

We'd used her own handcuffs to subdue her. She was sitting up now on the ramp and raving.

"She has a point," I said. "What are we going to do with her?"

Frank had climbed down from the roof of the plane to join us. He didn't seem concerned. "We'll deal with that in a minute. "EJ, I appreciate what you did. I knew you'd make the right choice."

"How are you still alive?" EJ asked. "I watched him shoot you."

"Luke is evidently full of parlor tricks," Frank replied. "Though most magicians warn their partners first."

"If you knew anything about guns you'd have seen it coming," I replied.

"Told you I never used the damned things. Still haven't, have I? We managed to resolve all this hoopla without shooting anyone."

"Thanks to EJ," I said. "And dumb luck."

"Nothing dumb about it."

"And the same can't be said about your girlfriend. She might still shoot us," I said. I turned to Lyla.

"I knew there was no way that woman was telling the truth," Lyla said. She'd stayed out of the scuffle with Gail but now approached us. "You and your son have a lot in common, Frank. Including your flare for the dramatic."

"You waited," Frank said. "I appreciate that. Half expected you to run off on me."

"Thought about it. Had the Uber app up on my phone three times. Wouldn't have done me any good though, would it? No diamonds."

"You don't seem too upset," Frank added.

Lyla sighed. "To be honest, I'm not sure I really wanted to go to Mexico and drink Mai Tais. It'd be a little dull after a while, don't you think?"

"You're feeling guilty."

"I've just been thinking, if you get so mad at someone that you want to shoot them to tech them a lesson, maybe that says something? About your relationship."

"You don't think you'd ever be mad enough to want to shoot me."

"I just can't see it. You're too much of a damned gentleman. Think you could ever want to shoot me?"

Frank shrugged. "Probably not."

Lyla wrinkled her nose. "I know. It was fun though, huh? I'll miss you, Frank." She slung her arms around his neck, stood up on her tocs and kissed him hard on the mouth. Then she let her fingers trail down his cheek. "See ya around, hon."

She gave me a wink too.

"Don't go just yet," I said. I walked around *Tropic Angel*, scaled the ladder, and reached inside the plane, returning thirty seconds later with Deacon's size fourteen basketball sneakers in my grip. I passed them to her. "In case you need a reconciliation gift."

"I *know* he's missing these." She hugged them to her chest, gave an impish grin, then turned and strode off toward the road, her phone already out to summon a ride. Frank watched her go.

"Deacon's rest and recuperation is about to hit a speed bump," I said. "You think they'll let her see him?"

"My money says she works it out," Frank mused. "She's a very persuasive woman."

"You all right?"

"I think so."

"Good. 'Cause I don't think we're done yet." I nodded toward the road.

Two Monroe County Sheriff's Department cruisers came into view. They sped past Lyla on the road without slowing, then pulled into the parking lot and came to a stop at the edge of the ramp.

"Ha!" Gail shouted. "What are you going to do now, Frank!"

I turned back to look at Gail. She glared at me with a smug grin on her face.

"This could be problematic, huh?" I said to Frank.

"Believe it or not, it's not our problem anymore," Frank said. He waved at the black SUV that was still idling in the lot. Except this time it wasn't the two Miami guys in the front seats that responded. The back passenger door opened and an old man stepped out. He moved slowly, but when he shut the door he did it with a force that showed he still had some power in his old muscles. The guy had to be at least eighty-five but strode forward with a kind of sturdy confidence. The walk of a cop. The deputies in the cruisers got out of their cars as well but stayed where they were.

Gail stared, mouth open. "Chief?"

Frank turned to me and EJ. "Guys, this is Deputy Chief Harlan Mercer."

"Retired," the old man added.

EJ just stared.

The older man walked forward and shook my father's hand. "Frank. It's been a long time. It was interesting getting your call."

"He's who you called from The Mooch's place?" I asked.

"Remember how I said there must be a reason The Mooch stayed out of prison all those years while I was in?" Frank said. "You're looking at him."

"Tony Brewer was a confidential informant for the department for a lot of years," Mercer replied. "One of mine. For good or ill."

"And he knew Harlan here was the guy who could do something about our situation," Frank said. "So here we are."

Mercer looked over at Gail. "Help me get my old protegé back on her feet, will you?"

Gail wore a shell-shocked expression on her face. "Chief, what the hell are you doing here? You can't be on *their* side of this."

EJ and I lifted Gail from behind so she was upright.

"You've wandered into a territory beyond your pay grade, Captain," he replied. "And you crossed a line. Couple of them now. Mr. Angel has done his time. Paid his debt to society as deemed appropriate by the courts. And in a few more private circles, he's been true to his word. And for those reasons he has earned my respect."

"What? He's paid you off? Is that it? You're gonna sell me out?" Gail's fury rose as she spoke.

Harlan breathed forcibly out of his nostrils. "Goddammit, Gail, when are you going to learn it isn't all about the reward? You were a good deputy. You always had drive. Ambition. One of the brightest trainees I ever had. Making your way as a woman inside that old boy network we had when you started sure wasn't easy, but you did it. I've always had a hell of a lot of respect for you for that. And I think you could have gone all the way to the top in the department if you hadn't taken matters into your own hands like you did."

"It put him away," Gail said. "*I* did what you couldn't."

"Couldn't and wouldn't are different things. You and me, and Frank here, we've been playing a strange game. We played fast and loose with a lot of rules in the Keys over the years, and I'll be the first to admit it. But one thing has stayed the same. The consequences were always real. We all knew the stakes. Frank found out, and he paid his price. Higher than most. But you've got to face what's due now too."

Gail bristled. "Tony Brewer was a crook. Frank's wife?" She jerked her head toward my father. "A crook. They all chose that side. We don't have to play by those same rules."

"I made my career on putting Frank Angel away," Mercer said. "And you were the one that made that happen. And I know you think I ought to have been more grateful. But the way you did it mattered, Gail. You broke a trust." Harlan frowned then, a resigned sigh escaping his lips. "I'm going to ride with you down to the station, see that you get every right afforded you by the law. But you've got a long road ahead of you. And I'm hoping by the time we're done talking today, you're going to see it. Sometimes justice is late, but it comes for all of us in this game. That part's never changed. And today is your day."

Gail stood defiant, but she didn't argue this time. She only shook her head. When the two deputies came to take her to the car, she went quietly.

Harlan Mercer stood with us while they went, then turned to Frank. "They found Tony where you said. José and the girl too. Tragic that. But you can be sure Gail won't get off easy for a triple homicide. Tony had dirt on nearly everything that went down in these islands. He had a file on me too, no doubt. Might be messy what comes out of all this."

"You worried?" Frank asked.

"I'm too old to worry," Harlan said. "Going the way of the dinosaurs soon. But this place is still my home and for what it's worth, I'll be glad it's over. It's been a long time coming. If you got your peace at the end of this, that's something too. I know it doesn't bring your wife back. But it's something."

Frank nodded.

"This is the famous plane, huh?" Harlan said then. "She's a beauty. I can see why you named her for Lucia." He shook Frank's hand again and nodded to me. Then he turned to EJ. "I knew your daddy a long time ago. Sorry to hear he passed. You gonna have something to say about all this with your aunt when it comes to it?"

"I think I will," EJ said. "You need me to come along?"

"Wouldn't hurt. They're gonna need statements from everybody eventually."

EJ turned to me. "Are you going to be all right? I'm real sorry for helping her, Luke. I swear I didn't know she was going to kill somebody. If I'd known . . ."

I extended my hand. "Thank you for looking out for me today, EJ. I'm sure your dad would be grateful too."

"You get so mad, it's hard to get unmad," he said. "I think mostly I'm just mad he's gone. Now Gail's going to be gone too. Losing all kinds of my family this week." He looked at me and Frank. "But Dad would probably say, not all of it, right?"

"Not all of it," I said.

Something about that thought seemed to settle him.

So he and Mercer walked back to the cars.

Frank and I lingered watching them go.

A plane buzzing overhead got our attention and we both looked up to watch it turn onto the approach for landing.

"That's a Cessna 185," Frank said.

"Look at you. Finally got one right," I said.

"I recognize the ones I've been in. Who's flying it this time?"

"Looks like you are about to meet my business partner," I said. "Come to rescue me."

"Good," Frank said. "Because we've still got some business to attend to. She's just in time."

FORTY-FOUR
SHORT FINAL

CASSIDY AND REESE parked the Cessna 185 alongside *Tropic Angel* and she shut the engine down. But neither woman was first out of the plane because the moment the door opened, a furry rocket launched from the rear seat and hit the ramp at a run.

"Murphy!" I shouted.

My dog came in at full speed and didn't stop till he'd made contact, nearly barreling me over. "Good to see you too, buddy," I said and gave him a good tussling of his fur for good measure. The dog gave me several good licks, then investigated Frank next, and once he was satisfied with the state of both of us gave a happy bark.

Cassidy and Reese approached at a slower pace, though just as welcome. I noticed Reese had come armed. On her frame, the bulge of a handgun at her hip was hard to hide.

"Looks like I was right," she said, nodding toward the departing sheriff's cruisers. "Too late for all the action. Knew I should have gotten here sooner."

"Sometimes shooting everybody is too easy," I said. "We wanted to do it the hard way."

"You're a tough guy to finish a conversation with lately," Cassidy said, looking me over.

"So you came to find me in person?"

"Only took three planes."

She looked good. Somehow the Archangel aviation T-shirts always looked better when she wore them. Not sure if it was the sun on us or the way she was looking at me, but I felt warmer all of a sudden.

"Dad, meet Cassidy. My ex-wife."

"Sorry I missed the wedding," Frank said, extending a hand. "Wasn't invited."

Cassidy laughed. "Would you have busted out for the occasion?" She shook his hand then looked back and forth between us. "God, you two do look alike. Now I see where he gets it."

"The irresistible charm?" Frank said.

"The audacity."

He smiled. "You could also blame his mother for that. Never missed a chance to speak her mind."

"Everything okay?" Cassidy asked. "Who's that?" She pointed to the black Nissan SUV. The two Miami-looking guys were still here and had emerged from their vehicle again.

Reese had clocked them too, regarding them warily.

"Those are some business associates of mine," Frank said. "If you can excuse me, I need to speak with them for a few minutes." He turned and walked that way, leaving me alone with Cassidy and Reese.

"You called him 'Dad'," Cassidy said. "Haven't heard that before."

"It's a recent development," I replied. "We'll see if it sticks."

"Did you find your buried treasure?" Reese asked. "There's a turn coordinator over there on the ground." She pointed.

"Yeah. Elsbeth might want a word or two with me about that. Gonna be another dent in the company budget. Hang tight and I'll give you the update."

Murphy followed me over to the boarding ladder for the Mallard and waited while I climbed aboard. I found my screwdriver in the tool kit and moved forward to the flight deck. After situating myself in the copilot seat, I used the screwdriver to remove the four brass screws holding the lowest instrument in the panel in place. The turn coordinator. The cannon plug was already off the back, probably because it was a different size. But the instrument had been close enough to the original to hide in plain sight. I pulled it loose from under the panel and held it in my hands. Only a slight haze from seawater still clung to the inside of the glass. Otherwise the instrument was just how I'd found it in Earl's Decathlon.

I climbed back out of the Mallard and descended the ladder.

As I reached the ramp, Reese winced. "So if that one is what I think it is, then that other one was. . ."

"Everything about this trip has been expensive," I replied. "I've lost track at this point."

Frank and the two Miami guys approached.

"You spotted it," Frank said. "Wondered if you would."

"Might not have if it hadn't dripped on my head first. Lyla never noticed the switch?"

"A little sleight of hand while she was figuring out the lav." He turned to his companions. "Hector and Mauricio, I'd like you to meet my son, Luke. And these are his partners, Cassidy and Reese."

The shorter of the two, who I took to be Mauricio, shook my hand. The big guy settled for a head nod. Reese and Cassidy got the same treatment.

"These gentlemen represent some friends of mine down in Mexico," Frank said. "They were instrumental in getting *Tropic Angel* back into flying shape. Landon has worked with them."

"We've met Landon," Cassidy said. "It was memorable."

"Haven't loved all of his friends," Reese added.

"I heard about how that meeting on Isla Pérez went," Frank said. "Regrettable."

"This is the shooter from Scorpion Reef?" Mauricio said, sizing up Reese. He then stepped over and offered her his hand. "You have a reputation. And my respect."

Reese took the offered handshake. "They weren't friends of yours then."

"Some were," Mauricio chuckled. "But respect, nonetheless." He turned to me. "You have distinguished friends."

"In some circles."

"These men would like to appraise my diamonds," Frank said.

I pulled the wrench from my back pocket and offered it to Frank. "You want to do the honors?"

"You got us this far. Go ahead."

I used the wrench on the nuts at the back of the turn coordinator, the same way I'd done it on the first. This time when I pulled the case off the back, a trickle of water escaped. And in place of the sturdy metal gyro and gimbal assembly sat a bag that had once been black but had taken on mottled gray spots in places. I tipped the soggy bag into my other palm and measured the weight of it. Felt like a lot of stones. I handed the frame of the turn coordinator off to Reese and untied the knotted cord at the neck of the bag. Carefully folding the neck over itself, I revealed the contents. Even after their stint underwater, the diamonds caught the sunlight and sparkled.

"Wow," Cassidy muttered.

Hector fetched a folding table, stool, and a rubber mat from the back of the SUV and set it up in the shade of *Tropic Angel*'s wing. Mauricio used a jeweler's loupe and spread the gems out on the mat. He called out numbers and values to his companion who typed furiously into his phone.

"Anything those things can't do?" Frank said, referencing the phone.

"Can't land a seaplane for you yet," I said. "Though I'm sure someone's working on it."

The process of assessing the diamonds moved along faster than I expected. Mauricio rapidly portioned off segments of the diamond cache into different value groups based on either size or quality. He and Hector consulted back and forth a few times. Finally Hector turned his phone around and showed a number to Frank. "This is where we're at on these. If it changes in your favor later we can let you know."

Frank only gave the number a cursory glance. "Good by me."

"We'll deduct what you owe," Mauricio said. "You still want your remainder in cash? You don't have an account number for us? Lots of dangerous people around here today. Might be safer."

"Your caution is noted. But I still prefer good 'ol 'efectivo'," Frank said. "Do you mind if I keep just one of these as well?" He plucked one especially sparkling diamond from the table. Mauricio noted which pile he took it from and nodded. "It's your money."

Frank smiled and palmed the diamond. "Lucia always hoped at least one would stay in the family."

The two men gathered up the other diamonds into baggies which then went into a locking case and were transferred to the back of the car. A few minutes later they returned with a briefcase and handed it to Frank. "Payment as discussed. That concludes our business, Mr. Angel. Unless you'd like us to stick around til you count it."

Frank unlocked the briefcase, took a brief glance inside, then latched it again. "I'm going to trust you."

"Buena suerte, Frank."

"Hasta la próxima vida, boys," he replied. He then turned to me. "See, just a little errand in the Keys. Easy, huh?"

I shook my head.

"I'm sorry about taking the plane earlier. Had to see this thing to the finish line. But I do have this for you." He carefully pulled a piece of limp paper from his back pocket and handed it to me. "It's handwritten, seeing that's all I had. But it should satisfy your federales. When we get back, I'll write another one I haven't taken swimming."

I carefully unfolded the soggy paper and found he'd written out the bill of sale. Smudged though it was, I recognized the stationery from Hank's boat that I stayed on. He'd left the amount space blank. But otherwise it was all there. Signed and dated two days prior. He must have written it out the night we'd come back from the beach. The night I'd first asked him for the plane.

"Your mother would be happy her airplane is staying in the family," he said. "Especially with you. I can't think of any better place for it."

My fingers tightened on the paper. He'd been good to his word.

I turned and showed the paper to Cassidy. She rested a hand on my shoulder, then rubbed a gentle circle on my back.

Frank smiled and extended his hand to Cassidy. She shook it.

Then he did something he hadn't since I was a kid. He pulled me into a hug. It surprised me, and while it was the last way I thought this trip was going to end, I didn't shrink away.

"I'm so sorry, son."

I was too. For a lot of things. But I didn't say anything. I just hugged my dad.

When I let him go, Frank sniffed and had tears in his eyes. This time I was eighty-percent sure he wasn't faking.

I wasn't either.

Frank Angel had a lot to live down and I knew there were plenty of reasons I could still find to hate him. But I didn't. I let them go in the warm summer breeze.

It was over.

Almost.

FRANK ANGEL HANDED me three big stacks of cash from his briefcase.

"The way I figure it, I owe you for a hotel, a scooter rental, some gas money, some landing fees, a turn coordinator. What else?"

"This more than covers it," I said, fanning the cash. I handed two of the stacks off to Cassidy. "Think that'll make Elsbeth happy?"

"Happy might be a stretch, but it should get her off your back for a while." She gestured toward the other stack in my hand. "What do you have in mind for that one?"

"I have a debt or two of my own to pay back. Incidentally, how much money do you think a Key West stripper makes in an average week?"

Cassidy arched an eyebrow. "How attractive of a dancer would you say she is?"

"My former-husband radar is picking that up as a loaded question. But let's say her professional charms are ample and she did me a significant favor at great personal cost."

Cassidy nodded. "Then I trust you'll give her what your heart tells you is right. In my experience, you always tend to make the right decisions in the end."

I tucked the money away in my back pocket and gave her wink. "We'll figure it out." I turned to Reese. "You three just got here. Someone recently told me it's a crime to fly all the way to the Keys and not have at least a little bit of fun. What do you say to a late lunch back in Key West? Early dinner? I don't even know what time it is."

"As long as it's somewhere dog friendly," Reese said. "Murphy is the best boy and he would like a snack."

"He and I both," I said. "How about Louie's Backyard? That's close to the airport. I even have a blind old lady's car we can all squeeze into to get there."

"Race you?" Cassidy asked.

"Last one there buys lunch," I said.

Cassidy brushed my arm with her fingertips, then she and Reese headed for the 185. Murphy didn't leave my side.

"Slowing me down already, huh?" I said. I climbed aboard *Tropic Angel* and located the folding air stairs to replace the boarding ladder and the second I had the stairs set up, Murphy bounded up them to get inside.

Frank and I climbed aboard and stowed the stairs away again, then I headed for the flight deck.

As I got settled into the pilot's seat, I noticed Frank had stayed in the back, buckling himself into one of the divans.

I leaned my head around the bulkhead and addressed him. "You know, this crusty old fossil told me that a Mallard is better as a two-pilot bird. Turns out . . . I think he was right."

"Sounds like a real smart guy," Frank replied. He unbuckled his belt and came forward. "Was he debonair and charming too?"

"He was a real pain in the ass most of the time. *Slow* swimmer."

"Can't be the same guy I'm thinking of then." Frank buckled in and found a headset. Cassidy already had the 185's engine running. "I think your girls are going to beat us there."

"I don't mind."

Murphy snuck into the flight deck and licked me in the elbow. Then he rested his muzzle on Frank's leg.

I ran through the checklist, calling out items, Frank responding from his side.

In a matter of minutes we had the two Pratt and Whitney radials thrumming on either side of us, the hum of their vibrations resonating through the airframe.

We taxied to the edge of the runway in time to see Cassidy lift the Cessna 185 into the air.

"Pressures and temps all look good," Frank confirmed after a review of the instruments. "Ready for takeoff."

"You want the honors?" I said, gesturing to the controls. "One more takeoff in your old bird?"

Frank considered the yoke in front of him but then shook his head. "I had my turn. And honestly, watching you do it is even better. She's yours now."

And when I rested my hand on the controls, I felt it. The history. The pain. But the way forward too. I pushed the throttles toward the horizon and the big engines revved and roared. *Tropic Angel* got rolling, faster and faster until she slipped Earth's grip. Her broad wings took us skyward over bright turquoise waters.

I banked left. The western Keys lay sprawled out like jewels ahead of me, Key West already coming into view. The dot that was Cassidy and Reese in the 185 had skirted north, perhaps dodging the Navy airspace, or just waiting for us to catch up. Either way, I followed.

It was going to be a short flight so I saw the value in extending it. At the moment, there was no place else I'd rather be.

Frank Angel smiled when he looked my way.

Murphy sat up and gave a happy bark.

"Me too, buddy," I said. "Me too."

FORTY-SIX

EPILOGUE

THE CAT on my lap was sound asleep. Curled into a semi-circle, her whiskers twitched occasionally and she made little chirping sounds as she dreamed. Perhaps she was chasing hangar mice. We hadn't seen any real mice in a long time thanks to her so I figured she was entitled to the dream.

Elsbeth hadn't appeared in my office even once this morning, and she'd sent me a cheery email referencing a zero balance from the account of one of our parts suppliers. She'd even added a smiley face to the email subject line. It was a banner day.

And it was Friday, payday. A pile of paper checks and envelopes sat on my desk awaiting signatures. Tyson, the youngest of my crew, complained biweekly that my refusal to implement direct deposit was "Giving Oregon Trail energy."

But I loved the feeling of walking around the hangar handing out paper paychecks. What was the point of being the boss if you didn't get to be the bearer of good news?

This week there was even an envelope with my name on it.

Cassidy breezed in the door looking entirely too put together for a lazy Friday. Her patterned blouse was loose and flowing, and her white shorts contrasted against the summer tan of her legs.

"Hey, I thought we were getting lunch on a lake today. You promised me water landings and chips and salsa."

"Still on my agenda," I said, checking my watch. "Can't leave yet though, I've got a cat on my lap."

"Good to know where your priorities lie."

"I don't make the rules in this relationship," I said, gesturing to the cat. But just then Blackjack opened her eyes, yawned and stretched. She dug her claws into my leg at the end of the stretch and then she was up, dropping to the floor with a flick of her tail.

"I take it back," I said. "I'm free now."

"Good. I'm hungry. By the way, I ran into your dad down there," she added, gesturing with a thumb toward the hangar entrance. "He's becoming quite the regular."

I looked out the window. "He shows up to tinker on the Mallard. Fixed the lav. Figured out why the bilge pumps were intermittent. He's actually kinda handy to have around."

Cassidy came over and stood beside me. "You thinking of taking him on?"

"We've been saying we want another mechanic."

"He *is* knowledgeable. But it would take thirty months to get him licensed," she mused. "You'd have to sign off his work till then. You think you two could stand each other that long? It's a big commitment."

"I had a call from my Aunt Margery yesterday. You know what she said? Someone paid off what she owed on the mortgage. And not just hers. EJ's ex-wife and kids got the same treatment."

"Frank did that?"

I shrugged. "He didn't say so to me, but I think it must have been his way of thanking Earl and EJ for what they did."

"Wow. Generous. You think he kept any of his haul for himself?"

"Can't be much left. Wasn't that big of a briefcase. So he'll need a job sooner or later, unless he was serious about becoming a borracho in Mexico."

Frank was chatting with Rip by the break area, my dog lingering nearby hoping for handouts.

"If you want to hire him, I'm willing to give it a shot," Cassidy said. "And if you don't, I understand that too. I support you either way."

"It feels strange," I said. "For all these years I've felt like I knew exactly who Frank Angel was, and it was easy to discount him. Now it's like I barely know anything about him—the real him."

"Sounds like a good place to start," she said. "Could be he feels the same way about you."

As we were talking, Frank looked up from the hangar floor, saw us, and waved.

I waved back.

"Family was never something I've wanted around," I said.

Cassidy took in the view of my crew down on the hangar floor. "Yes you have. You just didn't call it that." She bumped me in the arm. "Ready to go fly?"

"You're excited to add 'Grumman Mallard Captain' to your long list of flying accomplishments?"

"I'll go start the preflight," she said with a grin.

I followed her out the door, but paused at the top of the stairs while she continued down. The way the sunlight was shining, the way the hangar smelled of fresh motor oil and hot coffee, the shine of the airplanes and tools, the people gathered around chit chatting—all of it hit me at once. This place we'd built and saved was something I was proud of. Some part of me hoped that wherever she was, my mother, Lucia, could see it too. And if she could, I hoped she knew her sacrifices for our family hadn't been for nothing. We'd made something here. Something worth cherishing. And that was no lie.

Thanks for reading.

If you enjoyed this book and would like more, **please leave it a written review**! You can also follow Nate Van Coops on Amazon, Audible, or Goodreads to be notified of future books.

Luke's adventures continue. You can get exclusive extra chapters in this series when you sign up at NateVanCoops.com and download the bonus material.

It will also subscribe you to my highly engaging biweekly newsletter in which I discuss what's going on around Luke's airport, adventures with my family, and of course, book news! I look forward to sharing more stories with you.

-NVC

ACKNOWLEDGMENTS

Thanks for taking another flight with Archangel Aviation!

I hope you've enjoyed the ride. This series has been some of the most fun I've ever had writing, and the response from readers is a big part of why. Your willingness to communicate with me, leave reviews, and tell your friends about the books, has made these stories the most successful series I've produced.

I'm thrilled that my love letter to aviation has been met by such a strong response from the community. The amount of reviewers who have self-identified as pilots or aviation professionals has been heartwarming. I personally know the impact aviation fiction like *Where is Joe Merchant* by Jimmy Buffett had on me as young pilot. I'm pleased to hear that Luke Angel's flying adventures are finding a home with many of the same readers.

Luke's penchant for finding trouble will continue. If you want to keep hanging out with me in the meantime, I write biweekly newsletters that include what's going on at Albert Whitted Airport these days, flying adventures with my family, and of course, book news. You can join at natevancoops.com or by picking up any of the books' bonus epilogues.

Special thanks to my beta team, the TYPE PROS, who are my brave test pilots. A captain is nothing without a crew and this crew is amazing. Each one of you makes my books fly higher.

Thank you Marilyn Bourdeau, Julie DeStefano, Mark Hale,

Maarja Kruusmets, Judy Eiler, Eric Lizotte, Bill Lebus, Ken Robbins, Claire Manger, Yvonne Mitchell, Ginelle Blanch, Elaine Davis, Sarah Van Coops-Bush, and Bethany Cousins.

Sam, Acelyn, Luisa, and Kayleigh, thanks for being my co-working friends at COHatch. You make the day-to-day writing muy divertido! Thanks also to Matt Reichart and crew for your enthusiasm running the real life Hangar 4, and always making the airport such a fun place to hang out.

And to my writer friends, Lucy Score, Alan Lee, Cissy Mecca, James Blatch, Boo Walker, T. Ellery Hodges, Avery Maxwell, Tina Gallagher, and Amanda Traylor. You are a constant inspiration. Also a big thanks to the Tropical Authors group. When I found you guys, I felt right at home.

Thank you Scott Brick for using your tremendous talent to bring these thrillers to life in audio. I like these books, but they're better when you read them. And thanks to Gina Smith for making it happen!

To Stephanie, Piper, and Morgan: The sun in St. Pete shines brighter when I'm with you. Twenty second hugs forever. Better get used to it.

-NVC

ABOUT THE AUTHOR

NATE VAN COOPS is a commercial pilot, mechanic, and certified flight instructor in St. Petersburg Florida. His addictions to tacos and pickle ball wage a war for supremacy daily. When not writing, or flying at his favorite airport, you'll find him e-biking around St. Pete with his wife and kids. He also writes science fiction books under the name Nathan Van Coops. Learn more at natevancoops.com.

To say hello, or to inquire about the availability of film or television rights, send email to: inquiries@nathanvancoops.com